THE EMERALD TREE

BOOK II OF
THE CARROWKEEL SERIES

NINA ORAM

First published by Luna Press Publishing, Edinburgh, 2020

www.lunapresspublishing.com

ISBN-13: 978-1-911143-86-4

For Mum, Dad, Sam and Shell.

Thanks to everyone for their belief, love and support,
but especially Francesca and Luna, Coirle, Helen, Bill, Roy,
Kathryn, Denise, Brian and of course, Joe.

Contents

Chapter One

For Malachy, the light was blinding; even with his eyelids tightly closed it seemed to find its way into his eyes and into his head. Ellyllon had released his ankle and was moving by his side, his elbows and body bumping into him. Fearful of being left alone, Malachy grabbed at him, holding on to anything solid, only to be shaken off before grabbing again. There was a deafening roar and Ellyllon was violently pulled away, Malachy going with him. Despite the forces around them, Ellyllon shook himself once, twice, heaving Malachy from him and sending them both tumbling away in opposite directions. Malachy felt the faint breath of cool air and then he was out of the light and falling through darkness. Wind whipped at him, stinging his face and hands. He opened his eyes just long enough to see the white of sand before he hit the ground and everything went dark.

Malachy woke, feeling something cold, wet and sniffing loudly poking him in the chest, neck and face.

"Here; out of it. That's it. Let's have a look."

The voice moved closer as it spoke and he felt hands turning him over onto his back. He coughed, his throat raw, his body shivering with cold. He opened his eyes; a man, his face lined and weathered, knelt over him, his hat and clothes soaked by the light rain misting around them.

"Where did ye come from? Were ye out in that?"

The man instinctively looked up, as if surveying some kind of devastation, then returned his attention to Malachy.

"Have ye a name?"

Malachy coughed again. "Malachy. Costello." He managed his voice a deep rasp.

"Malachy Costello, is it?" The man squinted at him. "There be no Costellos round here. You're a long way from home, ladeen."

The man looked up again, thinking, then back at him, deciding.

"You'd best come home with me. Can ye walk? It's not far."

He placed his arms around Malachy, helping to lever him up first into a sitting position then slowly onto his feet. Malachy's head span and his body swayed. He could feel the man's grip on him tighten.

"I've got you. Now, we'll be taking it nice and slow. That's it. My name's Thady, Thady Padian."

They began to walk, Thady taking almost all of Malachy's weight, and all the time talking to him, encouraging, reassuring him. The ground beneath them was soft and their feet sunk into it, making the way hard going. Malachy's chest heaved and he coughed again. Looking down, he saw only sand, but he was too tired to question what that meant. At a hedge Thady stopped, letting them both catch their breath, and for the first time Malachy looked up. Ahead of them lay the usual green and brown of grass, hedge and track. A small cart sat the other side of the hedge, tied to a ragged looking pony. Malachy glanced back the way they'd come: behind them a huge bank of sand disappeared into the distance. Over to the right, something grey; it looked like part of a wall, or a tower, rose out of it.

"There's nothing we can do for the poor souls." Thady shook his shoulders softly but his face, looking in to Malachy's, was heartbroken. "Come ladeen, we need to get you home. Into the warm."

They stared at one another for a moment and then Thady led him through a gap in the hedge and out onto a track. Propping Malachy up at the end of the cart, Thady held him upright with his body, then, with a gentle push, used gravity to press him back into the bottom of the cart. He grabbed his legs, heaved them up and pushed him further onto the cart. Malachy put out his arms, trying to help, but they flailed helplessly. He didn't seem to have the strength.

"There," Thady said after few moments, breathing heavily.

Malachy's eyes were closed. With a shake of his head, Thady shrugged out of his coat and laid it over him. Shivering against the rain, he patted Malachy's ankle and moved around the cart to the seat. The cart dipped as he clambered heavily into it and, taking the reins, gave a loud whistle. His collie appeared, running furiously across the uneven ground, his tail flying. He bounded through the gap in the hedge and with one long, powerful jump, landed in the cart.

"Settle down," Thady admonished him and immediately he sat.

Brown eyes regarded Malachy curiously. He shifted forward and gently placed his nose next to Malachy's outstretched hand. Thady turned around, clicked his tongue and the pony moved off. The three of them were heading for home, taking Malachy with them.

Standing on the edge of the Bricklieve Mountains, Jasmine examined the landscape critically. It didn't look any different, although possibly fewer houses dotted the fields. It was hard to tell. She frowned. Maybe it hadn't worked…

…Eyes closed against the darkness, they spun until Jasmine's stomach heaved. Seamus' hand in hers never loosened its grip; she felt his Iomlan working with the power of the tomb, felt it pushing her on as she used hers to search for Malachy.

"Don't stop, keep thinking of him." Seamus' voice whispered. "Focus."

But there was no need for him to worry. Malachy filled her head, his face smiling at her, his eyes sparkling as he laughed at his own joke, the touch of his hand on her arm. She reached for him, yearned for him, not just with Iomlan, but with every part of her…

She rubbed her forehead. She'd thought out the other side she'd be able to sense him, and follow that sense like a beacon, but there was nothing there. It didn't work like that, Seamus reassured her; her connection to Malachy was more nebulous than that, more instinctive. Besides, it only worked inside the tomb, where she had the tomb's power to help her. But what if he were wrong, and it hadn't worked? Maybe they weren't even in the past; maybe at this very moment John was only just driving away. She shook her head irritably. She wasn't like Seamus, who seemed to be taking it all in his stride, as if time travel was the most normal thing in the world, like catching a bus. They couldn't be in the past, they just couldn't. Behind her, a pebble scuttled loudly across stone, and she turned to see Seamus approaching.

"Are you still feeling sick?" He asked.

"I'm OK."

He cocked his head. "Are ya sure?"

"Yeah, it's just, er…" She waved her hand at the view. "It doesn't look any different."

"Not from here it doesn't. But trust me, it will when we get down." There was a pause.

"Do you know what the name means? Bricklieve?" he asked.

"No."

"The speckled mountain." He looked back at the ridge. "It suits it, don't you think?"

"Yeah, I suppose."

He gave her a shrewd look. "He's here, and we will find him."

"But how can you be so sure?"

Seamus smiled. "Because that's why we're here. Why you led us here."

Jasmine looked down. Even after everything, he had such confidence in her. She wished she shared it. She took a deep breath.

"Do you know, er, when this is?"

"No, but I'm guessing we've not gone too far back. We weren't that long. Certainly not back to the time of the druids." He looked at his watch. "Almost ten. C'mon, we'd best get going."

"Our watches — they still work?" She peered at the dial on her wrist.

"Of course, why wouldn't they?"

Of course, why wouldn't they.

"I think that'll be the quickest way down." Seamus pointed right.

It was opposite to the way they'd come up. The slope was steep, the path little more than gorse and shrub flattened and parted by sheep, and narrow.

"What do we do when we get down?" She hadn't even thought about it, what they'd do out the other side; all the practical things.

But Seamus obviously had.

"First we need to find a settlement where we can find clothes — so we don't stand out — food and transport. Then we go find Malachy."

They set off in single file, Seamus leading.

*

Heads down, watching where they stepped, they walked in silence for twenty minutes. "Seamus?"

"Hmm?"

"If I can't feel Malachy, how do we find him? I mean, he could be anywhere."

Seamus shook his head. "I don't think so. If he came out of the void here — and there's no reason to think he didn't — then he'll likely come out in the place he went in."

She thought about it. "You mean Killaspugbrone?"

"I do. It's the best place to start."

*

The path meandered wildly where the sheep had followed the most solid ground, the best grass, it took them another half an hour to get down. Back almost to ground level, they stopped in front of a hedgerow, catching their breath while Seamus rested his leg and tried to get their bearings. To Jasmine, it seemed impossible. Each way looked the same:

green fields, hedgerows, clusters of trees. If there was a road out there she had no idea where it was. Next to her, Seamus closed his eyes.

She waited, expecting to feel his Iomlan, but nothing came. High above her head, the morning cloud was beginning to disperse, and it was surprisingly warm, given the time of year, and bright.

"I think it's this way," he said eventually, opening his eyes and grinning. "No need to use Iomlan when I can remember the lie of the land."

They skirted the hedgerow to a wooden gate, leading to a rough track. Seamus climbed up and over, swinging his body with ease despite his leg, Jasmine following.

"I'm hoping this will lead us to the village of Ballyfarnon. If it's there, or course," he explained as she landed beside him.

Still descending, the track led them past a tiny stone cottage, set low, like a cat crouched with its belly to the ground. Jasmine eyed it curiously, hoping to get a glimpse of the owner, but it remained quiet and empty.

They turned a corner and abruptly the track ended, disappearing into a junction and a slightly wider, muddy road.

"Ah, here we are. The village's not far now."

Finally, thought Jasmine, glad to be off the hillside and eager to get back to Killaspugbrone and start their search for Malachy properly.

*

The village was tiny; just a few houses, an inn and a shop along a main road thick with rutted mud. Outside the inn, a group of men milled about, seeing to horses, chatting, no one doing anything very fast. They were dressed in shirts and trousers, one or two of them wearing cloth caps. Seamus gave Jasmine a nudge to get her attention.

"I think we're sometime late in the nineteenth century," he whispered, even though there was no one nearby to hear.

Jasmine nodded vaguely, feeling very strange, as if she wasn't quite awake. They'd actually done it, travelled back in time. Abruptly, from behind, came a loud thundering. Jasmine turned to look, and in a whirl of sound and motion, a man shouted, Seamus grabbed her arm and pulled her sharply to one side and a coach, heavily splattered with mud and pulled by four horses, clattered by, its carriage swinging wildly. Jasmine had just enough time to glimpse the solitary passenger inside, his bottom bouncing as he hung on for dear life, and then it was gone, heading straight for the inn. It looked for a moment as if it was going too fast, that it must surely run down at least one of the men, but then, with a furious tugging of the reins and another loud shout, the driver brought it to a brief, shuddering stop.

"It's like a film!" Jasmine exclaimed, staring at Seamus in amazement, and he laughed at her.

"Come on. And try not to stare."

They walked up the main street, stepping carefully over puddles and thick piles of mud. Jasmine had to double step to avoid a large splatter of horse dung.

"A bit rougher than you see in films." Seamus' grin was ironic.

A woman stepped out of one of the houses, holding long skirts in one hand. She spotted Jasmine and her lips thinned with disapproval. And then turning away, she lifted her head and walked carefully but expertly across the street.

"What did I do?" Jasmine asked, put out by her look.

"She thinks yer after her purse."

"She thinks I'm a thief?!"

"Shhh, keep your voice down. To her, you look... unsavoury. Not a good Christian woman." He looked down at her, "She has a point; we really need to get you out of those clothes, or at least cover them."

"But how?" Jasmine looked up and down the street. "I don't suppose there's any clothes in that shop?"

"We won't need it to sell any." He stopped and drew her to him. "You know I'm not one for using Iomlan if we can avoid it, especially with other people, but sometimes it's the only way."

He glanced over at the inn. "We're going in there and I want you to stay still and quiet no matter what I do."

"But maybe I can help?"

"No." Seamus shook his head. "I'm going to be making this up as I go along and it's easier to do that on my own." He gave her arm a reassuring squeeze. "Let's get inside."

*

They reached the inn. The coach was empty; the passenger had gone inside for food and rest and the driver was chatting with the men outside.

Seamus stopped. "I've an idea. Wait here a minute."

He darted to the door of the inn and disappeared inside. A few minutes later he returned carrying a long, black coat. "Now, put this on."

Taking it from him, she shrugged into it and pulled the sides to. It was huge, the sleeves way too long, hung almost to her knees, but it obscured her clothes completely. Seamus' lips twitched.

"Now, I've found you a nice quiet corner in there. It's called a snug and it's away from everyone. It's where the ladies go. They're not allowed to sit with the men." Ignoring her indignant look, he quickly continued. "As I said, just keep your head down and stay quiet; don't draw attention to yerself. They'll be curious, but they'll think you're a gentlewoman travelling, so shouldn't approach you."

Opening the door, he glanced quickly around before ushering her in. The bar was big and wide, but made smaller by a series of tiny rooms sat along one wall. The snugs, as Seamus called them, were made from cheap, thin wood, their open doors pressed tight to their thin wooden walls. A fire roared in an inglenook hearth at the end nearest them, and a handful of men were standing at the bar. Sitting alone, at the table nearest the fire, the man from the coach drank what looked like whiskey out of a small, clear glass.

"Come on," Seamus whispered, putting his arm protectively around her shoulders and leading her to the snug furthest from the bar.

A bowl of stew steamed in the centre of a rough looking table, accompanied by a hunk of bread and a tall glass of Guinness stout. He propelled her into one of two high-backed chairs.

"I know it's early, but I thought you might like a small bite to eat while you wait. It might be a while before we get another chance. I'll be as quick as I can."

He darted away, and she watched as he walked across to the bar and, leaning in, began to talk quietly to the landlord. A man wandered past her snug and, glancing casually in, looked straight into her eyes. He stopped to stare at her, openly curious, and she quickly lowered her head. She waited, not breathing, for what seemed like forever, then cautiously looked up. The man had gone. She saw him then, standing at the bar with his friends, listening to the conversation. She breathed out. Seamus, meanwhile, had moved away, disappearing out of her sight.

*

With nothing else to do, Jasmine pulled up her sleeves and picking up the spoon, began to eat. The stew was delicious, and she was surprised how hungry she was. It must've been the walk down the hill. She took a sip of the Guinness and pulled a face. It was disgusting, the taste bitter, and she couldn't understand how anyone could drink it, must less give it its iconic status. Pushing it away, she turned back to the stew. Iomlan fluttered. Something was happening; she could feel it, like a slight draft, coming from somewhere to her left. It was Seamus; he was using his Iomlan, although it was very faint, very subtle. The men at the bar were all leaning to their left, all intently watching something at the other end of the room; something she couldn't see but guessed was by the fire. Slowly, unobtrusively, as if fearful of disturbing what was happening, they began to inch sideways. She lowered her spoon, and after a moment, got quietly to her feet and sneaked a look around the side of the snug. Seamus was sitting with the man at the table, the two of them sharing an already half-empty bottle of whiskey over a game of cards. As she watched, Seamus leant forward and slowly fanned his cards out on the table. The other man cursed and threw his hand down before reaching again for the whiskey bottle. He poured himself a drink, topped up Seamus' glass despite his protestations, and began picking up the cards. He said something she couldn't hear. Seamus nodded, as, with the last card collected, the man began to shuffle, preparing for another game. Stunned, Jasmine slid around the table and back to her seat. Seamus was cheating! And using Iomlan to do it. She sat down. She could barely believe it. After all his lectures, his constant moralising, telling her to use Iomlan responsibly, here he was using it to cheat at cards. A man at the bar grabbed the man next to him and whispered something in his ear. The other man laughed, a low, vicious laugh that could only be at someone else's expense. Jasmine frowned. Seamus was playing cards with the man whose coach had almost run her over. And the money he would win would surely help them get back to Killaspugbrone and find Malachy. She looked down at the stew. It would also pay for the bowl of deliciousness that was rapidly cooling in front of her. She pulled up her sleeve again, lifted her spoon, and, with a shrug, dipped it deep into the stew.

*

She managed almost half before her stomach gave out and she sat back, defeated. Seamus and the man were still playing cards, the men at the bar silent as they watched them avidly. It was hot in the big coat and she wished she could take it off. Yawning, she rested her head on the panelling behind her and gazed at the bottles lining the shelf above the bar. Light from the fire caught the glass. She imagined the flames. High up they danced, the heat spreading across the room, with a warm, cosy glow…

Malachy was standing in what looked like a yard, elevated above fields and grass with the sea far behind him. She was close enough to see his face and the surprising length of his hair, but he showed no sign of seeing her. A collie, all black bar his snow-white bib, ran across to him, jumping up towards his throat, his mouth wide, his sharp teeth gleaming. She recoiled, her breath hissing as Malachy staggered backwards and almost overbalanced with the weight of him. Laughing, he righted himself and began rubbing the fur around the dog's neck, under his chin, furiously...

...Jasmine stirred, blinking. The image of Malachy filled her head, as real and as solid as the chair beneath her. Then he was gone, lost in the moment between semi and fully awake. The men at the bar were clapping, shouting words of congratulations and approval. Seamus came into view, one hand stuffing something into the inside pocket of his coat. He nodded casually at the men then slipped into the seat opposite her. Almost immediately the landlord appeared, carrying another bowl of stew and bread, this time for Seamus.

"Thanks." Seamus smiled as it was placed down in front of him.

The landlord nodded. He flashed Jasmine a look she couldn't place before retreating back across the room. She watched him disappear through the door to the left of the bar.

"I've got the money we need," Seamus murmured, mouth full of stew.

Jasmine feigned innocence. "You did?! how?"

"Playing cards."

"Wow, you must be a very good card player!" She stretched her eyes to their widest.

She'd overdone it. Seamus gave her a suspicious look.

"I'm not bad." He paused to chew at a gristly piece of lamb. "But I had help. I used Iomlan."

He swallowed.

"Iomlan? You mean you cheated? You used Iomlan to cheat?"

He reddened. "No, I didn't cheat, I played the cards as they were dealt. Although I wouldn't put it past yer man to try and fix the dealing. No, I used Tionchar. Influence."

"Influence? I thought you didn't like it?"

"I don't, but sometimes it's the quickest and the most unobtrusive way. And I didn't do much. I didn't need to; the man's greed did most of the work. He just needed the smallest of nudges."

"But surely that's still cheating?"

Spoon lifted halfway to his mouth, he gave her a hard look. "That man is rich and unpleasant, and a small lesson in humility will do him the world of good."

"So it's OK to con people if they're not very nice?"

"Jasmine, you know well that's not what I'm telling you," he protested and she laughed, enjoying his discomfort for a change.

"I'm not the one who has a problem with it."

She laughed again and, deliberately ignoring her, he wolfed the last of the stew, wiping the bottom of the bowl with his bread. He lowered his spoon and looked at her bowl.

"Are you going to eat that?"

"I can't. I'm stuffed."

"Food'll be scarce here; you'd best eat it all when it comes along." Reaching over, he grabbed her bowl and replaced it with his own.

Behind him, the landlord was back, beckoning to him.

"I think he wants you," Jasmine said with a nod.

Seamus swivelled around and back. "It's about the horses. I won't be long."

Quickly, he finished her bowl and stood up.

"Horses? Are we getting a coach?"

"A coach?" Seamus shook his head. "Why would we get a coach? Horses'll do just fine."

"But, but, I've never ridden a horse before!"

"Then its time you were learning," he retorted, turning away.

*

Seamus spoke with the landlord briefly, handed over a small amount of the money and then said something to the rest of the men at the bar. Smiling broadly, they raised their glasses to him, one even clapping him on the back as he left. The landlord immediately began to pour a fresh round.

"That'll keep them happy." Seamus grinned. "C'mon, the landlord'll meet us in the stables."

She followed Seamus to the front door. Opening it, he waited, allowing her to slip through first and straight into the man from the coach. Swearing, he knocked her roughly out of his way with his shoulder and, with a final glare at Seamus, stalked over to the coach. He yanked the door open and climbing inside, slammed the door shut behind him. Almost immediately, his driver appeared, half walking half running from the far side of the inn and, after untying the horses, climbed awkwardly into his seat. The man in the coach stuck his head out of the window, shouting at the driver to get the horses moving, his tone bullying, heckling. Jasmine watched as the driver, smiling craftily, urged the horses suddenly forward, sending the man tumbling back inside.

"Idiot!" Jasmine muttered under her breath. "He deserved that."

Seamus laughed and patted his pocket with the money inside. "And to lose this. Come on."

The stables were behind the inn, at the far end of a cobbled yard. Seamus opened the stable door, once again stepping back to let Jasmine in first. Stalls ran down both sides; most were empty, only five having horses in them. Seamus walked over to them, running first a critical eye then his fingers over them, down their legs, checking their hooves, every inch the expert. The door opened again and the landlord walked in carrying a cloth sack. He nodded to Seamus and looked Jasmine up and down. There was that look again; she couldn't place it, but it wasn't good. Without a word he passed her the sack.

"Thank you," she said politely.

He nodded and moved over to Seamus and she peeked inside, seeing what looked like food wrapped in brown paper and a bottle of something black. Her heart sank. More Guinness.

Seamus was indicating two chestnuts, standing side by side. "We'll take those."

A flicker of dismay passed over the landlord's face and the haggling began in earnest. The conversation lunged and parried, and then, suddenly with a shake of the hands, it was all over. The landlord left, his face twisted with disgust, yet Jasmine sensed that he was quite happy.

"Nice horses," Seamus remarked, stroking the one nearest him. "I paid over the odds though."

"Why?"

"He's a good man. Oh, he wasn't best pleased when I picked his finest horses, but he gave in with good grace. Besides, he's happy now, and it's no questions asked. Now let's saddle those horses. I'll show yer how to do it."

Two saddles lay across the bar of the far stall. She watched carefully as Seamus picked up one of the saddles and placed it onto the first horse's back. It glanced curiously at him, but remained motionless as he bent over and, with deft fingers, quickly did the saddle up.

"Now, your turn."

He'd made it look so easy. Slipping out of the coat, she picked up the second saddle and, hefting it self-consciously, placed it awkwardly on top of the horse's back. Crooked, she tried to straighten it, but the horse kept shifting.

"Here." Moving forward, Seamus began to pet the horse, soothing it with his touch, his voice a soft, low murmur.

It worked; with an effort, she managed it. Luckily, the horses already had bridles on; she couldn't imagine getting that close to those teeth.

"Now, I haven't time to teach you to ride, so we'll going to have to do it the quick way," Seamus declared, taking her arm and guiding her to the other side of the barn. "It won't be perfect, but you'll have the basics."

"I don't understand."

"You will. I'm going to need you to trust me, to stand still for me and relax. Your first instinct will be to fight me, my Iomlan, but don't. Let me in. Now, ready?"

She nodded, swallowing. Coming in close, he raised his hand to her forehead and closed his eyes. She did the same, and immediately felt him probing, gently trying to find a way in. Automatically Iomlan flared, slipping around her mind, as if to protect it. She tried to stop it, to force it down, but as the probing intensified and Seamus' Iomlan became more insistent, it hardened around her, like a wall. Breathing deeply, she tried to force herself to relax, but it was all she could do to stop Iomlan fighting back. For a moment, the Iomlans jostled, equally matched. And then, with one, sharp jab, Seamus sent hers scattering and he flooded her mind with images. She saw herself getting on a horse, holding the reins, learning how to lift up and down with the movement of the horse, feeling the frustration as she tried to get the rhythm, the jar on her bottom and spine as she failed. More came, faster now, the speed of them making it impossible to know where one started and another ended. She was galloping for the first time, feeling the exhilaration, the wind in her hair, the wonder of a living creature moving effortlessly beneath her. Her head span, the pictures whirling crazily, and then they stopped dead. She opened her eyes, staggering slightly. Seamus caught her arm and led her to a thick wooden beam dividing one of the stalls.

"Here, sit down. It'll pass in a minute."

She breathed slowly, trying to calm her head. "What did you do?"

"I taught you how to ride; gave you the knowledge."

"But it was like memories, like I was actually riding."

Her head was singing with them, her body etched with emotions and feelings that she knew weren't her own. It was the strangest thing, they didn't feel like her, but still she felt them.

Seamus nodded. "Never forget we're emotional, feeling creatures. We learn best by doing and in the doing we feel, experience. The memories give you a connection and help the knowledge stick, as if you've really learnt to ride."

"So, I'll always have memories that aren't real?" She thought of something else. "Whose memories, are they?"

"They're mine." Seamus smiled, looking embarrassed. "It feels strange now, but that will pass as the memories fade, leaving the knowledge deep in your subconscious. But you must practice. Without practice, even the knowledge will fade."

Jasmine took this in. "Could you do it with anything?"

"Yes, I suppose so, but I'd have to have the knowledge." He paused. "Of course we can also take the knowledge from someone else, if they're willing that is, but it could be dangerous for them."

She thought about it. "So potentially I could learn anything, any language, in minutes?"

Seamus nodded, smiling. "Potentially, but I haven't tried. Well, except for Spanish."

"You speak Spanish?" Her eyes brightened. "Will you teach me?" she asked eagerly.

He laughed. "Maybe, one day. Now, time to go."

She climbed back into the coat and they led the horses out of the stables.

"Here, I'll give you a leg up," Seamus offered, letting go of his horse's reins.

Jasmine grabbed hold of the saddle and reins and pulled as Seamus heaved. The coat caught around her legs, but to her astonishment, she landed squarely in the saddle, her legs neatly astride. Seamus, seeing the expression on her face, laughed loudly. He was still laughing when he climbed on his own horse.

"Are yer ready?" he asked, grinning.

"I think so," she answered dubiously, still uncertain.

"Let's go."

He clicked his tongue and set off, turning his horse to the way out of the yard. Jasmine pressed her legs into the horse's side and moved the reins to follow him. Seamus looked back at her, grinning broadly. She stared at the horse's neck in front of her; she could hardly believe it. She was riding.

Chapter Two

They rode north, under a high sun, following the rough dirt road that would one day become smooth and tarmacked. There were a few houses along the road, or dotting the hills to their left, but mostly the landscape seemed quiet, untouched. To Jasmine, it seemed like another place, another country almost, but every so often she saw something she recognised; a bend in the road, a wood to her left, and she knew exactly where she was. It was, she decided, feeling slightly odd, two completely different things at the same time, and yet neither of them feeling quite right.

"How long do you think it'll take? To get to Killaspugbrone, I mean." Jasmine mopped her forehead.

The afternoon was surprisingly warm, or maybe it was the stupid coat. Once again, she found herself wishing she could take it off.

Seamus squinted. "Most of the day, I think."

Most of the day. It seemed like eternity. They continued.

"Seamus?"

"Hmm?"

"I was thinking. I know you don't like using Influence, and I understand why, but with that man, er… it's just, if it works so well, surely there are worse things?"

There was a pause.

"There are," Seamus agreed. "But Tionchar's the ultimate manipulation. It takes the feelings and frailties of others, their hopes and dreams, their love, their fears and weaknesses and uses them to satisfy our ends. Does that remind you of anyone?"

"Ellyllon."

"Exactly. He's a master of it. You know the pain of being lied to, of being manipulated. Not just by him, but by me and John, lying to you—"

"But that's different," she interrupted him quickly. "I understand now why you and John did it. You waited until I was ready; you did it to protect me."

"But does that make it any better? I was so certain I was right, but now I'm not so sure." He shook his head, as if to clear it from unwelcome thoughts. "No, Tionchar's dangerous. With it, we whisper into a person's ear and change what they do, what they think, maybe even what they believe in. That's a terrible power, and seductive, not least for us. If we use it too often and too lightly, who knows what we will become?"

"Like Ellyllon?"

"Yes." His smile of approval was tinged with sadness. "Like Ellyllon. Hollow, empty, with nothing but a burn for power."

*

They rode for more than two hours. For Jasmine, the novelty of riding was beginning to wear off. Seamus might've planted the knowledge of how to ride in her mind, but he hadn't been able to do anything for her muscles or bottom, and they were starting to feel very sore. She almost asked if they could stop so that she could get down and stretch, walk about for a minute, but was afraid she'd never get back on again. The road undulated; they climbed the last slope and, as the ground levelled out, the trees opened out and she saw it. Knocknarea! And behind it, Benbulben, its narrow, chiselled length like the upturned hull of a ship. They were almost there. She gazed at the familiar green and grey slopes, the distinctive flat top, as if someone had lopped the top of it, and there, at the far end, the outline of Queen Maeve's tomb, a darker grey against the fading blue of the sky. Her heart lifted. Malachy was there; she knew it suddenly, inexplicably, waiting for them just the other side.

"Seamus, look, we're almost there!" She pointed excitedly.

"Ah, we've a way to go yet. It's just the perspective makes it look closer."

It was true, she realised, her smile dropping. She'd lost her bearings, got confused by what seemed an endless journey. Constantly visible now by the flatness of the land, Knocknarea remained stubbornly in the distance, almost as if it were teasing them by moving back as they moved forward. And yet, slowly, imperceptibly, it grew closer.

Abruptly, Seamus stopped his horse and turned to look at her.

"There's a crossroads up ahead. Left takes us around Knocknarea and on to the coast. But we're close to the river. It's over there." He pointed right. "We should stop, rest the horses and ourselves. Do you want something to eat?"

Jasmine looked at her watch. Half past four. She thought of Malachy.

"If we're that close, can't we keep going?"

"We should rest the horses, and if you don't stretch yer be stiff in the morning."

"I'm already stiff."

Actually, she was beyond stiff. She'd lost feeling in her bottom some time ago.

"It won't take long, and they need to drink."

He clicked his tongue and he moved off to the right, and reluctantly she followed him.

*

They followed the road around Knocknarea's lower slopes. Jasmine twisted her head to look upwards at the exposed granite, cut and sheared by the elements. To her left, just visible through the gaps in the trees, the ocean twinkled in the early evening sunlight.

"We've not got long now."

Knocknarea dropped away and the whole of the peninsula was revealed, the ocean beyond it.

Staring, Seamus reigned in his horse. "That's odd."

"What?" Jasmine came alongside him.

"Look, you can see the church tower; that's Killaspugbrone, but I can't see any houses."

Jasmine shielded her eyes with her hand. The only houses she could see were a few tiny white cottages dotting the land away from the coast. "Won't there be sand dunes?"

"No. If I've got my history right, and I think I have, the sand hasn't overtaken the village yet." He frowned. "Let's go. I want to see it up close."

Moving off, he pushed his horse into a fast trot. His sudden urgency was alarming. Jasmine followed, her stomach fluttering.

They reached ground level and the church disappeared behind a small wood. The land was rough, the grass thick, looking as if it could barely sustain the few houses they passed. All was quiet. The wood retreated and the church tower came into view again. They passed a white stone cottage on their left and saw a man digging in the field next to it. Hearing them, he stopped work and looked up. Seamus raised his hand and shouted in greeting, but he didn't answer, just watched them, his eyes dark. Continuing, Jasmine looked back a couple of times. He was still staring at them. She shivered. Ahead of her, Seamus stopped abruptly.

"Seamus, what is it?"

"The track. It's gone."

He was right. It just stopped, disappearing into sand. Dismounting, keeping hold of the reins, he skirted the edge. Jasmine watched him nervously.

"Seamus, where's the road gone?"

"More than that, where's the village? Killaspugbrone should be just ahead."

She scanned the horizon. Apart from the top of the church tower, a section of the church wall and a tall, High Cross, the same High Cross Ellyllon had leant against, there was nothing but sand.

"Oh my God, Seamus, what happened?"

He stared back at her, horrified.

"The village was overtaken with the sand, about four months back. It was a storm. Most of them didn't have time to get out."

They turned towards the voice. The man had tracked them, following them unnoticed from the other side of a wall. He leant on it.

"There was no warning."

"That's not possible," Seamus protested quickly. "What storm could do that?"

The man crossed himself. "The Devil's."

There was a pause.

"How many?"

"Thirty-eight, almost half young 'uns." Jasmine's hand flew to her mouth, but he ignored her, his whole attention fixed on Seamus. "What business have ye here?"

Seamus bowed his head for a moment, thinking.

"Did you see a lad about the place?" he asked then, his voice light and deceptively casual. "A stranger?"

The man's head lifted slightly, his cold eyes becoming even more suspicious, more hostile.

"And what's that to thee?"

"He's kin. We've been looking for him this past time."

"You'd best try the cottage down yonder." He indicated with his head "'Bout a mile back."

Seamus followed his gaze.

"But isn't that's the Padian house!" he exclaimed in surprise.

"Aye, Thady Padian's." The man's face softened slightly, but not by much, "Yer not local."

"No, I'm not local. Thank'ee for yer kindness."

The man's nod was almost imperceptible.

They rode in silence, the man's words echoing after them.

"Seamus," Jasmine spoke first, swallowing hard. "Was that me? Did I do that?"

Seamus wouldn't look at her. "I don't know, but I can't think what else, other than the void, could have so much power."

She felt sick. She could almost hear those people in her head: men, women and children screaming, choking, suffocating. Iomlan stirred inside her, agitated.

"You weren't to know," Seamus said softly.

Jasmine didn't answer, didn't trust herself to speak. It was as if the horse she was riding had kicked her.

"This wasn't you. It was Ellyllon."

"But I helped him."

She couldn't deny it and neither, if he were honest, could he. Without her, Ellyllon would have been powerless to open the void and thirty-eight people would still be alive.

"But you didn't help him willingly; the intent was all his." He sighed. "You mustn't blame yourself. That way lies madness."

Jasmine looked at the ground. She knew what he was saying, but it made no difference. She'd killed those people as surely as if she'd taken a gun and shot them. She felt contaminated, as if her guilt stained and marked her, like a brand.

"Jasmine, look." He rose up, his legs ramrod straight against the stirrups, and pointed to a chimney, with smoke coming out of it, just visible over the curve of the land. "There. That's Padian's."

*

The house lay at the base of Knocknarea, just beyond the point where the land rose. Darkened by the cast of Knocknarea's shadow, it was tiny, no more than two rooms beneath thatch; the musky scent of burning turf filling the air around it. The track up to it was steep, stony, so they dismounted and led the horses by the reins. It was hard going and, stiff and tired, Jasmine's legs ached. Her heart thumped, the sound loud in her ears, but she didn't slow. The stranger had to be Malachy. He was up there, a few metres from them, maybe in one of the rooms inside. The thought made her dizzy. They reached a yard, framed by the house and outbuildings on two sides, a gate, leading to fields, and land the other. It was empty; the only sign of life the turf smoke and the door to the house left wide open.

"Wait here." Seamus passed her the reins of his horse, and walking over to the house, stuck his head inside. "Hello?"

Jasmine shifted impatiently. Abruptly, a man stepped out of the shed, his head stooped to avoid the low door frame, making her jump. Spotting her, he froze.

"Can I help ye?"

Seamus' head reappeared. "No, Thady Padian, but ya can help me."

The man turned to look at him, "Do I know ye?"

Seamus smiled, coming forward. "No, but I knew yer father when you were just a boy. Me name's Seamus, Seamus Higgins."

An exclamation came from inside the shed, followed by a loud clatter. A scruffy, mud encrusted collie, all black but for a patch of white on its neck and between its front legs, ran out, followed by a young man dressed in shirt and trousers. Jasmine's heart stopped. It was Malachy. He saw Seamus, then Jasmine, and went pale. He looked thinner, leaner, the clothes hanging off him. His hair had grown long, the ends curling. He made a sound as if trying to speak, and before she knew what she was doing, Jasmine dropped the reins and ran over to him, shrieking his name like a person demented. She threw her arms around him, almost knocking him to the ground.

"Mal, it's you, it's really you; you're alive!" she gabbled.

*

Iomlan ran down her body and spilled outwards, covering Malachy with tiny jolts, like electricity, as if it too were glad to see him. He looked down at her, as if seeing her for the first time.

"Mal, it's me, Jasmine. What happened? Are you OK?" Concerned, she let him go and took a step back.

He nodded slowly, his eyes enormous. "I think I need to sit down."

"Oh." Looking about, she spotted a woodcutter's stump. "Here." She guided him to it, hovering anxiously as he stared blankly into space. "Mal?"

A hand pressed her shoulder. It was Seamus, his touch soothing, reassuring.

"Jas, he's in shock. Take a breath and give him a minute."

She did as he said, watching as he squatted down in front of Malachy. "Malachy, it's good to see you. Sorry it took us so long."

It was a strange thing to say; it hadn't been *that* long, just over a day.

Malachy turned to look at him. "I thought I'd be here forever; that I'd never get home."

"But you must've known we'd come and find you!" Jasmine protested.

"I didn't know if you could." He shook his head. "After four months you give up."

"Four months? But that's not possible!" Open-mouthed, she looked at Seamus and he shrugged, spreading his hands wide. She turned back to Malachy. "We'd never have left you. I thought you were dead. I thought I'd killed you."

It was too much; her voice broke, tears threatening, and she swallowed hard, trying to keep them at bay.

"Do I look dead?" he asked her suddenly, plaintively, something of the usual Malachy coming back.

"N-o," she gulped.

"I know I don't look great. It's these curls." He flicked his hair with his hand. "It was either that or let Thady loose with the sheep shears."

Grinning, he stood up, and he was back and they were both laughing and hugging, and this time Jasmine let herself cry.

*

She was still crying when Thady came over to them, his movements hesitant, as if he was reluctant to intrude. They broke apart and Jasmine quickly wiped her eyes.

"This is Thady." Malachy's smile was bright with affection, "He saved my life. Thady, this is Jasmine."

"Saved your life?!"

"Malachy makes too much of it, and now he takes care of me."

His smile, with two of the front and most of his back teeth gone, was shy, quiet. There was a gentleness about him, a kindness that seemed to emanate from the light in his pale grey-blue eyes. Jasmine liked him instantly.

"Malachy, why don't you take Ja-Jasmine inside, next to the fire. Make a bit of tea, a bite to eat. It's getting late."

Malachy nodded and led her across the yard. At the door she glanced back, Seamus and Thady were in the same place. They hadn't moved.

"We're right behind ya," Seamus called reassuringly, and she followed Malachy indoors.

*

Thady's cottage had just two rooms. The larger living room, which, being true to its name, was where everything but sleep was done, and a small bedroom through a low door on the far side of the hearth. It was a plain room, basic, but neat and surprisingly warm despite the white, empty walls and bare stone floor, with the heat coming from a turf fire in the hearth. Between the door to the bedroom and the far window was a dresser. A small, rough looking table lay under the window, a Sligo chair next to it. A second chair, a discoloured, high-backed Windsor one, was sat in front of the hearth. The only decoration was a handful of crockery sat on the dresser and a small, cream coloured china cross given pride of place. A heavy looking iron kettle was attached to a ring over the fire.

"We usually eat about now, so the kettle's already on," Malachy explained. "But it takes ages, so I'll try to speed it up." Using a poker he gave the fire a heavy stoke before adding more turf.

"Sit down." He waved one vague hand and she sat in the chair next to the fire.

She watched, marvelling, as he busied himself, getting everything ready in the way his great grandparents would've done without a second thought.

"How did you find me?" Malachy asked, not looking up.

"The tombs at Carrowkeel. They have some kind of power. You can move through time, like a conduit."

That made him look. "Shit!" He laughed softly, incredulously, "But how did you know where to find me?"

"We didn't. It's hard to explain, but basically, I, er, I mean, we, focussed on you, and the tomb took us to you."

She looked down, afraid she'd given herself away. She needn't have worried; Malachy seemed too busy to notice. Stacking the crockery on the dresser, he carried it to the table and began to place them: plates, cups, almost all chipped or cracked and discoloured with time.

"If you can use the tomb to travel through time, why didn't Ellyllon use it?" he asked suddenly, looking up.

"Seamus says the power's protected. The druids did it to stop people like Ellyllon using it."

"But I thought the tomb was much older than the druids?"

"It is, and the power is, but I guess the druids didn't want it misused." She sighed. "Seamus explains it better."

There was a pause.

"So, how, er… what's it been like, living here?"

"Odd, at first. There were so many things I missed; me family, food, I mean our food, I still dream of chips, proper chips from the chipper." He paused, smiled dreamily. "The internet, music, TV that sort of thing, and of course, an inside toilet." He snorted. "But it's amazing what you get used to. And after a while you stop noticing."

The kettle began to steam, and Malachy dashed over to it, lifting it off the hook with a stained and discoloured cloth.

"Can you tell Seamus and Thady it's ready?"

"Sure." She got gingerly to her feet, feeling the muscles in her thighs protest, and went back outside.

With the yard empty, there was no sign of either Seamus or Thady. The shed too, was empty, but now she could hear voices, talking softly. It took her a moment. They weren't inside the shed, they were behind it. She followed the sound to where Seamus and Thady were standing, their backs to her and Knocknarea, looking out across the land to the sea, watching as the sun set. She stopped, the beauty of the view catching her unawares.

"I thought he'd be soft with those hands, but he's not; he's a hard worker. Got used to him about."

It was Thady speaking, and as Jasmine watched, Seamus' head turned towards him.

"We came here to find him. His people are looking for him."

Thady nodded. "Good family?"

"Yes-s, you could say that." For a moment, Jasmine thought Seamus was going to say something more, but he changed his mind.

"I thought so. Ya can see he's used to a different kind of life." Thady sighed. "When will you leave?"

"As soon as Malachy's ready."

"Then you'll stay the night. Set off in the morning."

There was a pause. Jasmine knew she should say something, do something to let them know that she was there, but she couldn't help herself. She continued to listen.

"You never asked Malachy how he got here?"

"At first he was sick with the fever. Then, later, I thought if he wanted me to know, he'd tell me."

"He was lucky it was you who found him and took him in."

"Ah, anybody'd do the same."

"I'm not so sure. I heard they called it the Devil's storm."

"The Devil's storm!" Thady snorted. "But if I'm honest, there have been a few looks, alright. That's not just superstition," he quantified quickly. "It's the way the lad talks sometimes. Ya can tell he's different. But I've kept him close and no one dared say anything to him in my hearing."

Seamus turned suddenly. "Jasmine?"

She flushed. "Er, the tea's ready."

"We're coming now," Seamus replied, and something in the way he looked at her told her that he'd known all along she was there.

*

Jasmine took a small sip of her tea. Dark, stewed and tasting faintly of metal, it was all she could do to keep it down, but the last thing she wanted was to insult Thady. She took another sip. No one spoke. There was a sad, mournful air to the room, despite the blazing glow of the fire and the food. She'd been given one of the chairs, Seamus taking the second as a guest, only reluctantly.

*

Later, with Seamus and Thady sharing a smoke by the fire, Jasmine and Malachy washed and cleaned the crockery in a bucket just outside. Malachy had brought out a candle but the sky was clear, without a cloud, the moon bright, illuminating the ground as effectively as the floodlights in a stadium.

"You said Thady saved your life."

"Yeah, he found me. I remember him kneeling over me; I think it was the next morning. Thady said that it rained bad after the storm, and I'd got a chill. He nursed me for over two weeks. I was so weak; he did everything for me, just like yer mam would." He looked away, embarrassed. "It wasn't until later I realised that he took me in when nobody else would've."

She thought of what Thady had said. "They're horrible. You could've died out there."

He took a plate from her. "No, Jas they're not horrible. Look, it's hard for us to understand, but they don't have our education, and to them that storm was unearthly, supernatural, evil; it caused the death of thirty-eight people. And then I appear just after it, strangely dressed and odd, and no-one knows me or knows where I've come from. So they think I had something to do with it. In a way, they're right."

She stared into the bucket, at her hands as they reached for a cup at the bottom. "I can't imagine what it's been like. So many people gone in just one night."

He tapped her shoulder, getting her attention. "Jas, you can't blame yourself for what happened."

She looked at him, but his face was unreadable. "Who else can I blame?"

"Just a guess, but maybe Ellyllon?"

She sighed. "Oh, I know. He loaded the gun. But it was me who fir—" She stopped, flapped one hand irritably. "The only thing I can do is help Seamus stop him."

It's the only way I can begin to make amends, she told herself silently.

"But how are you going to do that?"

"I don't know," she admitted. "But I have to try. Seamus thinks he's going back to the time of the druids… to get his revenge on them, or worse."

"So you're going back there too?"

"Yeah. After we take you home, of course."

She passed him the cup.

"Of course," he repeated, wiping it furiously.

Chapter Three

Jasmine climbed into bed. She'd been reluctant to take it and leave the three men on the floor in the sitting room, but Thady had insisted. It didn't seem fair, especially given Thady's age, or Seamus' even, but her protests had fallen on deaf ears. There was no way, Thady had said, his jaw sticking out determinedly, he'd allow a woman in his house to sleep on the floor or in the same room as the men. She pulled the blanket tight. Ironically, she'd've been warmer in the sitting room. Even with the fire Malachy had lit in the small fireplace, the room felt cold. Pulling her knees up towards her chin, she closed her eyes and willed sleep to come.

...Standing atop Knocknarea, she faced Maeve's tomb. It was huge, bigger than she'd been expecting, made up of layer upon layer of black stones. Framed against bright blue sky above, and the ocean mirrored below, they glistened in the sunlight. She moved closer. The sides were flawless, unbroken. There was no opening, no doorway, and yet she knew exactly what to do. She reached the end of the path. The top of the cairn loomed high above her; she was too close now to see its peak and Iomlan stirred. It fluttered up through her stomach, a sensation like tickling that set her teeth on edge, and up towards her throat. She spoke, just one word, from a language she'd never heard before, and the stones of the cairn shifted and blurred. She found herself looking at an entrance similar to the one she'd seen at Carrowkeel. With a quick glance around her, the smallest of hesitations, she stepped inside.

It was pitch-black, cold. Only inches from daylight and no light or warmth penetrated the air or illuminated the way. She shuffled forward cautiously. Part of her wanted to turn, to spin around and flee, back in to the warmth and the sunlight, but she couldn't. It was as if something was pulling her, drawing her on, step by step, into darkness. Instinctively she raised her arms, hands, trying to use them as a guide, but they stretched out into nothing, touched nothing. She took another step, then two more, and stopped, some instinct telling her that she was in the epicentre of the cairn. Almost immediately there was a small flicker of light, off to her right. It brightened, growing quickly until it permeated the darkness and showed her a long stone coffin that lay nestled along one wall. Even in the half-light she could see the intricacy of the etchings that covered the lid and sides, swirls and spirals in ones and threes, strange looking animals, shapes that reminded her of the carpenter in Sligo, the Croi. She shifted her weight and was preparing to step closer for a better look when she felt the warmth of soft breath on her neck and caught the scent of heather, peat, grass. She turned.

The face of an old woman pressed close to hers, framed by a black hood. Her skin was thin, so pale that Jasmine could see tinges of the blue veins underneath, the cheeks etched with a crisscross of thick, deep lines that stretched from the cheeks' hollows downwards to a chin hanging loose and upwards to the sockets of her eyes. White hair, grown wispy, poked out from under the hood. But it was her eyes that drew Jasmine. They were opaque with age, the colour almost but not quite leeched out of them, the irises underneath kept bright with a vivid emerald. The woman's mouth opened, showing teeth thin and brittle, threatening to crack and split like sun warmed slate, and she spoke. It wasn't English. Bewildered, Jasmine shook her head, and the woman spoke again, frowning impatiently.

"I don't understand." The words were on her lips but nothing came out. Then the woman spoke again, her voice urgent.

Abruptly, her eyes began to change, the opaqueness clearing as the green of her irises burned and melted it away. Jasmine gasped and took a step back, but the old woman grabbed her wrist, held it tight between bony fingers. She tried to pull away, but the woman was too strong, and in desperation she summoned Iomlan. Nothing happened. Her mind whirling, she tried again, and this time Iomlan responded, but sluggishly, as if it were unwilling to move. The woman was still talking, now saying just one word, over and over. The hand holding Jasmine's wrist twisted, the nails digging in as a second hand grabbed the back of her neck, forcing her head forward. Green eyes glowed, the mouth closing onto hers. She tried to turn her head away, to get Iomlan to do something, anything. Their lips touched. She felt the rough taste of cold hard stone, the tickle of soft, green moss and her mouth was forced open. Stone filled her mouth, forced its way into her throat, cutting off the air. She coughed, her throat convulsing, choking as she tried to swallow something too hard, too solid, and then the hand released its grip and she was falling backwards and away . . .

*

Jasmine woke. Sunlight shone in through the thin curtain, brightening the small, dark room. She swallowed, feeling the rawness of her throat, as if the sides had been scratched and scraped. Last night's dream was still with her, still vivid; she could almost smell the old woman, her scent that was earth, leaf and stone. It had seemed so real. She swallowed again. She must've been shouting in her sleep, her mouth working silently, drying out her mouth.

"Jasmine? Are you awake?" It was Malachy, knocking lightly on the door.

"Yeah." She sat up.

"Seamus said we need to go soon."

"Oh, OK." She pulled back the blanket. "I won't be long."

*

They ate breakfast together, porridge cooked with buttermilk.

Seamus stood up, draining his cup. "It's time we were going. Thady, I want you to take this."

He put his hand into the inner pocket of his coat and brought out almost all the money he'd won and placed it into Thady's hands. Thady stared at it in amazement.

"But, but, this is a fortune!" he spluttered.

"Not quite." Seamus grinned. "I want you to use it for the people, the families left behind after the storm, to help them start again. But keep something back for yourself. Call it payment for caring for Malachy if ya will."

"But Seamus!"

"It's not mine. It was given me from someone who has so much he feels no loss of it." The flecks of auburn in Seamus' eyes gleamed suddenly; the colour of fire. "You'd be doing him a good turn; help him save his soul."

Thady laughed at that. "In that case, I'll take it with thanks. We'll use it to build a new village, away from the sea."

They shook hands.

"Come on, Jasmine, we'll get the horses ready." Seamus looked meaningfully at Malachy and Thady.

"Yeah, course." She got up and walked over to Thady. "Thank you, for everything."

She raised herself up slightly and kissed him lightly on the cheek. He gave her his shy smile and nodded and she left quickly, Seamus following.

They waited for Malachy outside.

"The village, away from the sea. That's Strandhill, isn't it?" Jasmine asked Seamus curiously.

"It is." He nodded, smiling. "Much later, they build the promenade there."

"Because of you."

"Ah." Shaking his head, he played with the horse's bridle.

But it was true. By giving Thady that money, he enabled the rebuilding of the village. It was a comforting thought, as if somehow Seamus was making amends for what she'd done. And now it was her turn. They *had* to find Ellyllon and stop him. Malachy appeared in the doorway, wearing his old clothes.

"I'm ready," he said as he joined them.

They all looked at one another.

"OK, then. Malachy, you're going to have to ride with Jasmine. I know it's not the best for the horse, but we've not got far to go and we can take it slow. There's a Neolithic site just the other side of Knocknarea. We can use that. Have you ridden before?"

Malachy nodded. "Yeah, but it's been a while." He saw Jasmine looking curiously at him. "Me uncle has horses on his farm, down in Cork. He taught me to ride."

"That's grand."

"You can be in front," Jasmine offered quickly, glad of the respite. She held out the reins.

Malachy looked down at them, but he didn't take them.

"Seamus, I've been thinking," he said slowly. "When I was in the void with Ellyllon… at one point we were sort of fighting, and then we were pulled apart. He went one way and I went the other. Couldn't he be here, now, in this time?"

Seamus rubbed his chin, his eyes narrowing. "It's possible, but I don't sense him here, and I'm sure Jasmine would've felt him when we were in the tomb. Besides, if you were parted there's no telling how far apart you both fell; it could be centuries. But you're right; he could be anywhere, in any time, or he could be exactly where he intended to go. It doesn't change anything though; we still need to get to Carrowmore."

Malachy nodded and, taking the reins from her, stepped close to the horse, stroking and touching its face and neck, talking softly, introducing himself. He eyed the stirrups critically, adjusted them expertly then climbed on with one easy movement. He glanced down at Jasmine and grinned.

"Are you coming?" He offered his arm, took his foot out of the stirrup.

She replaced her foot with his and, grabbing his arm, used it as a bolster to heave herself upwards. Once more she landed neatly.

"Not bad," Malachy said admiringly. "But don't forget to hold on."

She did as she was told, leaning in so that she could hold him around the waist.

"Wait!" It was Thady, running awkwardly across the yard, his collie running alongside him.

Breathing heavily, he reached up one hand towards at Malachy. "I couldn't let thee go without giving ya this."

He pressed something small and shiny into the palm of Malachy's hand.

"Thady!" Malachy protested, lifting up his hand to look. A silver chain, small, and delicate, slipped out from between his fingers. "I can't take this. It was your father's!"

"And intended for my son." He smiled faintly.

"But…?" Malachy reached down, forcing Jasmine to let go, and gave Thady an awkward half hug.

She looked away. They'd got so close so quickly, and yet Thady had been long dead, even his gravestone old and decaying, by the time Malachy was born.

"Ah, now, Malachy," Thady was saying, as he pulled gently away.

Malachy straightened, his hand with the chain still in it going to his eyes. Jasmine, slipping her arms back around his waist, felt him gulping for air. She pressed her cheek to his back and squeezed him once, trying to let him know she understood, but if he noticed her he didn't show it.

"Goodbye Thady." Seamus raised his hand in salute as he turned his horse, and slowly walked it back down the track.

Malachy took one long look, as if trying to memorise Thady's face, then urged his horse after him. He didn't look back, but Jasmine, swivelling awkwardly, did it for him. Thady had raised his hand and was holding it upright, like the hand of a man drowning. She lifted hers, but the curve of land deepened. For a moment, he was cut in half, only his torso and head and shoulders visible as he held his hand up high. Then he was gone.

*

Reaching the road, they turned right, following it north as it skirted around the slopes of Knocknarea. The air was fresh despite the growing heat, and a gentle breeze played across their faces and bodies, bringing with it the faint trace of salt carrying all the way from the sea. Malachy hadn't spoken since they'd left and she left him to it, knowing there was nothing she could say. Encircled in her arms, his body was warm, his back moving against her, following the step of the horse. For a moment, the urge to press, to tighten her grip and mould her body to his was overwhelming. She imagined him turning, his face lowering, his lips slipping over hers, his tongue… she pushed the thought away.

"Hey," Malachy said, half turning. "Don't let go."

"I'm not," she lied quickly. "I was just getting stiff."

She took a deep breath. She was being silly. Malachy saw her as nothing more than a friend, and worse, had just said goodbye to the old man he'd come to love. She wasn't just being silly, she was being selfish. Finding Ellyllon should be her only concern. Squaring her shoulders, she looked up at Knocknarea, wanting the distraction. It was strange, but she'd never really looked at it before. Studied its lines and contours. Or noticed the myriad of colours, the subtly changing shades of green. Now she was looking at it, she realised there was a softness to it, despite the coarse, hard stone and sheer cliff face lacerated by falling water. Maybe it was the lower slopes that made it seem so lush with greenery, or the faint purple tinge to the grey granite.

The road twisted left, then right. The horses continued, their step slow and even and their heads nodding rhythmically. It was so quiet. Jasmine yawned. The sun, hot on her back, was having a soporific effect. Unbidden, Iomlan swirled lazily inside her. She knew she should push it down, but couldn't seem to summon up the energy. It was so good to be in the sun, she thought dreamily, feeling the heat on her skin and seeing the blue sky high above her so completely empty of clouds. Her head floated. Knocknarea was friendlier than she remembered, comforting, like a reminder of home. Against the blue sky, the cairn perched on the edge of the flat summit cast a wide, dark shadow. She thought of her dream and wondered idly what she'd find inside. Would it be the dark, inner place, empty but for the stone coffin? Or the old woman? The old woman; she had such green eyes. They seemed strangely familiar. But that was dreams — your mind took reality and warped it, melted it like a pocket watch in a Dali painting.

*

"There's Carrowmore," Seamus called back at them, pointing ahead.

Jasmine gazed over Malachy's shoulder and saw nothing more than a large, uneven field. Iomlan stabbed, the pain in her stomach sharp as it was sudden. An image flashed through her head, and without thinking she followed it.

Around her, men were fighting, their voices grunting, shouting and screaming. She heard the clash of weapons, the scrape of metal, saw the grass around her red with blood, patches of sliced flesh and hacked limbs. Something moved behind her. She span, seeing a man jump towards her, his thick, heavy-looking sword raised high in both hands. He was too late. She thrust. Skewered him expertly in the stomach, then twisted. He screamed and fell backwards, and she helped him go, watching dispassionately as his body slid off her sword, leaving the metal smeared with red. Her head whirled, the noise fading, as if someone had turned down the volume. She blinked and the men vanished.

There was no battle, no weapon in her hand or blood on the grass. The pain in her stomach, like the twang of a stiff muscle, was gone almost as soon as it came. Rubbing her belly, she wondered what had caused it, where the image had come from. She'd read somewhere that ghosts were imprints of traumatic events. Was it possible that Iomlam had picked up and replayed a battle once fought here? She thought of asking Seamus, but he had enough to think about.

"Is that it?" Malachy was asking. "Where's the tombs?"

"Most of them were destroyed through one thing or another. But the main one's over there, just the other side of the ridge. Come on."

He dismounted, Jasmine and then Malachy following.

"They're all around there." He pointed again as he walked. "See the stones?"

Some, she realised, were buried; others, the walls and roofs gone. Close up, the monument was much bigger than it had looked, with an intricate series of connected grassy mounds, low standing stones and circles. It must have been a place of great importance. Maybe that was it, Jasmine decided quickly; Iomlan was reacting to the power within it.

"Now, we want the central tomb," Seamus explained distractedly, looking around him. "It's been a while since I was last here."

"What about the horses?" Malachy asked.

"We'll leave them free, I'm sure someone will find them, but if not, they'll be fine."

"We should've left them with Thady. He could do with them."

"I never thought of that," Seamus admitted, flushing. "Still, he has the money now to buy his own."

*

With Seamus still leading, they reached the top of the ridge. At the bottom, built into the side of the ridge, was a tomb. Or rather, half a tomb. One side had fallen away, leaving slabs of stone lying higgledy-piggledy across the grass.

"It's broken," Jasmine exclaimed.

"That's OK. It doesn't need to be intact," Seamus said as he started down the ridge.

Reaching the tomb, he got down on his haunches and, muttering a curse, clambered awkwardly inside. They followed, the three of them manoeuvring to give one another room.

"Now, Malachy, take my hand and Jasmine's. That's it." He took Jasmine's hand in his other. "Keep a good hold of us. We don't want to lose you again. Jasmine, it's the same as before, only this time think of home, focus on going home. Now, are yer ready?"

"I think so." Malachy swallowed noisily, looking from one to the other.

Jasmine smiled to reassure him, then closed her eyes.

"Wait!" It was Malachy. Jasmine, feeling him let go of her hand, opened her eyes in surprise. "I don't want to go home, I want to come with you."

"But you can't. It's too dangerous." Seamus shook his head. "And yer parents are waiting."

"I know, but — I can't go home and leave you two looking for Ellyllon. I know I don't have any power, but I can help. I know I can."

"You're right, you don't have any power," Seamus agreed bluntly. "And that makes it even more dangerous for you than for us. It also makes you very vulnerable to Ellyllon."

"Oh, and you and Jasmine aren't vulnerable to him?! Surely the whole point is that Ellyllon manipulates, and he can manipulate you two as much as me. Maybe less so, because he wouldn't bother with me."

"No, he'd just walk through you!" Jasmine retorted angrily. Immediately, she was sorry. "I'm sorry, Mal, I shouldn't've said that."

"It's true. I know it's a risk, but it's my risk to take." He stared at her, exasperated. "I can't just go home and leave you both here and pretend nothing's happening, I just can't! And you shouldn't expect me to."

"Well, you can if we won't take you, and we won't, will we, Seamus?!" He didn't answer. "Seamus?!"

"I think Malachy has earned the right to choose."

"What? You can't be serious!"

"It's Malachy's decision to make." Seamus' face was grim. "But in making it, Malachy, I want you to remember this. You aren't just more vulnerable to Ellyllon, you make us, Jasmine and me, more vulnerable, because he can use you to get to us." He sighed. "But you may be right, and your lack of power is also your strength. It's your choice."

There was a pause.

"Then I'm coming."

"Agreed." Seamus looked hard at Jasmine, silencing her before she could protest again. "Now, Malachy, take hold again, and Jasmine, focus on Ellyllon."

She closed her eyes, toying with the idea of focussing on home instead. Once they were there, surely Malachy would have no choice but to stay?

"Remember, Jasmine. Focus on Ellyllon."

He'd done it again, read her mind, or maybe simply guessed. Sighing inwardly, she did as he said and focussed on Ellyllon before summoning Iomlan. The spinning began, slowly at first and then gathering speed, and she was lost in the moment, forgetting everything but her desire to find Ellyllon.

Chapter Four

The spinning seemed to last much longer this time. Feeling sick, Jasmine just wanted it to end, but somehow she kept her focus. Finally the whining in her ears lessened and the tomb slowed to a stop. Instantly, she knew Ellyllon was there. They'd found him. She opened her eyes. Seamus was looking at her and she knew he felt him too. Malachy's eyes were still closed. His face was very pale, and he swallowed convulsively. His hand in hers, she noticed suddenly, was slick with sweat.

"Mal, it's over."

He opened his eyes and heaved.

"Shit!" Snatching his hands away, he covered his mouth.

Still heaving, he crawled out of the tomb and scrambled shakily to his feet. He disappeared, swaying as he tried to run. She and Seamus looked at one another.

"And how are you feeling?" he asked.

"Sick, but better than last time. I don't think I'm going to throw up."

"You must be getting used to it." Seamus unbent his legs, his knees creaking. "Let's get out of here."

They climbed out, Seamus going first then turning back to help her to her feet.

"He's here. You felt him."

She nodded, although it wasn't a question. "I don't know where exactly, but I know he's here."

"I feel the same." He gave her a solemn look. "Before Malachy gets back, I need you to promise me something. Don't use Iomlan unless you really have to, or unless I tell you to."

"I know." She nodded. "You don't want people to know."

"No, it's not that. Not just that. You know Ellyllon can sense us, sense our Iomlan. There's a way to hide our presence, deflect his senses. It's easy enough, if we don't use Iomlan, but using it, it's like a beacon. And the younger we are, the less experienced, the bigger the bloody beacon." She went to speak but he waved her away. "Oh, he'll know we're coming. Even if he doesn't sense us, he knows I'll try to stop him. I just want to give him as little warning as possible. Agreed?"

"Yeah, I suppose. But what, if, you know, it slips out?"

"Then we'll deal with it. But try not to let it."

They looked about them. Everything looked exactly the same; the stones, the field, the bright sun and blue sky. Except everything looked bigger, bushier, greener. And hotter, much hotter.

"It's summer," Seamus concluded as Malachy reappeared, wiping his mouth self-consciously.

"Do you know when we are? What century?"

Seamus shrugged. "No idea. But the best thing to do is to aim for Sligo." He gave Malachy a speculative look. "How are you feeling?"

"Better. Is it always like that?"

"Inside the tomb? Yes, but I think it gets easier. Are you up to walking?"

"Of course."

Seamus smiled. "Then we should get going. It's not far to Sligo, but we've only got our feet."

"You know which way to go?" Malachy asked.

"I do. It's this way." He nodded.

They began to walk, Seamus slightly ahead, Jasmine and Malachy behind, falling naturally in step together.

"Are you sure you're OK?" Jasmine asked.

"Yeah. But I wouldn't want to do that too often. It's like being on a fairground ride; you want to get off as soon as it starts."

It was the perfect description.

*

They walked for over an hour, across grassland mostly, although they could see trees, the edge of the woods ahead of them, off to the right.

"This is all so weird. I can't get my head around it. First it was spring, and now it's summer, and just two days ago it was winter." Jasmine glanced at Malachy. "You had Christmas with Thady. What was it like?"

"Different. I hadn't long been up and at first it was quiet and a bit depressing, but Thady seemed so happy to have the company..." He shook his head. "I think the quiet was the hardest thing, but in the end, all I missed was people." He grinned. "I even missed my sister."

They laughed. "But on Christmas Day, two of Thady's neighbours joined us. Tommy played the whistle, Mick the bodhran, I tapped my feet and Thady sang." His eyes misted. "He didn't have the best voice, but the feeling he put in it..."

He shook his head in disbelief then smiled again. She listened, fascinated.

"You should've seen the night of my birthday. When Thady heard it was my eighteenth, he invited the neighbours. Most of them didn't come, but a few did. Mrs Kelly even made me a cake, and there was poitin. God, that stuff is lethal! My head the next day… I thought I was going to die."

"Shit." She stopped in midstride. "I've just realised. If it's summer, I've missed mine."

"Missed what?" Malachy stopped two paces ahead of her.

"My birthday. My seventeenth."

"Oh, happy birthday. Sorry I forgot your card." He waited for her to catch up. "But maybe it doesn't work like that. I had my birthday; I was actually, y'know, somewhere. But with you, maybe, I dunno, your birthday's floating somewhere in time."

"What? Does that even make sense?" She shook her head at him, disgusted by his logic. "Does any of this make any sense?"

He laughed, spreading his arms wide. "But happy birthday anyway."

"Thanks." It was her turn to grin. "Have you got me a present?"

"Yeah; I've got it with me, been carrying it around with me for a few centuries."

Seamus looked over his shoulder at them. "Less talking would help ya walk faster."

"How long will it take to get to Sligo?" Jasmine asked.

"Another hour, probably." He turned back, upping the pace, and forcing them to do the same.

*

Seamus was right; it was almost an hour later when they saw the roofs of Sligo in the distance, but it took them another half an hour to reach the city wall. Dark grey, thick and incredibly high, each corner was punctuated with towers for lookout and defence. They could see the main gate, the portcullis up, the doors open wide. It was busy, chaotic with people, animals, horses and carts. Over the top of the wall flags fluttered in the wind and behind them they could just make out the towers of a square castle. Jasmine and Malachy stopped in midstride and Malachy's mouth fell open. A voice in Jasmine's head told her not to stare, but she couldn't help it. Sensing they were no longer with him, Seamus turned around. He sighed and then, coming back, led them sideways into the shadows of the trees and out of clear view.

"Give yerself a minute." He turned back to the castle and studied it intently.

"I didn't know Sligo had a castle," Jasmine whispered to Malachy.

"It doesn't. Well, it hasn't for a long time."

"I think this might be the fifteen-hundreds," Seamus announced suddenly.

"So Malachy was right; he knocked Ellyllon off course?!"

"It looks like it, and it might just give us an advantage." He gave a Jasmine reflective look, "How well do you know Irish history?"

"We're doing later history, but John went through the basics with me."

"Then you'll know it's a turbulent and bloody time; the English are trying to bring the Irish chieftains to heel, but they're fighting back. It's not the time to advertise the fact that you're English. You only have to meet the wrong person. Yer going to have to learn Irish."

"But it'll take ages for her to learn Irish. Mine's not that great either," Malachy interjected.

Seamus smiled. "Oh, I think we can find a quicker way."

*

Seamus was inside the castle walls. He was using his Iomlan. Jasmine could feel it, although it was very soft, very subtle. Surely, wherever Ellyllon was, he couldn't possibly feel that?

"How are you feeling?" she asked Malachy.

Sat in amongst the trees, their backs against a tall, thick oak, they were hidden from view.

"Like my head been squeezed it in a vice. You?"

"Oh, I'm OK. Having Iomlan helps."

"It's so weird. I have all these memories that I know aren't real."

"It is, isn't it? But as Seamus said, they will fade. It was the same with riding, I had all these memories of learning to ride, but I've already forgotten half of them."

Malachy nodded, then winced, his hand going to his head. "Aw, I shouldn't've done that."

Pressing his head back against the tree trunk, he closed his eyes. After a moment, Jasmine did the same.

"Jas?"

"Yeah?"

He nudged her with his shoulder. She opened her eyes.

"I'm feeling better."

"That's good."

"Why don't we try it? C'mon, say something in Irish."

"Like what?"

"Anything. The first thing that comes to mind."

"Cead mile failte."

He laughed. "Everyone in the world knows that! Say something else."

"Ta me lag leis an ocras."

"I'm starving too. Not bad. It's almost right; your accent must be getting in the way."

They practiced, keen to keep themselves busy. Easy for Malachy, but for her it was much harder. Especially the pronunciation. She heard the words in her head, as clear as a bell, but when she tried to fit her tongue around them it didn't seem to want to go.

"Hey, there's Seamus." Malachy scrambled to his feet, Jasmine following.

Leading three horses, each one carrying a bag made out of cloth, he stopped when he saw them. He'd changed his clothes and was wearing a shirt, jacket and trousers that looked more like leggings under a long brown, cloak.

"Don't say anything," he warned, seeing Malachy and Jasmine grin.

"No, of course not." Malachy's grin widened. "Oh great and mighty sorcerer."

"Very funny," Seamus replied acidly, moving to one of the bags and untying it with quick, deft fingers. "Laugh away; you'll be wearing this next."

"Oh, great." She paused. "You were ages; we thought something had happened."

He frowned. "Nothing happened. Only... I felt something, some power. I thought at first it was Ellyllon, but it was different." He shook his head. "It was too faint, almost as if it were being deliberately hidden. I couldn't find it."

"What do you think it was?"

"Not a clue." He shrugged. "It's not important. We need to go."

"Where are we going?" Malachy asked.

"South. People were reluctant to talk at first, but with a bit of persuasion—" He paused. "It might not be him, but I very much doubt it. He's been up to his auld tricks. Here." He handed her a bundle of clothes. "Be as quick as you can."

Slipping behind a tree, Jasmine changed into the shirt, fitted trousers, with a strange, front opening panel, like a hatch which could only be for one thing, and a sort of jacket-cum-waistcoat that she guessed might be called a doublet, leather shoes and cloak. She folded up her clothes.

"What shall I do with these?" she asked, stepping back out.

Malachy was stuffing his old clothes into one of the cloth bags, his cloak swaying with the movement.

"S-e-x-y!" She laughed.

Malachy threw her a look over one shoulder. "You don't look any better."

"No, I suppose not."

"Put yer clothes in the bag and this is your horse." Seamus lifted up a pair of reins." And have you got something to tie your hair up with? Right back, so with a hood you wouldn't see it. You'll attract less attention if you look like a boy."

"I don't think so." She examined her clothes as she put them away, looking for something that might do.

"Just pull it back. It'll do, for now." He looked from one to the other. "Rule one, from now on we speak Irish, even if there's no one else around. I'm not happy about your accent, Jasmine, but there's not much we can do about it. Maybe, for the moment, try to avoid talking around strangers unless you have to. There are differences in the Irish in this time to the Irish we know, but the dialect changes from area to area, so that will explain it. Rule two, do exactly what I say, when I say. Now, are yer ready to go?"

They nodded. Mounting their horses, they followed Seamus as he led them back towards the castle, then left, onto the road.

*

They travelled south. Wending its way through the trees, the road was narrow, just wide enough for a coach and horses, and rough, its surface little more than grass and soil worn down by centuries of passing. Near Sligo it was surprisingly busy, with the hustle and bustle of business drawing people in from the surrounding countryside, like blood flowing from capillaries into arteries. But not for long; already the flow was lessening, the gap between each traveller stretching out further and further. Apart from the twitter of birds and the soft rustle of the breeze through the trees, the forest was quiet, peaceful. Gazing upwards into their lush, green, heights, Jasmine marvelled at their size. It made her sad to think that in her time, something so vast, so solid would no longer be there.

*

The afternoon lengthened, the forest giving way to grassland. Still hot, the sun was almost too warm without the dark, cooling canopy. They stopped for food by a river and ate chunks of bread with a hard, yellow cheese, washed down with water. And then they were moving again, following the road as it skirted the river's wide meanderings.

Half an hour later and roofs appeared, the outline of a small village rising up through the grass.

"I think we should take a look," Seamus suggested. "We might learn something about Ellyllon."

Turning into a rough track, they crossed a wooden bridge built over the river and approached the village. Silent, with no sign of life, it looked empty. They reached the boundary.

"You two, wait here," Seamus ordered, pulling up his horse and dismounting.

"But–" Malachy stopped, silenced by Seamus' look: rule number two.

"I won't be long. Look after the horses."

Leaving them to dismount, he stepped through the boundary and walked into the centre of the village. Almost immediately, a man appeared, his body short and stocky. They talked for a while and then, as Jasmine and Malachy watched, the man indicated the house nearest them and waved Seamus inside.

"This might take a while," Malachy said dryly.

*

They sat on the grass, the horses grazing beside them, and watched the village, waiting for Seamus' return. The sun was hot on Jasmine's hood, the dark cloth absorbing its rays. She was tempted to pull it down, but who knew who could be watching? Maybe there were eyes just the other side of those dark, empty looking windows, watching their every move. A door creaked and a young boy stepped through the doorway of the house closest to them. Almost immediately a girl, maybe one or two years older, appeared behind him and quickly pulled him back inside.

"Do they seem a bit nervous to you?" Jasmine asked. "I mean we're not exactly threatening, are we?"

"No. But like Seamus said it's turbulent times; maybe they've got good reason to be afraid of strangers."

"Yeah." She sighed. "I hope he's not too long."

*

Jasmine yawned. Malachy was lying flat, his arms under his head. Jasmine's stomach fluttered as Iomlan shifted slightly.

She looked up, like a dog sniffing the air. "Seamus's using Iomlan."

Malachy sat up. "Do you know why?"

She frowned. "No. I don't sense anything bad, but I dunno, it's hard to tell. Maybe we should go and check?"

"But he said to wait here."

They stared at one another, then Malachy flapped his hand impatiently. "Give him ten minutes, then we go in."

Three minutes passed.

"It's OK, he's stopped. He's not using it anymore."

"O-kay." Malachy blew out his cheeks. "What do you want to do?"

"Wait until the ten, then see?"

Fifteen minutes later and they were still debating when Seamus and the man reappeared. Coming closer, the man was older than she'd first thought. Muscle and fat jostled in a body used to hard physical labour but beginning to slow. And his light brown hair was flecked with grey around his ears and temple and along the crown.

"How are ye?" he greeted them with a nod, rewarding their answer with a ghost of a smile before saying something to Seamus in a low voice.

Seamus murmured something in return and then the two of them embraced as if they'd known each other for years. With a last nod at Malachy and Jasmine the man turned and walked back towards the centre of the village. He didn't look back.

"Do you know him?" Jasmine asked curiously.

"No, why would I? He's a good man, though."

"Why did you use—?"

"Did he tell you anything?" Malachy interrupted her impatiently.

Seamus nodded. "Pretty much the same as in Sligo. But now I'm certain it's Ellyllon. And, oh, they did tell me where to find him."

"Where?!" Jasmine and Malachy said in union.

He grinned. "He's allied with Grainne Mhaol. Grace O'Malley."

Malachy's eyes widened. "Granuaile? The pirate queen?!"

Seamus nodded. "She was meant to have been a very clever woman, amazingly astute. You'd think her instinct would warn her against Ellyllon, but then greed's a powerful motivator."

He shrugged. "Her territory stretches along Clew Bay. She has a castle there, so that's where we need to go. We've gone too far south; we need go back a ways, to the crossroads we passed." Putting his hand in his pocket, he pulled out a thick, woollen thread. "Here, that's for your hair."

"Thanks. Seamus, why did you use Iomlan?" Bunching up her hair, Jasmine carefully tied it back.

"They needed help, so I gave it. It seemed only fair after what they'd told me."

He climbed onto her horse, waited for them to join them, then pressed his knees. They moved off and it was only later that Jasmine realised he hadn't actually told her.

They backtracked to the crossroads and, taking the left fork, followed the road back into the forest. They continued along it for as long as they dared, but the evening was drawing in, the light fading. In the end they had to stop for the night, sleeping under a leafy canopy, with the stars high above twinkling; a safe distance from the main road.

*

When Jasmine woke the next morning both Seamus and Malachy were already up. She washed in a nearby stream, wincing at the coldness of the water, then dressed quickly. They had breakfast and a drink of what Seamus called 'small beer', which was beer diluted heavily with water, before setting off again. The road was quiet and they rode undisturbed for most of the morning. Another break, this one to avoid a small group of riders and to rest the horses, and the forest receded, giving way to wide, open bog. Gorse dotted the landscape, growing in thick, spiky clusters, its flowers brilliant flashes of yellow and orange against the duller green and brown. Off to the right, water shimmered, the lake's surface a cold, smooth platinum despite the warmth of the day. The road twisted first one way and then the other. They passed another lake, and then another. A breeze tugged at Jasmine's hood, rippled the white fluff of the bog cotton, like a million rabbits waving their bottoms in the air.

Bog flowed into forest, and mountains appeared over the tops of the trees, and then back to bog. The land began to undulate, the ground dipping and rising into hillocks and hills. Slowly, surreptitiously, the mountains moved closer; Jasmine could see the roughness of the rock, the weathering of the stone in the jagged, granite outcrops.

"How much further do we have to go?" she asked, stretching and wriggling, trying to alleviate the ache that was spreading across her backside and into her lower back.

Seamus stopped his horse and examined the countryside.

"I'm not sure. I think we're getting close." He glanced at her. "Is there a problem?"

"No, I'm just stiff."

"Then we should stop and give you chance to walk. Look." He pointed towards the next hill. "See that outcrop of rocks? It's the perfect place to stop. Behind them, we won't be seen from the road. It can't be far, about a mile?"

It looked further away than that. Sighing quietly to herself, Jasmine nodded.

*

They reached the outcrop. Smooth, grey stone towered as Seamus led them around to the other side.

"God, Mal, me arse is really sore," Jasmine muttered. "I can't wait to get off this horse."

He laughed. "So's mine. I don't know how Seamus does it; he doesn't seem to notice it."

"Oh, I notice alright," Seamus said, looking all around them. "I just don't keep complaining about it." He frowned. "I don't like this; something's wrong."

At that moment, all hell broke loose. Men, shouting, their arms swinging wildly, ran at them from all directions. Spooked, Jasmine's horse backed into Malachy's, sending it rearing. She fought for control as men swarmed all around her. They snatched at her, trying to grab her legs, her arms and pull her to the ground. Malachy was already there, his body heaving as he fought against the men holding him. A hand caught her cloak, another her leggings; she screamed and tried to push them away, and then Seamus' Iomlan roared past her, knocking the men from her and sending them flying. More men appeared; Seamus' Iomlan flashed again, but it was too late. There were too many. They grabbed her, using their weight to topple her and press her body to the ground. She turned her head, searching wildly for Seamus, the movement sending her hair, already loose, tumbling inside her hood. A man with thick, black hair and narrow face behind a beard and moustache moved towards them, carrying a sword in his right hand. Behind her the men were cursing, shouting at each other in Irish to hold him down, and she guessed Seamus was on the ground but still fighting. The man with the sword stopped in front of her, and the men holding her let go. He studied her for a moment, his eyes narrowed suspiciously, and then, taking a step back, flicked his sword. The blade glistened in the sunlight. Another flick, and he thrust it downwards, straight towards the centre of her face.

Chapter Five

Iomlan flashed, ready to strike, but centimetres from her face, the sword shifted, catching the edge of her hood and pulling it away. She closed her eyes, breath coming out in a rush, and when she opened them again, the sword was gone, re-sheathed into the scabbard hung down the man's side. Iomlan swirled, but she forced it down as the man growled something she didn't catch and the men lifted her roughly to her feet. She pulled against them, straining to get her arms free, but their grip was too strong. They held her as the man stepped in close, so close she could smell the sourness of his breath, and then, first with one hand and then the other, he grabbed the neck of her tunic. His fingers tightened and his arms and shoulders flexed, ready to pull and rip.

"Duggan, enough! Take your hands off her!"

A new voice, low with a slight husk, crackled with authority and the men instantly fell away.

A woman, dressed in the male clothes of a warrior, strode purposefully toward them. She was stunning. Tall, taller than many of the men around her; her Viking heritage was clear in the length and curve of her limbs and stature and the long, golden auburn hair pulled off her face and plaited. She carried a sword on her belt, next to a dagger, and it swayed gently with the motion of her hips; the lushness of her body and her femininity were strangely heightened by the masculinity of her clothes and the men around her. Strong, well-defined features belied the perfect beauty ascribed by modern myth makers, but there was a quality to her face, a regularity of form and quick, intelligent beauty, that drew the eye and held it.

"Who are you? What do you want here?" she demanded, coming close.

Jasmine stared at her, her mind refusing to move.

"What is your name?" she repeated, frowning, her hand slipping to the hilt of her sword. "Answer me."

"Jasmine."

"Jas-mine?" Her lips lingered on the sound. "Jasmine. A strange name. Jasmine. But of what family?"

"She is of no family, my lady."

It was Seamus who answered, his voice muffled by the men who had given up trying to hold him and had simply sat on him.

Her eyes narrowed, and the men around Jasmine froze. For a moment, no one spoke and then, with a quick, elegant spin, Grainne Mhaol turned to Seamus.

"Release him."

They did as she said. Those that held Malachy did the same and both he and Seamus got shakily to their feet.

"No family? Then tell me why would a young girl be travelling, dressed as man, with only a man and a boy for protection, if not to hide her identity? And why would a girl without name or family do so?"

"Surely there are other reasons to hide? Either way, there's no gold to be had from her, my lady, Grainne Mhaol, or from us."

Grainne stiffened slightly. "You know who I am?"

Seamus bowed lowly, theatrically. "Your name precedes you, my lady. But even then, I fear it does not do you justice."

She laughed once, the sound hollow. "What need have you for gold when there is silver in thy tongue?" Her smile vanished and she took a step towards him. "But you haven't answered me. If you know me, you know this is my territory, and should know better than to enter it."

"We're just passing through. Jasmine is my granddaughter, and Malachy here is her brother. When their parents died, I raised them. We're looking for someone, a man." He waved one hand, the picture of innocence. "Perhaps you've seen him?"

"A man?" She looked meaningfully at Jasmine. "It is an old, tired tale. Tell me, what are you: protector or avenger?"

"Protector," Seamus answered firmly. "The man we're looking for has a certain persuasiveness, a power almost, to make people do what he wants, even against their own nature, but he has not touched her."

Grainne tilted her head thoughtfully. "This man with the charm of the devil, does he wear the garb of a priest? His face pale, his eyes deep, almost black?"

Seamus nodded. "It sounds like him. Do you know him?"

"Perhaps." Her voice was light, but Jasmine caught the deep throb of controlled anger.

"Would ye know where he went?"

"What it is to me where this man went?!" She shrugged.

There was a pause. No one spoke; the only sound was the tap of Grainne's nail against the hilt of her sword. They waited.

"I see you have no weapons," she said eventually. "And this is dangerous country for an old man and children to be wandering through. Come, my castle's not far. I offer you my hospitality, the hospitality of the O'Malleys; food and a warm bed for the night."

She turned to the man, Duggan, and drew him aside with a nod of her head. They talked for a moment, their voices too low to be heard. Duggan said something, his face urgent, and Grainne lifted her head in surprise. Almost immediately, she lowered it again and, talking quickly, touched Duggan's arm in a strangely placatory gesture. He bowed slightly, taking his orders, but still he looked unhappy.

"My men will walk beside you. To protect you, of course." She waved one hand carelessly, then taking the reins of her horse from one of her men, climbed on in one fluid motion.

Their horses appeared beside them, and Seamus, giving Jasmine and Malachy a look that said just do as I do, mounted first. Jasmine and Malachy followed his lead as hands helped them on. With all the riders mounted, Grainne turned her horse, and the company set off, moving as one.

*

They travelled northwest, the pace slow to allow for the men walking. Croagh Patrick lay to the west, its distinctive triangular peak unmistakeable even from this distance. To the right, the mountains of Nephin Beg loomed as green grass slopes gave way to thick brown gorse and stony peaks with a lunar like bleakness. They rode in silence, Jasmine, Seamus and Malachy in single file, Grainne's men riding either side of them. To Jasmine's right rode the hugest man. Built like a bodybuilder, his width seemed almost half his height. His face, too, was wide, with long, thin lips and flat, ruddy cheeks and nose. Fair hair had been cut short, but his beard was long and bushy, giving him a wild, ferocious look. He was the perfect captor or jailor, she decided; you wouldn't get far if you tried to escape. He'd flatten you with one hand, and not even a punch, just a negligent flick of his wrist. She looked away. A bird flew past them, heading, like them, to the coast. Its wings were huge, their beat slow and powerful. A lone heron, returning to the water to fish. She touched her stomach, pressed it lightly. Why hadn't she felt Iomlan when Grainne's men had attacked? It had almost responded to Duggan's sword, following her instinct, her desire to protect herself, but why not the men? If it had, the two of them would've easily overcome Grainne's men and escaped. But to where? Grainne's castle.

OK, maybe it wasn't so bad; they were going exactly where they wanted to go. But it still didn't change the problem of why Iomlan hadn't responded.

They reached the coast. Jasmine gasped, seeing Clew Bay for the first time. Ringed by mountains, and framed by long stretches of golden yellow sand, dark blue water glistened.

"Galanta." The huge man lifted his right hand and pointed. *Gahallinn*. Beautiful.

Across his palm was a long, thin scar as if he'd tried to defend himself from an attack with a knife or dagger. She nodded, too afraid to speak, but, still gazing at the view, he didn't seem to notice. But even if they were going where they wanted to, Grainne didn't know. Maybe, the more important question was, what did she want with them?

*

They skirted the bay, following the coastline into an inlet and away from the sea, then turned left at a crossroads. Ahead, a wooden bridge lay over a wide, shallow river and, crossing that, they turned left again, riding across lush, green flatland. Water rippled in the distance. They were, Jasmine realised, returning to the coast, and had only moved inland to negotiate the inlet. Up ahead, perched on the flat, black rock at the sea's edge, was a grey tower. Grainne's castle. They rode closer. Tall and narrow, it had none of the walls and parapets Jasmine had been expecting. Behind it, a sixteenth century ship lay anchored in the bay, its sails tightly furled; close enough to the land for protection but far enough out to avoid the rocks. Jasmine stared at it, at the beauty of its wood and richly coloured hull and thought of The Victory she'd seen on a school trip to Portsmouth. A village lay a hundred metres or so inland. Low to the ground and tiny, its houses were basic; clay walls topped with thatch. Smoke drifted lazily upwards, carrying with it the sweet, aromatic scent of turf and wood.

They reached the tower and dismounted, and not even burning turf could cover the stench of daily life; unwashed bodies, rotting meat and human waste. Jasmine coughed, placed her hand over her nose and then pinched it, seeing Malachy cover his with part of his cloak. She was tempted to try and use Iomlan, to somehow keep the stench at bay or use it to desensitize her nose, but she knew what Seamus would say.

"My home." Half turning, Grainne swept her arm towards the tower.

Speeding from the village, a group of children ran up to them, jigging around the men, calling out to them and eyeing her, Seamus and

Malachy curiously. The women followed more slowly, wiping hands, leaving fires and tasks to greet their menfolk. Jasmine realised that this wasn't just an army, it was a small community, made up of the families of Grainne's men. With more stares, they reached the door of the tower. Grainne disappeared inside as Duggan organised the men.

"Come," he told them when he'd finished.

Flanked by four men, Jasmine and the others followed him into the tower.

*

Inside was one enormous room. Parts of it had been partitioned into small sections, designed for storage and the housing of horses and animals. A huge fireplace had been built along one wall, the hearth filled with a thick, iron grate. Of Grainne, there was no sign. Or of a staircase, or any way up to the other floors.

"Come." Duggan gestured towards a rope ladder hanging unnoticed from a small opening in the wall next to the fireplace.

They looked at one another.

"You want us to climb up there?" Seamus asked.

Duggan eyes gleamed. "Unless ya wish to sleep down here with the pigs."

Seamus went first. Climbing quickly despite his bad knee. As he disappeared through the hole, Duggan looked at Jasmine. It was her turn.

She climbed. It was harder than Seamus made it look. Every time she tried to take a step, the rope ladder moved away from her, jackknifing her body. Breathing heavily, she reached the top, hearing Duggan order Malachy onto the bottom. The rope ladder bucked, then settled and with one last, final, effort, she hauled her body off the ladder and into the hole, her arms protesting. The tunnel was narrow, just big enough to allow her onto her haunches. Ahead, flame flickered, illuminating a stone wall. She crawled towards it. At the end Seamus stood waiting with one of Grainne's men. Seeing her, he grabbed her arms, helped to pull her out and up onto to her feet.

"Are you OK?"

She nodded, still breathless. They were in a corridor illuminated by torches, the only natural light coming from a thin slit of a window at one end. Malachy was already coming; they turned to help him, moving away from the tunnel when Grainne's man told them to.

Duggan came next, followed by the huge man, who was too big to crawl and had to wriggle, then the last two. Watching, Jasmine thought how easy it would be to overpower them with Iomlan, but if Seamus had the same idea, he showed no sign.

Duggan led them to a stone staircase. Narrow, twisting, they climbed dizzily up past one floor and onto the next. Tucked in behind Seamus and Malachy, with the huge man behind her, Jasmine's head span.

"In there." Duggan nodded Seamus and Malachy inside. She went to follow but he barred her way. "Yer in there." He pointed to the room next to it.

The room was small and empty apart from a high, narrow bed, overhung with a worn, dusty canopy, and a chest in one corner. A fire, hastily made, was just beginning to catch. The door slammed shut behind her, making her jump. A key turned in the lock.

"Some guest," she muttered, going to the window.

The window was set unusually low, so she had to stoop slightly to see out of it properly. Her room faced out onto the sea; the only land she could see was a thin strip off to her right. The tide was on the way in, toying with the rocks as it ebbed and flowed towards them. With the sun beginning to lower, the light was amazing; it gave the little she could see a warm, almost golden glow. She thought of her mum, imagined her seeing the view and wanting the inevitable photo, and suddenly wished she was at home, sitting with her and John. Arguing even, over something that would now seem so silly and unimportant, but then would've been everything to her. She sighed. When this was all over, she'd return home and everything would go back to normal. But she knew it wouldn't, for how could it?

A tree caught her eye, in the centre of the thin strip of land. Small, narrow, its limbs twisted from the winter storms, it looked almost black against the fading light. Around its base something flapped, like a piece of cloth caught by the breeze. She moved closer, squinting to try and get a better view. There was nothing there, nothing but a single, old tree. She was getting paranoid, imaging things that weren't there. What did she think? It was Ellyllon, peering comically from behind a tree? She straightened and, turning her back on the view, went over to the bed. Sitting perched on the edge of the bed, she threaded her arm around the bedpost and rested her cheek on it. What did she want with them? It wasn't for Ellyllon, she was sure of it. She'd felt Grainne's anger, her fury when they'd talked of him. And despite her paranoia, he wasn't here; she'd've felt him, or at least Seamus would've felt him and he'd hardly have come so meekly if he'd thought there was any danger from Ellyllon. Her stomach growled suddenly. She lifted her cheek, wondering when she might get something to eat. Maybe not when, but if. She returned her face to the post. Either way, it would only be at my lady's pleasure. So here she was again, back to the same question; why was it my lady's pleasure to bring them here? Maybe she wanted to help them? Almost immediately, she dismissed the idea. According to Malachy, Grainne was a pirate, and a pirate was violent, ruthless, no matter how romanticised the legend. She frowned. But Seamus believed she was more than just a cutthroat, that she didn't kill for killing's sake, and everything this highly intelligent, ambitious but pragmatic woman did, she did for a reason. Jasmine sat up. That was it, that was the crux of what was bothering her: what on earth could Granuaile have to gain by bringing them here?

The room darkened as outside the sun began to set. Jasmine shivered, feeling the cold come creeping. Without the sun's rays, any heat in the thick, stone walls was rapidly disappearing. Pulling her cloak tightly around her, she got up and shuffled over to the fire. It needed more wood. A small pile had been left in a willow basket next to it, so she added a few pieces. Immediately they took, the fire licking and curling around the edges. She sat, manoeuvring her body until she was leaning against the wall. Pulling her cloak back around her, she folded her arms beneath it, and closed her eyes.

She was choking. Sand filled her mouth and forced its way down her throat. She coughed, spluttered, fighting for air. She could hear the cries of children; their voices shrill with terror...

The sound of a door swinging heavily open woke her and she opened her eyes. Duggan was stood in the doorway. Outside, the sky was black, and from somewhere below her feet, voices talked and laughed.

"Out," Duggan growled, his face unreadable, as she scrambled to her feet.

Taking her arm, he propelled her towards the stairs.

"Where are we going? Where's Seamus?" she demanded, finding her voice, but he ignored her.

Going first, he took her wrist and began to pull her down to the next floor, and off balance, her cloak flapping around her feet and ankles, it was all she could do to keep from falling. A few steps down a short corridor and Duggan led her into a vaulted hall. Running the length of the tower, a monstrous hearth lay in the centre of one wall, big enough to sit in. The fire had been lit, and the flames, burning brightly, were almost a foot high. Torches hung around the room, bringing both light and shadow to the room, distorting the faces of the people sat around a long, dark oak table. Plates and bowls held remnants of food, chunks of bread and bones, gnawed and licked clean, all that was left of a huge feast. At the centre, her back to the fire and her hair loosened into thick, long locks, sat Grainne. She turned towards Jasmine and her face broke a soft, almost motherly, smile.

"Jasmine, come join us. Sit beside me." She indicated the empty chair next to her.

Duggan let her go. Rubbing her wrist, Jasmine looked around the table, but there was no sign of either Seamus or Malachy. She hesitated.

"Jasmine, come," Grainne repeated, still smiling. "You must be cold, and hungry. Don't worry; the others will be joining us shortly."

Beside her, Duggan shifted impatiently. Reluctant, but not knowing what else to do, Jasmine did as she said.

As soon as Jasmine sat, a girl appeared, carrying a metal jug so heavy with drink that she had to balance the lip with her other hand. Grainne's cup was poured first; she lifted it, waiting for the rest, then raised it further in a toast. Dutifully the other guests raised theirs. Jasmine watched as everyone took a drink.

"Jasmine, I have a drink especially for you." She lifted her hand, and a second girl appeared, carrying a smaller jug. "It's very rare."

She waited for it to be poured. Brown with a tinge of yellow, like water from the bog, swirled as Jasmine lifted her cup. She stopped. Don't drink it, a voice inside her warned.

"Go on." Grainne beamed encouragingly. "It won't harm you; I prepared it myself."

Jasmine pretended to take a drink. "Hmmm, lovely." She swallowed theatrically.

Grainne threw back her head and laughed. "You're no actress. But didn't your grandfather teach you that to refuse hospitality is to insult the host?" Her face hardened. "Drink, Jasmine, I insist."

There was nothing else to do. Jasmine took a tentative sip. The first flavour was green, like a smoothie made from spinach, followed quickly by orange, cinnamon and clove. It wasn't bad. She took a larger sip and felt it warm her throat. Soothing, it reminded her of Christmas. Around them, people began to talk, suddenly.

"Do you like it?" Grainne asked, taking a drink from her own cup.

"Yes, it's very nice. What is it?"

"A wine, of sorts." She shrugged. "From a plant that grows on the shores of the bay. The giving of it to an outsider is considered to be an honour.”

“Thank you,” Jasmine replied awkwardly.

She looked at the other guests. They seemed engrossed in their conversations, but Jasmine sensed the tension in them, like dogs alert to the whims of a fickle mistress. Without thinking, she took another drink, larger this time and the warmth moved down her throat and settled cosily in the bottom of her stomach. Grainne placed her cup on the table beside her and leant in towards her, her manner conspiratorial, like old friends. Her breath smelt sweet, tinged with the scent of rosemary.

“Your grandfather is an interesting man. So confident. Almost as if he had no fear, no reason to fear.” She laughed lightly, the sound intimate, for Jasmine’s ears only. “Here, inside a tower with a bunch of cutthroats and he seems almost unconcerned. A rare man indeed.”

She straightened suddenly, her face luminous as she lifted her cup. “A toast, Jasmine, just between you and I, to your grandfather.”

They clinked cups, and this time Jasmine drank deeply.

“Tell me about him.”

The warmth was spreading through her, radiating out from her stomach, making her fingers tingle and her head woozy. She felt so happy, so content; her earlier doubts of Grainne seemed so unfair, so silly, especially as she was showing her such kindness. She looked into her face, at the expectancy waiting there, and wanted nothing more than to fulfil it. But there was that voice again, coming from deep inside.

“He’s… he’s, a farmer,” she heard herself say.

“A farmer?” Grainne repeated, her eyes narrowing.

She reached over and poured what was left in the jug into Jasmine’s cup, smiling, at ease once more. “You tease me; he’s no simple farmer. Here, enough of him. Drink and tell me about you.” She watched as Jasmine emptied her cup then, reaching over, rested her hand on her arm. “You are as strange to me as he is.” Sliding her fingers upwards, she played delicately with the folds of Jasmine’s sleeve. “So quiet, so obedient, and yet I sense something in you. An air, a confidence, as if you were born to something more than this. You intrigue me.” Her fingers moved higher, danced lightly across Jasmine’s shoulder and touched her face. “Even in these times, when a woman can hold such power, the power of a whole nation, still they have to prove themselves not just equal to men, but more.”

She paused, then tilting Jasmine’s face, looked deep into her eyes.

Jasmine's head swam; it took all her concentration to follow Grainne's dialect.

"When I was young I went to sea. I dressed as a man, I fought as a man. Slowly, I earned their admiration, their respect and finally their loyalty. When my father died, I inherited his ships. As a woman I was denied my birthright as the head of this clan, but still they follow me. I, Grainne Mhaol, Grace O'Malley, the leader of the O'Malleys, their one true chieftain. They follow me now not as a man, and not because I'm as good as a man, but because I am the best of all of them. And if that best is a woman; why should I deny it? Why then, Jasmine of the unusual name, do you? Tell me, who are you?"

Her face was close that Jasmine could see every fleck of colour in her eyes, feel the heat of her breath on her face, sense the heat from her body. A shout of laughter from somewhere behind her but she ignored it; Grainne was all she could see, was all she wanted to see. She had become her whole world.

"Tell me. There is so much I would like to know about you, so many questions." She stroked Jasmine's cheek. "I think friends should be able to tell one another anything, don't you?"

Jasmine nodded, watching her lips curl delicately around her words. Her face felt hot, flushed.

"But first, tell me about your grandfather." Grainne's fingers moved to the top of Jasmine's arm, her shoulder, the fingers pressing into her skin.

Jasmine opened her mouth. Seamus flashed through her head, his Iomlan probing, as if he were searching for her. She closed it again.

"I want to help you," Grainne continued, her eyes huge, earnest. "I know more than you think. I know what he can do. I saw what he can do. But what does he want here? What does he want with Ellyllon?" Her fingers flexed and tightened. "Tell me about his power. Who is he? What is he?"

Seamus had gone. Lost, entranced without him and desperate to say anything, do anything that this stunning woman asked of her, Jasmine opened her mouth to speak.

Chapter Six

"Leave her be!"

It was Seamus, his voice cutting through the talk and the laughter and into the confusion in Jasmine's head. He walked calmly into the hall, his boots echoing across the floor. Malachy followed a pace or two behind. All eyes were on them.

"Who are you to order me in my own castle?!" Grainne roared. "How did you get in here? Where's Duggan?!"

At that moment he appeared in the doorway, two men behind him. Breathing heavy, as if he'd been running, a small cut was visible just below his hairline. Spotting Seamus, he drew his sword.

"Don't be silly, Duggan." Seamus dismissed him with a wave of his hand, his eyes fixed on Grainne. "Call yer Rottweiler off. We need to talk."

"I think you should learn some manners, old man. Maybe we should teach you some."

"Go on then, give it a go," Seamus countered, throwing himself into the empty chair opposite her.

Uncurling, Grainne flew out of her chair, her hand to her side as if reaching for her sword. "I gave you no permission to sit!" She gestured to her guests, her face red with fury. "Out, out. Get out, I want you gone!"

For a moment, they looked at one another, and then, without a word, got to their feet and began filing from the room. Breathing heavily, Grainne pressed her hands to the table, as if to steady herself.

"You dare too much, old man." She looked at Malachy and, catching her meaning, Duggan moved towards him.

"As do you!" Seamus spat, sitting bolt upright. "You say you know what I can do. D'you really think I'd let him get within two paces of Malachy? Are you looking for a new lieutenant?"

Grainne stared at him for a moment, then waved her hand at Duggan. "Perhaps not."

He responded instantly, stopping and sheathing his sword, the men behind him following suit. Malachy quickly joined Seamus at the table, sinking into the chair next to him, trying to look unobtrusive.

Grainne watched him impassively, then faced Seamus. "I know the lies your kind speaks. She would have told me anything I wanted to know."

She lowered her hand and very gently took hold of a single tress from the side of Jasmine's face, sliding it between her finger and thumb.

Seamus snorted. "It's said that yer an intelligent woman, quick-witted and cunning; I have yet to see any of it. Jasmine, take my hand."

Reluctantly, she did as he said, reaching out across the table. She felt his Iomlan, cold, chilling against the heat in her body. It poured over her and she gasped, feeling as if she'd fallen headfirst into ice-cold water and jumped back, her strand of hair slipping through and out of Grainne's fingers.

"How did you do that?" Grainne breathed; her eyes wide and very bright.

"It was nothing. Jasmine, are you OK?"

"Yes, I think so."

Her mind was crystal-clear, the fog lifting, but she remembered everything; Grainne's voice, soft and seductive, her fingers stroking her cheek, and her own helpless infatuation. Flushing, she glanced furtively across at Malachy, but he was too busy watching Grainne. She sat slowly, her eyes still wide, as if she were in shock, but Jasmine sensed her mind racing.

"So, what do you want of me, sorcerer? Or should I call you devil?"

"Neither. Me name's Seamus. And you invited us."

"I did," she conceded. "I wanted to know why a sorcerer should be seeking Ellyllon. And why he consorts with the English." Seamus opened his mouth to reply, but she stopped him with a wave of her hand. "Duggan heard her speak English. She speaks Gaelic well, but her accent gives her away. Do you deny it?"

"That Jasmine's English? Of course not, but consort?" He sighed. "She's one girl. Would you blame her for the actions of a Queen, or the men who serve her?"

"No, but I would die to protect my lands, and my people from slaughter."

"Then you have nothing to fear from us. We have no wish for land or wealth. All we want is Ellyllon." He leant forward. "Tell me, why did you bring us here? It was more than idle curiosity. What did Ellyllon take from you?”

Grainne started, this time her eyes widening in genuine surprise. “Something very precious.” She lowered her gaze. “I thought to use you to get back what was stolen.” She sighed heavily, sadly, the picture of regret. “I can see I was wrong. Forgive me.”

“Stop that,” Seamus ordered irritably. “It won’t work on me.”

“It was worth a try,” she retorted, grinning. “You said you wanted to talk, sorcerer, so talk.”

Seamus leant forward. His face was serious, but his eyes, staring directly into Grainne’s, were sparkling. Jasmine shifted uncomfortably. She was obviously trying to manipulate Seamus now. But was it possible the old man was falling for it?

“If I tell you what you want to know, Grainne Mhaol, will you promise me it will not be spoken of beyond this room?”

“I will.”

“And what about him?” He jerked his head towards Duggan.

“He is as my right hand. You can trust him as you trust me.”

“That much?” It was Seamus’ turn to grin. “Agreed.”

“Agreed.” They clasped hands across the table.

“Sorcerer or no, if you break your word, I will find you and cut your throat.”

“Fair enough.”

They let go.

“Has anyone told you yer a remarkable woman?”

She gave a short laugh. “There’s that tongue again. Duggan, join us.”

She waited until Duggan had taken the seat next to Jasmine. Immediately, the girl appeared with another jug of beer.

“You say you’re no sorcerer, no devil,” Grainne said seriously, the time for games and manipulation obviously past. “What are you? Where do you come from?”

“I’m a man like any other. And we’ve travelled from O’Connor’s lands.”

“O’Connor? You’re an O’Connor?”

“We’re from no clan. Well, no clan you’d know. Thank you.” He beamed at the girl serving him. “My kind, people with what you call magic, are found in all peoples, all lands and countries.”

Grainne was frowning, “What you say seems strange to me, and yet, on a ship you see many strange things. And there is one——-” She stopped, as if thinking better of it. “Why do you seek Ellyllon?”

He took a swig of his beer. “To stop him. To prevent him from doing any more harm."

"And how is Ellyllon known to you?"

"We're old enemies. He was once a man, but now he's beyond that. The power, the magic, he steals it from my kind and uses it to gain more and more power. In time, no one will be able to stand against him."

"His power is so very great?"

"He has the potential to amass more power than anyone has ever had. The only limit is what he can consume."

"Consume?" Grainne's fingers gripped her cup. "You say he steals from you. What happens to those whose magic he steals?"

"They die."

"Die!" Her fingers tightened, her knuckles paling. She shared a look with Duggan. "This magic, what you call power, how does he know how to find it?"

"He feels it. Or smells it, like a dog. Why?"

"The precious thing Ellyllon stole was more than wealth, more than lands." She took a drink, swallowed it with a gulp. "He stole my nephew."

"Your nephew?"

"Yes, Cormac. He is the only son of my sister. She was my younger, by years, the water to my fire, and even though we were so very different we were close. I was her protector." She sighed heavily. "But I could not protect her from the will of God; she died giving Cormac life."

"I'm sorry for your loss."

"It was a long time ago." She shook her head irritably. "I stayed away at his father's demand; he is a pious man and does not approve of me. But when Cormac was ten years his father began to see things in him, a magic, and he sent him to me, begging me to protect him. I did this for his mother's sake, in her name. He is not easy; he has not the grace to make others like him and that gives him pain, but he has the soft heart of his mother and the light of her in his eyes. He has become like my own son."

Seamus nodded slowly. "Without someone to guide him, he'd be vulnerable to Ellyllon. Ten is very young, too young."

"Ellyllon arrived at the gates of my castle offering his help, his allegiance, but I know now it was Cormac he came for. They became close almost immediately and, thinking he could help, I encouraged them. But it wasn't long before I noticed changes in Cormac; he became more solitary, suspicious, thinking that I cared nothing of him beyond using his power for myself. I learnt too late how this devil had whispered into his ear, poisoning him against me. I tried to keep them apart, using force when all reasoning failed, but nothing worked. Cormac left with him when I was at sea."

Seamus rubbed his chin, thinking. "Do you have any idea what Ellyllon wanted Cormac for? I mean, him in particular?"

"To steal his magic, his life, of course! He may already be dead!"

"No, forgive me. Ellyllon can only steal the power when it's new. If he took Cormac, it's because he wants to use him, to use his power."

"I don't understand."

"If he controls Cormac, he controls his power. He needs him."

"Then he lives." She closed her eyes.

Silence. They waited.

"I know where Ellyllon went, where he took Cormac." She opened her eyes, and the light in them burned. "He went to MacDermott, the chieftain who rules the land to the east. I need your help; I cannot bring Cormac back, cannot make him see the nature of the thing he left with, but maybe you can. If it was magic that corrupted him, then maybe magic can restore him."

"Maybe we can help one another. Ellyllon has an army, and to defeat him, we need an army ourselves."

"If you help me, I give you my word I will do everything in my power to help you stop Ellyllon." Standing up, she held out her hand again. "What do you say, old man?"

Seamus joined her and, reaching out, clasped her hand. "And I will do anything in my power to bring your Cormac back to you." He let her hand go, and grinned. "I'll say it again, yer a remarkable woman, Grainne Mhaol. If only I was thirty years younger—"

"What matters thirty years, when there is still fire in your belly? Enough. You have not eaten; you must be hungry. Duggan, bring them food."

Duggan disappeared and, at Seamus' suggestion, he and Jasmine swapped seats, and almost immediately he and Grainne fell into a deep conversation. She watched them talking, their heads bent together, their voices low, planning their next move. Seamus said something and Grainne laughed, her fingers playing with a loose thread on his sleeve and Jasmine's jaw clenched.

"Jas, are you OK?" Malachy asked next to her. "What did she do to you?"

"I'm fine." She shook her head. "I'm not sure, but I think it was in my drink."

"She drugged you! But—" He stopped as Duggan appeared, moving swiftly as he returned to his seat.

A woman followed more slowly, carrying a large clay bowl. Behind her, one of the serving girls carried smaller bowls and a willow basket containing a small, round loaf of bread. She placed the bowls down, one in front of each of them, then put the bread basket in the centre. Going to Duggan, the woman served him first, ladling a thin, watery looking soup or stew into his bowl. Jasmine's nose twitched unpleasantly. Fish. The woman moved to Seamus and filled his bowl. Grey lumps floated.

"Jes—" Malachy bit back a curse.

The woman moved next to Malachy and the scent of fish was overwhelming. Jasmine's stomach lurched, and then it was her turn. Seamus was already eating, wolfing down alternative spoonfuls of stew and thick mouthfuls of bread. She glanced at Malachy. He was trying to swallow, his throat convulsing, but he kept his lips carefully closed. The woman moved off and now it was Jasmine's turn to try. Dipping and lifting her spoon, she eyed the grey lumps. From the other side of the table Duggan watched her, his lips twisted into something resembling a smile. Annoyed, she took a deep breath and closed her eyes. The stew hit the back of her throat. She gagged, fighting the urge to bring it back up again, and finally swallowed.

"Oh, God, Mal, I can't eat this!"

"Yeah, it's worse than my sister's cooking!" He was staring at the stew as if it were a snake.

She lifted another spoonful, then noticed the jug to his right. "Could you pass me that?"

"Good idea." Pouring himself a drink, he reached over and poured her one too, and for the first time, she saw the right side of his face and the dark red mark that lay across his cheekbone. It looked as if he'd been punched.

"Mal, what happened to your face?"

"It's nothing." He stroked it gently. "I'd forgotten it was there."

Duggan lowered his spoon. "It was I. We caught them breaking out of the room." He grinned. "He fought back." He lifted his chin at her and she saw a small red mark, just to the left. "Even a wren will defend its nest."

Ignoring the rest of her stew, Jasmine nibbled at a piece of bread. Onto her third cup of beer, she was beginning to get a taste for it. But then, she told herself, the taste of beer was bliss compared to the rancid flavour of Grainne's fish stew. Finishing his, Duggan had already left, with a stiff nod of his head and a bow to his mistress. Seamus was talking, his hands gesturing, while Grainne listened, her face enrapt. Jasmine yawned and, placing her elbow on the table, rested her head in her hand.

"Yer drunk!" Malachy grinned.

"No, I'm not, I'm just tired," she retorted. Her elbow slipped and her head nodded violently, jarring her neck. "Ow!"

"Yeah, right." Malachy's grin widened. "Come on, I'll help ya to bed."

Grabbing a candlestick and holding her around the waist, he helped her upstairs. With the torches long dead, the stairs and corridors were dark, empty. Candlelight flickered, made strange shadows on the wall, the stone beneath their feet. All was quiet.

"Is it me or was she flirting with Seamus?" Jasmine whispered, turning her face into his.

His eyes gleamed in the candlelight. "There's life in the old dog yet."

"Yeah, but which one!" She burped loudly.

"Thanks for that." He laughed, turning his face away. "That's a bit harsh; remind me not to upset you when you're drunk. Here we are." He let her go.

"I'm not drunk!" she retorted, swaying slightly. "Besides, he'd be safer with a python. She'd eat him whole."

"Yeah, but what a way to go." He gave her an appraising look, then, opening the door, grabbed her around the waist again. "C'mon, let's get you into bed."

"OK, mummy," she giggled, allowing herself to be led.

Inside, the fire was only just going. From the empty box next to it, it looked as if the wood and turf had been topped up while they were downstairs but had burned down to glowing embers. The room was freezing. Malachy propelled her to the bed.

"Here," he said, lifting the covers and manoeuvring her gently down.

"Shit, it's cold," she shivered.

He sighed. "OK then, budge up."

"Whatcha y' doing?"

"Warming the bed. When it's warm, I'll go back to my own room." She smiled up at him. "Thanks Mal."

He curled in behind her, pulling the covers up around them both. Jasmine closed her eyes.

His stomach growled suddenly, loudly. "I'm starving! And that stew was putrid."

"I don't want to think about it. I'm not sure I ever want to eat again."

"You say that now, but what would you do if I offered you a curry?"

"Bite your hand off," she replied dreamily.

"It's OK for you; you've only been a couple of days without decent food. Imagine what it's like after a couple of months! I'd have chips with salt and vinegar. Or chocolate, or a burger, with extra cheese, or pizza. Or me mam's apple tart — no one makes it like her—" He paused. "I wonder what she made tonight for dinner, me mam, I mean."

He sighed again.

Jasmine opened her eyes and turned so she could look at him. "Are you worried about her?"

He nodded. "A little. She pretends not to, but I know how much she worries about us all. I can't imagine how she feels, wondering what's happening to me, if I'm alright."

"You could still go back. I could take you back, if you wanted me to." Her heart sank at the thought, but she ignored it.

"Yeah right, think of the trouble you'd get into without me." He gave a short laugh and turned onto his back.

"Yeah." She closed her eyes, and tentatively rested her head on his shoulder.

"Two more minutes and I'll go." He laid his head next to hers.

"OK," she murmured, already half-asleep.

Chapter Seven

Jasmine woke early the next morning, disturbed by the light and the sounds of life coming through the bare windows. Laid on his back, Malachy was still there, must've fallen asleep next to her. She watched him for a moment, liking the way his long hair curled across his face. For a moment, the temptation to snuggle into him was overwhelming. But it would only make things awkward. Sighing to herself, she slipped out of the bed and across the room. The tide had turned in the night. She could see the sand beyond the black, slate-like rock, and to her right, the deep rock pools of salt water. In the distance, the ocean mirrored the sky's overcast pale grey. It seemed to match her mood.

"What time is it?"

She spun. Malachy stretched and rubbed his eyes.

"Oh, almost half seven."

"Early yet."

"Yeah, but I think everyone else is already up."

Malachy dropped his hands. "And Seamus?"

"Probably. Why?"

"Shit!" Throwing back the cover, he flew out of bed.

"Malachy, wait, what is it?"

Too late. Bundling out the door, he was gone. She moved to the bed and sat down. She knew exactly what it was. He didn't want Seamus to wake and see his undisturbed bed and know he'd spent the night with her, even though they hadn't actually done anything. But would that really be so terrible, she asked herself miserably? Was she really so repulsive?

"He's not there," Malachy said as he came back through the door.

Jasmine straightened her shoulders. "He must be having breakfast."

Malachy smirked. "Yeah. He's probably starving after last night."

"Like me." She threw him a suspicious look. "What's so funny?"

"Oh, nothing. C'mon, let's go and get some breakfast."

*

As she predicted, Seamus was sat in the hall, having breakfast.

"Yer up, finally." He pointed at a large, earthenware bowl and wooden spoon placed in the centre of the table. "Help yourself. It's porridge, and there's milk in the jug."

Including Seamus, the table had been set for four. They sat opposite him, leaving the chair next to him vacant. Jasmine grabbed the wooden spoon and filled her bowl before passing it to Malachy.

"Grainne will join us soon," Seamus said, taking a drink from his cup. "She's making the final arrangements with Duggan."

Jasmine's spoon froze halfway to her mouth. Grainne?!

"Arrangements?" Malachy asked, his mouth already full.

"Yes, we're going to MacDermott's. We planned it all last night. Ellyllon went to great pains to manipulate Cormac away from Grainne. Why?"

Jasmine and Malachy looked at one another. "I give up." Malachy shrugged.

"I don't know, meself. But whatever it is, it must be important. If we persuade Cormac home, Ellyllon will surely follow, and then we'll have him."

Jasmine took her spoonful, swallowed it, musing. Seamus' logic made sense, but his plan hinged on them being able to trust Grainne. After what she'd done to Jasmine last night, was that really so wise?

"But how are we going to persuade Cormac to come back?" Malachy was asking.

"I'm not sure," Seamus admitted. "But I have a couple of ideas. We'll have to wait and see; it depends on Cormac and how strong Ellyllon's hold is on him. Ah." He turned his head, his whole face lightening up. "Here she is."

Grainne was stood in the doorway, her long hair plaited once more. How long she'd been there was impossible to know, but Jasmine was sure she'd been listening. Immediately, Grainne stepped lightly towards them, her hand balancing on the handle of her sword.

"Good morning, Jasmine, Malachy. I hope you're enjoying breakfast?" Smiling broadly, she glanced at Seamus and her blue eyes sparkled.

She looked, Jasmine had to admit, radiant, as if she were glowing from the inside out.

"Yeah, it's great," Malachy enthused, unable to take his eyes from her.

"That's good." She rested one hand on Seamus' shoulder and, bending over him, reached for his cup, her breasts all but grazing his face.

"That's mine!" he protested, grinning.

She took a drink, letting her lips linger on the edge of the cup, then lowered her face to his. He grabbed the back of her head and they kissed, long and passionately. Stunned, Jasmine glanced at Malachy. He was staring at them, his mouth hanging open. Realising, he shut it with an audible snap.

"Hmm, it's a shame we have to leave so soon," Grainne murmured, her smile wide with pleasure.

"It is," Seamus agreed.

They kissed again.

"Perhaps, Seamus, we are too keen to leave? Jasmine and Malachy are still eating."

Pulling away, she stretched, arching her body, like a cat.

"That's true." He watched her, his face flushed. "And there's the horses."

"Ah, yes, the horses."

"But, but—" Jasmine stopped. They turned to look at her. "You two?!"

"Yes?" Seamus' eyes narrowed, the flush receding.

"But, you're o—"

"What? Old? Sex isn't just for the young, ya know."

"Especially when the lover is so accomplished," Grainne agreed, smiling, but her eyes were vicious.

Now it was Jasmine's turn to flush. Grainne laughed and, giving Seamus a meaningful look,

returned the way she'd come, hips sashaying even more than usual.

"Y'know, she really is a remarkable woman." Seamus sighed, his eyes full of her as he watched her go. "And what an appetite. Enough to wear a man down; if he didn't have Iomlan, that is."

"Oh, God, Seamus, please stop!" Jasmine protested, holding up both hands to him.

"Jasmine, for someone so young yer a bit of a prude. We're both adults; what harm?"

He stood up. "Maybe you should give it a try. It might improve yer form."

Following Grainne, he shot across the hall, his steps bouncing with anticipation like an eager young man, and then he was gone.

"Can you believe that?!" Jasmine looked at Malachy, but he was still staring at the doorway, as if willing Grainne to reappear.

"What?" He dragged his eyes away.

"Seamus and her. He slept with her, is sleeping with her."

"So?"

"You knew?"

"I guessed." He shrugged. "The bed in our room hadn't been slept in."

"Oh, yeah, right." She scowled. "That's why your jaw hit the floor."

"It's not that." He reddened. "It's just… her."

"What about her?! Like I said, she'll eat him alive and spit out what's left."

"I don't think so. Seamus knows what he's doing."

"No he doesn't, he's infatuated! She's using him, manipulating him, just like—" She stopped, not wanting to say what was in her head: *she did me*.

"No, Jas, you're wrong." Shaking his head at her, Malachy turned his attention back to his breakfast.

There was a silence. Jasmine toyed with her porridge. It wasn't fair. Malachy was reacting as if she was the one with the problem.

She thought of what Seamus had said, and her own night, lying next to Malachy. "But you know I'm not a prude, right?"

He scooped up a huge spoonful of porridge and lifted it to his mouth. Milky globs slid off both sides and fell back into the bowl.

"I wouldn't blame you if you were, not the way your father was," he said, opting for what he must've thought was an understanding tone.

"What's my dad got to do with it?! It's not that. I just don't trust her. She's ruthless and will do anything, use anything, to get what she wants, and now she's got him eating out of the palm of her hand."

"I don't think so; not Seamus. He's not stupid."

She ran her hand through her hair. "Everyone's stupid when it comes to someone as clever and manipulative as her."

"So even after everything he's done, you think he'd let that happen? You don't have much faith in him, do you?"

"I told you, it's not Seamus I don't trust, it's her."

"Yeah, but yer not listening to me. He wouldn't do anything to jeopardise finding Ellyllon. It's just — a distraction, a bit of fun." His mouth closed on the spoon. He swallowed, then slowly, nonchalantly, licked the edges. "I mean, Jas, she's a real-life legend. She's Granuaile, The Pirate Queen. After years of plundering English ships, she manages to get a pardon from Elizabeth I, one strong, powerful woman to another. And look at her; can yer honestly say you blame him?"

"Fine! Whatever," she snapped, pushing her bowl away and jumping to her feet. "I need the loo."

"Downstairs, second door on the right!"

Muttering to herself, she followed Malachy's directions and found herself in a room just big enough to climb into. At the furthest end, near the wall, was a rough wooden box with a hole in it. She peered tentatively into it. Far below, past the smears, the remains of matter she'd rather not think too much about, hay surrounded a pile of earth and waste. She straightened. But there was no choice, especially after that stew; she had to go. Pulling down her leggings and knickers, she crouched over the hole, trying not to let any part of her touch the wood.

Watch out down below, a voice inside her sniggered. *Jasmine*, she told herself firmly, *this is no time for jokes.* She shut her eyes.

Finished, her first thought was to go back to her room, but her feet carried her on towards the tunnel. Her instinct told her she should go back, wait with Malachy for Seamus and Grainne to be finished, but she'd had a bellyful of Malachy's real-life legend. "*And look at her; can you honestly say yer blame him?*" He might not be so keen, if he saw her sat over a hole in the floor, her crap free-falling down the side of a castle. That thought made her feel better. Bending down, she climbed into the tunnel and crawled towards the rope ladder.

*

Back on the ground floor, men moved about her, too busy with their preparations to take much notice of her. The noise of the village echoed through the stone walls, the sounds of daily living strangely enticing. Weaving through the men, she slipped out of the tower and, turning away from the sea, walked towards the village. A few moments later, a figure stepped out of the shadow of the tower, and slowly, carefully, began to follow her.

Jasmine ambled through the village, unable to shake the feeling that she'd wandered onto a film set. Sights and sounds assaulted her: the loud metallic ring coming from the blacksmith's, a hawker selling his wares, surrounded by women in long dresses or brightly coloured skirts, their hems kissing the ground, a basket weaver, a small, brown scruffy looking dog, and chickens, sheep, horses. There was so much to see. Two children ran past, one tugging the other by the sleeve. A third, tall and gangly, caught her shoulder, knocking her sideways. She stopped as he ducked his head apologetically and ran on, following his friends. She lifted her head, sensing sudden movement behind her. She spun, but all she could see was villagers. Shaking her head at herself, she continued. Behind her, eyes watched her from under a hood. The figure straightened.

*

In the centre of the village, three women stood next to a well. They watched her as she approached, the one to the right lowering her head and murmuring. Jasmine recognised her immediately as the older serving woman, the one that had brought the fish stew.

The middle woman stepped towards her, stopping her in midstride. "You're the girl staying with Grainne Mhaol?"

"Yes, I'm—"

Throwing her head back, she spat. Spit caught Jasmine in the face, sprayed across her left cheek. Shocked, she raised her hand to it as a figure raced past. It grabbed the woman's arm and, with a growl, propelled her backwards.

"Have yer lost yer mind?" A voice hissed, "Go home, and pray no one speaks of this to Grainne Mhaol."

With a final push, he let her go and, with a shake of his head, turned back to Jasmine.

It was the huge man who'd rode beside her.

"Come." He grabbed one arm, as if he were planning to force her, like some wayward chicken, or goose, back the way they'd come. "We must return to the castle."

Jasmine finished wiping her face with her sleeve. She wanted nothing more than to get to the well and to wash and scrub her skin clean, but around them people had stopped and were staring.

"It's not safe." His eyes were surprisingly soft; he seemed to be pleading rather than ordering.

She nodded.

They walked through the village, the man hovering protectively around her, his bulk parting the villagers like the thick, heavy metal hull of a ship parting the waves. Word was already carrying; she could see it the nudges, the stares. Some were curious, others, she thought, were dark with hostility, but after being spat on, that might be just her imagination.

"Thank you," she said as they reached the last house/ "I'm sorry, I don't know your name."

"Brennan." He gave her an assessing look. "I merely followed Grainne's orders."

"Her orders?"

"To protect you."

She stopped. "It was you? Following me? But why? I don't need protecting." He looked at her cheek and she flushed. "Why did that woman — why did she — spit on me?"

He didn't answer.

"I'm not going anywhere until you tell me."

"Very well." He sighed, then lifted his arm again. "But we must go."

"OK."

They continued.

"She comes from a town east of here. A year ago, it was destroyed, burnt to the ground, and those that tried to escape were killed, slaughtered as they ran."

"Oh, God, who would do that?!"

"English soldiers."

It was her turn to look away.

"I — I–" She stopped; there was nothing to say, nothing she could say. Other than it was history, it wasn't like that anymore, but it wasn't, it was happening right now and it was her people doing the killing.

They were almost at the castle. Horses and men were stood waiting for Grainne's reappearance and the order to leave. Reaching out, Brennan touched her arm, stopping her.

"I do not have the right to ask, but will you speak of this to Grainne?"

"No, why should I?"

"As Grainne's guest, you lie under her protection; an injury to you is an injury to her. A clan member has insulted you, insulted her, and that cannot go unpunished. You have only to request it."

"No, I couldn't. It wouldn't be fair. No." She glanced at him. "What if someone else tells her?"

"She would be honour-bound to punish the insulter, both for the insult and her defiance of Grainne's word."

"Then you can't tell her. Promise me you won't."

He smiled faintly.. "Would ye have me lie to my chieftain? My Queen?"

"No, of course, not." She thought fast. "But as her guest, I'm asking you, no, requesting, that you never, ever speak of it. Surely to speak of it would only compound the injury? And you were ordered to protect me."

He laughed, and to her surprise, bowed slightly. "I am at your command, my lady."

"Jasmine! Jasmine!" It was Malachy. Coming from the direction of the beach, he ran towards her.

"My thanks." Brennan's eyes held hers for the briefest of moments, and then he was gone, lost amongst Grainne's men.

"Where have you been? I've been looking for you; it's time to go."

"Just to the village."

"C'mon, the horses are ready. Seamus is here; we're just waiting for Grainne."

Right on cue, Grainne appeared, stepping through the castle doorway. She moved to her horse and they followed her, climbing hastily on, and then, with Grainne and Duggan leading, the company moved off, away from the castle. With their backs to the village, no one noticed the figure that stepped out from behind a house. Dressed in a long, black cloak, its face obscured by a hood, the figure twitched once, then disappeared.

*

Clew Bay receded as they travelled east then south, going back the way they came, the land returning to the more familiar forest, tree and bog. This time Jasmine was riding alongside Malachy, just behind Seamus, Grainne and Duggan. She looked for Brennan and spotted him near the back, riding with a man with Malachy's size and colouring, but with a thick, black moustache and neatly trimmed beard. They stopped at midday for a rest, drink and a little food, then turned east, along the road Jasmine and the others had travelled only yesterday. As the afternoon lengthened, the wind picked up, blowing the white, fluffy cumulus away, and the darker, heavier rain clouds in.

"It's gonna rain," Malachy remarked, looking upwards.

But, amazingly, it didn't. Still dry, they rode into early evening until Grainne called a halt on the edge of the forest. Dismounting, Jasmine and Malachy sorted their horses while Grainne's men got the camp ready, their movements swift and efficient despite the rough banter, the laughter and the catcalls, running between them. Seamus went to one side with Grainne and Duggan, the three of them once more falling into a deep conversation.

*

With their horses sorted, there was little for Jasmine and Malachy to do.

"Let's get some firewood," Malachy suggested, shivering slightly. "It'll help keep us warm."

Leaving the camp, they followed a rough path into the forest. Still bright, it looked dark in there, full of shadows. The wind caught the leaves, making them rustle. Malachy went first, Jasmine second. The trees closed over them.

The ground was soft, the earth covered with a thick, springy moss that made Jasmine's feet bounce. Without the sun to warm it, the air was cold, the wet and damp from the ground and bits of fallen, rotten wood, rising upwards. Moving apart, but keeping each other in sight, they gathered wood. Jasmine picked up a piece of branch, but it broke into two, so she dropped it. It shattered, the bark crumbling like hollow, diseased bone. She tried another, but that was rotten too. She continued, scanning the ground, hearing Malachy somewhere off to her left.

The forest was silent. She lifted her head, realising she couldn't hear Malachy.

"Mal?"

No answer. Spinning, she looked for him through the trees, the undergrowth. He wasn't there.

"Yeah?" His voice carried faintly, still to her left.

His head appeared over the top of a bush. He must've been bent down, picking up some wood.

"Oh, nothing."

A tree, fallen sideways, lay across the forest floor, thick, its trunk covered with whorls of grey-green lichen, and it called to her. Placing the wood carefully on the ground next to her, she perched on the edge and, pulling up her knees, hugged them. It was nice to have a quiet moment, away from everyone else, bar Malachy. So much had happened; it was hard to take it all in; Seamus and Grainne, the woman spitting in her face, the look of hatred in her dark eyes, and Brennan's story. How could anyone do that? Murder innocent people, men, women and children, watch their bodies burn? The terror they must have felt. Just like the villagers in Killaspugbrone, suffocating on sand. She rubbed her face. Who was she to talk? She'd killed thirty-eight innocent people, killed them as surely as those soldiers who'd set the houses on fire. She stared at the ground. Green leaves lay on top of brown, the half-mulched fall of the previous autumn. Iomlan moved inside her, not so much a stir, but like a little hand waving. Here I am. It was strangely comforting, like the touch of a pet's nose, an inquisitive paw. Before she could stop it, it began to float upwards, its touch light and soothing. It filled her, bathed her in a glow like the warm, early morning sun. And then, slowly, leaves began to lift up from the floor of the forest. Unable to help herself, she added more, watching as they floated into the air in front of her and began to spin. They span around one another, twisting and turning until greens, browns and yellows merged into one fluttering cascade. Her heart swelled.

"Wow," Malachy breathed from the other side of the clearing.

She hadn't even heard him come. Edging carefully around the spinning leaves, he joined her on the tree trunk. Entranced, his arms cradling the collected wood, his eyes flicked as they tried to follow the leaves, their pattern.

"Ah, that's beautiful, Jas." He smiled at her, his eyes shining. "And you made it."

They stuttered. She tried to keep them going, but she couldn't. Her focus was gone, Iomlan slipping away from her. They dropped, scattering.

"Damn, I was enjoying that." His face fell. "Jas, Jas? What is it? Was it what I said, this morning?"

She wiped at her eyes. "No, it wasn't that. You were right; why shouldn't Seamus have a bit of happiness?"

"So, what's wrong?"

"Nothing." She gave him her best smile. "Just feeling bad for being a cow."

"She did drug you, to be fair. Of course, she was just trying to find a way to get her nephew back." He nudged her and grinned. "But it's OK, it was one night. I don't think they're planning on getting married just yet."

They wandered back, their arms full of wood. The camp was already finished. Fires had been lit, each one satellite to Grainne's in the centre, the men sat around them eating and drinking. To their left, the undergrowth rustled. A hand appeared, a head ducking under a branch. The figure straightened. It was Brennan. Seeing them, he touched the front of his leggings, as if checking he'd closed them properly, and then, giving Jasmine a small smile, strode over to where his friend, the man with the black beard, was sitting by a fire.

"Jasmine, Malachy, you must eat," Grainne called, beckoning them over. "Here."

Immediately Duggan stood up, indicating they should have his blanket. Dropping the wood near the fire, they sat and a man they didn't know passed them two cloth bags, one small, the other larger. Inside the small bag were dry hard pieces of what looked to have once been meat and in the other, two small, round loaves of bread.

"It's pig," Duggan explained, moving away.

Jasmine took a bite of the meat, pulled hard with her teeth and twisted, trying to get it free. It broke and she chewed on it.

"We should get to MacDermott's by tomorrow evening," Seamus told them, taking a drink from what looked like a bottle of ale.

Duggan was pulling something from the pack on his horse.

"Duggan has something he wishes to give you," Grainne said to Malachy.

"Me?"

Duggan drew out a sword and sheath, "Yes. You have no weapon, no means to protect yerself."

"But I don't need anything." Malachy glanced across at Seamus.

"But what if you became separated?" Grainne asked, archly.

"Here." Duggan held it out. "Take it."

Malachy did as he said. The hilt was surprisingly decorative, and the metal of the blade shone as if it had been carefully tended.

"Thank you." He hefted it awkwardly.

Duggan eyes widened. "Have ya ever used a sword before?"

Malachy flushed. "No, not really."

He rolled his eyes. "I'll teach ya all I can. Enough to make yer opponent pause." He shook his head. "I'd best teach yer to hold it first."

*

They spend an hour together, Duggan giving direction and watching Malachy's efforts with a harsh, critical eye. Slowly they drew a crowd, the men fascinated, amazed at the ignorance of someone his age. One or two of them laughed openly at him, but it didn't last long. He was applying himself too hard, following Duggan's instructions too diligently and without complaint for them to not to take him seriously.

"Jasmine?"

Seamus had come up behind her. Engrossed in Malachy's lesson, she hadn't noticed. He joined her on the rough blanket, stretching out his bad knee awkwardly.

"You used Iomlan."

"Yeah, I know, sorry. I shouldn't've."

"No, you shouldn't've." He leant in. "Unless, it was urgent?" He knew it wasn't.

"I'm sorry, I didn't mean to. It just happened."

He sighed. "Let's just hope Ellyllon didn't sense it."

"I know," she agreed miserably. "I really didn't mean to."

He gave her a shrewd look. "Is something wrong?"

"No, not really." She paused. "I guess I was just thinking about Iomlan. When Grainne's men attacked us, it didn't react, well, not at first, and I was wondering why."

"Shock, probably. It all happened so fast." He patted her knee. "And that's it? There's nothing else?"

"No," she lied quickly.

"That's good." Pressing down with his hand, he used her knee to help himself up, "I must get back. But, please, try not to use it again, especially as we're getting close."

"I promise."

"Grand." He flashed her a smile before returning to Grainne.

She watched them for a moment. She still didn't trust her, but she knew Malachy was right. There was no way Seamus would jeopardise their hunt for Ellyllon. If she couldn't trust Grainne, she had to trust him, trust he knew exactly what he was doing, which was more than she could say of herself.

Chapter Eight

Dawn brought rain. A light misting at first, by the time they'd finished breakfast and were ready to leave, the wind had picked up and it had started to pour. Back on her horse, following Grainne and Duggan as they led the group back to the road, Jasmine lifted her hood and pulled her cloak tight around her. The men followed suit, their heads bowed to keep them covered. They drudged through the rain, silent but for the occasional low curse, their mood as low as the thick, grey cloud. The road turned to the left, headed for the trees and then they were in the forest, the canopy high above keeping off the worst of the rain.

By midday, the rain had stopped, the sun burning the last of the clouds away. Disliking the feel of the heavy, damp wool, Jasmine pulled off her hood and folded her cloak back off her shoulders. Next to her, Malachy flicked his over one shoulder, revealing the sword and belt strapped to his waist. Her lips twitched. He looked so strange, like an extra in a Lord of the Rings film. He glanced self-consciously at her and, not wanting to hurt his feelings, she smiled what she hoped was a supportive, encouraging smile.

*

Another mile and, swapping forest for grassland, they stopped to rest the men and horses. Immediately, Seamus joined her and Malachy.

"Can I have a word?" Cocking his head, he led them away.

"Right." He began in a low voice, looking all around them. "I wanted to talk to you alone. Grainne thinks there might be a spy in her camp. Loyalties and allegiances can be easily swayed, especially for money, and I don't want Ellyllon or MacDermott knowing our plans." He took another look around. "We'll be dividing soon. MacDermott's castle sits on an island very close to the lake's south shore, Grainne will set up her camp about half a mile away, but we won't be joining her. A small band of us will enter the castle to rescue Cormac while Grainne keeps MacDermott occupied."

"How?" Jasmine asked, imaging the pitched battle.

"She's already sent word to MacDermott, requesting an audience to negotiate the return of Cormac."

"But Ellyllon's hardly going to let him do that," Malachy scoffed. "And what if Cormac doesn't want to be rescued?"

"We'll kidnap him. But Grainne's meeting with MacDermott is just a ruse, a pretence of a formality. It's complicated. As far as chieftains go, MacDermott and Grainne are fairly evenly matched. Mostly, the chieftains have been left to pretty much do what they want, but now the English are trying to force them to pay taxes direct to the Crown, and they're not happy about it. For the English, any infighting would be a gift, the old tactic, divide and conquer. The Anglo-Normans were masters at it. No, let's just say that politically, neither of them will want to enter into a full-scale war. So we have posturing."

"But what about Ellyllon? He'll know we're here," Jasmine asked.

"I've been hiding our presence as much as I could — not using Iomlan has helped." Jasmine shifted uncomfortably. "But as we get closer, he will sense us, so I'll try to muddle our presence so he won't be able to pinpoint exactly where we are. By the time we're in the castle and he finds out what we're doing, it'll be too late. MacDermott won't be able to get back to help Ellyllon, and Ellyllon's not powerful enough to withstand both of us."

Malachy frowned. "But surely Ellyllon will just disappear, like he always does?"

Seamus grinned. "Either way, we'll have Cormac. I'll've kept my bargain with Grainne, and now we'll have something Ellyllon wants. He'll have no choice, he'll have to come to us."

Jasmine looked at Malachy. If Grainne was right and there was a spy, then possibly Ellyllon already knew they were coming and would have made his own, slippery plans. She sighed to herself. Back in her bedroom, when Seamus had told her what he was going to do, it had sounded so straightforward: find Malachy and stop Ellyllon. So far, finding Ellyllon had been easier than she'd thought. The hard part was stopping him. Seamus' plan was similar to the one he'd used with her, only this time Cormac would be the bait, and look how that one had turned out. And yet, how else could they get close to him? Let's face it, she told herself darkly, catching Ellyllon was like trying to catch a fish with your bare hands.

They returned to their horses. Most of the riders were already seated. Brennan, Jasmine noticed idly, was stood fiddling with the straps to his saddle. Almost, immediately, he finished, and with an affectionate pat on the horse's rump, climbed on.

*

Continuing east, the land began to rise, gradually at first, with deep undulations that sent them down and then up and down again, but all the while climbing. Grassland gave way again to forest. The road narrowed.

They entered a clearing; Grainne raised her hand and the group stopped. Nudging her horse, she moved in close to Seamus and, leaning over, kissed him softly on the lips. "You have my best, and most trusted. Good hunting."

He cradled her head in his hand. "And ye."

They kissed again. Grainne straightened and, with a nod towards Jasmine and Malachy, swung her horse around. She and her men moved off, streaming past Seamus' group and onwards, along the road.

*

It was just the six of them. Seamus, Jasmine and Malachy joined by Duggan, Brennan and his black haired, bearded and moustachioed fellow rider, Morain. Duggan led them through a break in the trees and into the forest. They weaved slowly between the trunks, ducking to avoid overhanging branches and foliage. The forest was quiet, silent apart from the rustle of hooves in the leaves, the odd jangle of metal. No one spoke.

"Off," Duggan murmured suddenly, gesturing with one hand.

They dismounted quickly, following his lead as he tied his reins to the nearest tree.

"The lough." He pointed through the shrubbery.

Jasmine squinted but could see nothing but green. Crouching low, Duggan crept through the foliage, with Seamus, then Malachy, Jasmine and Morain following, with Brennan bringing up the rear. Brambles and stinging nettles grew thick and tall. Already Jasmine had two scratches across one hand. After ten minutes, Duggan raised his hand and stopped, crouching down on his haunches as the group gathered round him. The edge of the lake was less than a metre away, the water visible through the trees. Duggan pulled back a branch. Straight ahead, a few hundred metres out, lay MacDermott's castle. Covering most of the island, the castle was huge. Thick stone towers rose higgledy-piggledy upwards, accentuated by the high, Gothic windows. Behind, a turreted stone wall surrounded a round courtyard. A large boat lay moored along a wooden jetty, surrounded by a few smaller ones.

"Wow!" Malachy breathed.

Hearing the word, Duggan gave him a quick, suspicious look, before continuing his scrutiny of the castle. A small boat appeared, coming from the shore, two men rowing in quick, athletic strokes. A man appeared on top of the tower nearest them. He saw the boat, pointed and shouted as Duggan let the branch go.

"They're scouts, warning of Grainne's arrival. Let's get back to the horses. Brennan, Morain, meet us there."

He cocked his head at the two men, and without a word they crept away, each circling the shore in different directions.

Returning to the horses, Duggan untied a pack. "We'll leave when it's dark. We should eat, rest."

The undergrowth rustled. Duggan whirled, his hand going to his sword. A hand parted the thin, narrow branches of a willow and Morain appeared. Jasmine breathed out.

"Brennan?" Duggan snapped.

"Here." Brennan stepped out from behind a bush. "I found a boat."

Duggan lowered his hand, his shoulders relaxing. "Show me."

*

They waited for night to descend. Battle hardened, Grainne's men drank and ate, then threw themselves down to rest. Jasmine watched them enviously. Eyes closed, their bodies relaxed and their breathing deep and even, in comparison, she was a bag of nerves, her stomach fluttering. The shadows lengthened. A few minutes later, Duggan opened his eyes and sat up, Brennan and Morain following. They drank again, passing the beer from one to the other, talking and laughing in soft, low tones, and this time she felt the tension in them, tightly sprung like a coil, or a cat waiting to pounce.

*

Night, and dark clouds shut out even a glimmer of moonlight. Going slow, their feet and hands searching in the darkness, they carefully picked their way back to the lake. In the silence, they seemed to Jasmine to be making the most horrendous noise, but she knew the forest, like a blanket, would smother them. They reached the shoreline. Stepping down onto a gravel beach, Duggan skirted the trees. At the far end was the boat Brennan had found. Presumably owned by a local fisherman, part of one side was rotten, but the bottom looked sturdy enough. Together, they gently eased it out onto the water, Brennan and Duggan holding it as the others climbed awkwardly in. One hard, heavy push and the boat lurched forward. Duggan and Brennan jumped inside. Morain took one of the oars, Brennan the other. They dipped, the water around them rippling gently. And then slowly, steadily, the boat began to move across the lake, towards the castle.

Silently, they skimmed the water. The wind was getting up. It tugged at Jasmine's hair, fanned the torches illuminating the sides of the castle, sending the light dancing across stone and the dark water far below. The castle moved closer. Shadows shifted across the front towers, the dark outline of the men keeping watch. There was little cover on the island; even in the darkness, as soon as they stepped out they would be exposed: it was the perfect defence. Jasmine bit her lip and looked at Malachy, but he only had eyes for the castle. There was the soft pad of the paddle into water, the creak of wood on metal, as the oars slipped and turned and the castle's dark grey walls loomed.

"Jasmine," Seamus murmured, and the men stopped rowing, pulled the oars in and waited.

Earlier, as Grainne's men had rested, Seamus had told her what he wanted her to do. Out on the lake, the time to hide Iomlan would be past. They would have to rely on Seamus, his ability to misdirect, to confuse Ellyllon. But this was down to her. She focussed.

The boat lurched and quickly began to glide smoothly, silently through the water. She could feel Grainne's men watching her, feel their eyes fixed on her face, but she ignored them. She needed all her focus to land the boat exactly where Seamus wanted, at the far end of the beach, the furthest point from the towers and overshadowed by a grassy slope above it. They were almost there. Duggan glanced at Seamus.

"Trust me, they can't see us," he whispered.

The boat bumped gently against the floor of the lake a metre from the shore and they clambered out, gasping against the cold, the grey, freezing water that reached up to their knees. Shoulders strained as they pulled the boat up onto the beach and away from the water, then dashed for the grassy overhang.

Huddling together, they crouched under the grassy overhang, the flash of a helmet on top of the tower the only sign of life. Abruptly, the clouds parted. Moonlight bathed the castle, the grass slope.

"Shit," Malachy hissed.

They looked at one another. And then, moving slowly, stealthily, his eyes fixed on the tower, Duggan climbed on to the grass slope, and broke into a run.

"Go," Seamus mouthed.

Jasmine scrambled, her feet sliding on loose, muddy soil. And then she was on the grass, running as fast as she could, feeling her heart beating wildly, her breath coming in huge, cramping gasps. The helmet on the tower flashed again; she saw lights in the windows, imagined a face pressed against the glass, its eyes widening as it stared straight at her and then it was turning back into the room, opening its mouth to shout… she reached the wall, felt the rough stone under her hands and cheek. The blood in her ears thumped, her breath ragged, but inside the castle all was quiet. There was no shout, no pounding of feet as someone raised the alarm. Seamus was right; they couldn't see them. She closed her eyes with relief, feeling a body bump into her. It was Malachy, joining her next to the wall. Then came Seamus, Brennan and Morain. Duggan nodded his head and, skirting the tower to their right, led them around the back of the castle. He followed the wall, his hands tracing the stone under thick clumps of ivy, looking for a door. He stopped.

"Here," he whispered, beckoning.

They joined him, standing all in a line, their backs pressed against the wall. Seamus sent his Iomlan out, gently probing the door's lock. Jasmine's back prickled. He couldn't do it all, confuse Ellyllon and hide them from MacDermott's men and unlock the door. If one of them looked out, they'd see them. Duggan shifted impatiently. Metal scraped loudly against metal, and then, with a smile and a nod, Seamus took a step back.

Duggan flexed his shoulders and pushed. The door swung open. He poked his head through, then entered with a quick, light step. They waited.

His head reappeared suddenly. "Come."

He disappeared again.

*

They stepped into a huge courtyard. A wooden structure hugged the wall, similar to a veranda, the struts holding the thatched canopy in place. Used for storage, and to house the craftsmen necessary for life in the castle; the blacksmith, the weapon maker, the potter and tailor, now there was no one here. Even the turrets, spaced evenly across the top of the courtyard wall, were empty.

"MacDermott will want to give Grainne a show of force, but he would not leave the castle undefended. Where are the guards?" Duggan asked Seamus, frowning. "This is the weak point in the castle's defence. How can they not defend it?"

"I don't know." Seamus shook his head.

Jasmine and Malachy looked at one another; she could almost read his mind. *I don't like it.*

Neither did she.

Keeping in the shadow of the canopy, they made their way to the nearest tower. Jasmine's foot caught on a raised cobble and she fell to her knees, one hand catching a small barrel balanced on top of another and sending it crashing. Grainne's men leapt forward, shielding them with weapons raised. They froze. Nothing happened. Duggan lifted his hand, *wait, wait.* Still nothing. Together they took a breath, the men lowering their swords as Malachy helped her to her feet.

"Are you OK?" he whispered as the others stepped past.

She nodded. "I think so."

He turned away and, as she went to follow, a movement from the back side of the courtyard caught her eye. She reached out to tell Malachy, but he'd already gone. There it was again. Pale, coming out of the shadows, it looked exactly like an arm lifting. She took a step towards it. It was still there. She took another.

"Jasmine!" Malachy hissed, appearing suddenly. He grabbed her arm. "Come on."

He tugged at her, but she resisted. She looked back, but it had gone. With another hiss Malachy tugged again, and this time she let herself be led.

Two narrow steps led up to a small door. Darting forward, Duggan turned the handle. It clicked and the door swung open.

"Unlocked," Seamus said grimly.

*

The tower was dark, the only light the moonlight coming in through the narrow windows and the open doorway. A stone staircase curled up one wall, the steps disappearing into shadow. The room was cold, the air damp. Shivering, Jasmine drew her cloak tight around her. Her hands, she noticed with surprise, were shaking.

Duggan moved towards the staircase, but Seamus put out his hand to stop him. "Remember what we agreed. No one is to be killed. If we see someone, I'll handle it."

There was a pause, and then Duggan nodded. He took a step back, lifted one hand and grinned. *After you.*

"Thank you," Seamus responded dryly.

Slowly, cautiously, he began to climb.

They reached the first floor. There was only one door, leading into the main house. Seamus grabbed the handle and, turning it ever so slowly, pushed the door open into a wide corridor. Torches lay down both sides, bright against the white walls and the dark, narrow floorboards. There was little decoration, just one small, wooden chair and an empty iron candlestick. The windows to the right were shuttered, keeping out the night and the cold breezes coming up off the lake. At the far end, a staircase led up and down, its dark, gleaming wood intricately carved. Tiptoeing silently, they crowded inside, Seamus turning to close the door behind them just as footsteps echoed on the staircase. In a flash, Seamus pushed the door to; he and Duggan readied themselves as Brennan and Morain shrank back into the wall. Malachy followed, grabbing Jasmine's sleeve and pulling her with him. They waited, listening, barely breathing as the footsteps came closer. They reached the first floor. Jasmine imagined the owner turning, one hand stretching towards the door handle. Flinging the door open, Seamus sprang forward. The man had time for just one, startled little cry, and then Seamus' hand was on his forehead and his eyes closed and he fell. Metal clattered, but Duggan was already there, the two of them holding him up to prevent any more noise.

"Quick." Duggan gestured to Brennan and Morain. "Take him. Hide him downstairs, then come join us."

Lifting the man's body, they did as he said, carrying him awkwardly down the narrow stairs.

"Let's find Cormac and get out of here," Seamus muttered.

A few steps into the corridor and they reached an open doorway. Through it, voices echoed, talking loudly. Duggan unsheathed his sword, and a watching Malachy did the same. Duggan tensed, and then, with a quick, sharp nod, he leapt into the room, the others following.

*

The upper hall, the dining hall for entertaining only the richest, the most select guests, was enormous. Thick, heavy beams crisscrossed a high, vaulted ceiling, and at the far end sat a suspended gallery built for musicians to come and serenade the diners. Wooden panelling had been fixed to each wall, lined with woven tapestries in luxurious blues, reds and oranges, and ceremonial weapons rich in encrusted jewels. Halfway along the right wall, a fire roared inside a huge, stone fireplace, large enough to spit a whole cow in, the MacDermott family crest chiselled into the stone. A long table and chairs dominated the centre of the room, but unlike Grainne's rougher, paler wood, this was a deep, dark mahogany. A middle-aged woman, and two young men about Jasmine's age, were sat in chairs next to the hearth, their clothes rich and opulent, the woman's neck and dark green headdress dotted with jewels. Seeing them, the young men started, while the woman got to her feet and calmly and deliberately threw back her head and screamed. Immediately they heard footsteps, and six men appeared, coming through the door at the far end of the hall. Seeing them, MacDermott's men took out their swords and, as the scream faded, crept slowly towards them.

Chapter Nine

Grabbing the two young men, the woman pulled them in towards the wall as MacDermott's men moved past her. More footsteps. Jasmine whirled to see three more men appear behind them, and then, with a yell, Duggan leapt forward. Seamus' Iomlan flashed, knocking two off their feet and sending them flying. Behind them, two men stalked Malachy, the third moving towards Jasmine. She darted away from him, around the table, as Seamus sent Iomlan across his back. Stumbling, he fell to his knees and, without thinking, she grabbed a candlestick from the table and hit him hard across the top of his head. He crumpled. To her right, Malachy's back was against the wall. He had nowhere left to go. One of the men raised his sword and lunged, and he parried desperately, using the technique Duggan had taught him, but with a quick twist of his wrist, the man ripped the sword from him, sending it clattering. Smiling, he raised his sword. Jasmine's Iomlan flashed. Catching him just under the ribs, it lifted him off his feet and sent him crashing into the stone wall. There was a loud crack and his body slid to the floor, his neck at an unmistakable angle, his eyes wide and staring. She looked wildly for the third man, but he was already backing away. He turned to flee but now Brennan and Morain were there. They lunged mercilessly, one catching him in the stomach, the other in the chest and he fell, blood pumping. Still alive, Jasmine watched, appalled, as his hands grabbed at the floor as if he were trying to crawl away. Without a word, Brennan darted forward and, holding his sword in both hands, lifted it high into the air then plunged it down, like a dagger. The man's hands stopped, his fingers uncurling and relaxing. Feeling sick, Jasmine looked away. Beside her, Malachy had retrieved his sword and Seamus and Duggan were stalking the only man left standing. Duggan disarmed him quickly, efficiently, holding him at swordpoint until Seamus could reach over and touch his forehead. Unnoticed, one of the young men had moved away from the wall and was standing in the centre of the hall.

"Jas!" Malachy shouted.

A knife whistled through the air, coming out of nowhere, heading straight for Seamus. Jasmine reacted before she'd realised, deflecting it harmless into a tapestry.

"What?!"The young man turned to look at her. Fair, shoulder length hair framed a round, boyish face and soft rosebud lips. Iomlan flowed through him, swirling impatiently, as if desperate to strike. *Cormac.*

He slashed his right hand and a second knife flew off the wall, this one heading straight towards her. She knocked it away, but more were coming. Knives, a sword, the lethal spiked metal of a mace. There were too many; panicking, she sent Iomlan out in a wave and the weapons dropped.

"Jas!" Malachy shrieked.

A battle-axe hurtled towards her. Almost too late, she caught it a metre from her face. It hovered, refusing to drop. Cormac still had hold of it; she could feel his Iomlan pressing, his lips tightened, and the battle axe inched closer. She looked at the blade, the sharp, shiny edge and swallowed. She mustn't lose her focus. The axe stopped again.

"Jasmine," Seamus' voice said warningly, and she knew instantly what he was trying to say.

This battle with Cormac was down to her. She was on her own. She clenched her hand into a fist, and the axe dipped.

"No!" Cormac shouted.

His hand was shaking now, his eyes wide as he forced the axe upwards. Jasmine tried to hold it down, but she couldn't stop it. The blade straightened. Cormac groaned, and the blade slipped closer. Too close. Shrinking back, Jasmine jabbed hard with Iomlan, twisting desperately. It broke Cormac's hold, the axe clattering to the ground. With a gasp, he dropped his hand, his Iomlan fading and dying. With a calmness she didn't feel, she stepped towards him, Seamus approaching from the other side.

"Cormac, I'm called Seamus," he said gently. "And this is Jasmine, Malachy. We've come to take you home."

Breathing heavily, Cormac stared at him, his eyes dark. "Ellyllon spoke of you." His gaze shifted to Jasmine. "And you."

"Did he now? And why would he do that?"

Cormac laughed. "He knew you would come. He foresaw an alliance between you and my aunt. Tell her I will not return; my home is here, with Ellyllon."

Seamus' eyes narrowed. "Where is Ellyllon? Why doesn't he show himself; is he afraid?"

"He fears nothing. His power is too great."

"If his power is so great, why does he need you? Trust me, Ellyllon is not who you think he is. Jasmine can tell you what he is, what he does. How he manipulates, uses everyone he touches."

Cormac looked at her briefly, then turned back to Seamus, who was still taking small, almost imperceptible steps towards him. "Why should I believe a stranger who has done nothing for me over one who has done everything? I—"

"Because you did it once before," Duggan interrupted swiftly. "Yer aunt took you in, raised you, loved you, as her own, and yet you turned from her, turned from your kith, your kin." He waved his hand. "But all that is forgotten. I've come to bring yer home, to where you belong. Yer aunt loves you still." He paused and, to Jasmine's amazement, smiled softly. "As do I. Cormac, remember, did we not always know who you were, what yer could do, and did we ask anything of you?"

For a moment, Cormac eyes softened, and Jasmine thought Duggan had done it, but just then the woman spoke. "My husband will have you disembowelled for this outrage, Duggan. This boy asked for our protection, and we gave it freely, without greed or self- interest. We ask nothing of him in return, not like the whore you serve."

Cormac's eyes hardened and he turned away. "I will stay here."

Duggan looked at him sadly, then nodded to Seamus. Quick as a flash, he jumped forward, his hand outstretched, Cormac saw him and lifted his arm, a fraction too late. Seamus' hand touched his forehead. He stepped back and Cormac fell into Duggan's waiting arms.

"Brennan, take him," Duggan ordered.

Coming over, Brennan crouched while Duggan slipped Cormac over his shoulder. Cradling his legs, he stood up.

"Duggan!" Morain shouted, and they turned to see the second young man dashing out of the door. "I'll get him." He ran after him.

*

Seamus looked at MacDermott's wife. "My apologies to you and your house, but the boy belongs with his family. Grainne Mhaol is a woman of honour and her love for Cormac is strong. Once he is free of Ellyllon, he will remember that."

"You won't get far," she sneered. "My son will raise the alarm. You should choose your allegiances with more care, sorcerer. Duggan is a serpent; he serves no one but himself, as does his whore of a mistress." She spat on the ground at his feet. "Honour!"

"And so should you," Seamus shot back. "Ellyllon destroys all he touches. He'll suck the life out of your husband and leave you with nothing." He bowed slightly. "Enjoy it while you can, m'lady."

They turned to leave.

"Wait!" Her face cold, MacDermott's wife lifted one hand. "You wish to know where Ellyllon is? I will tell you. He stands where he should be, next to my husband, beside him when he destroys your whore and the rest of her clan."

Duggan darted forward. "What?! What are you saying?"

"Did you not ask why the castle was so unguarded?" Smiling, her eyes hard, she drew herself up. "Your kidnap of Cormac serves nothing but your own destruction. His heart cannot be changed; he *will* remain loyal to Ellyllon and my husband. And when his aunt and her men are slaughtered on the battlefield that is the south shore, he, like us, will lift up his cup and rejoice."

There was a roar, the sound of a loud explosion, and light flashed, illuminating the castle. It came from across the lake.

Duggan ran to the window and looked out. "Cannons!"

She cocked her head, her eyes glinting, "Cannons. That is the power of my husband. With Ellyllon at his side, he will destroy the O'Malleys, then O'Connor and the great and mighty O'Donnell, and then every lord and chieftain that reigns across Eire. And when he has finished, when every clan member bows their head to him, swears fealty to him, he will chase down the English and drive them from our land." Her chest heaving, she raised her hands and lifted up her voice until it rang out, across the hall. "And he will be MacDermott, the High King of Ireland, greater even than Brian Boru, for he shall be the one and only king, and I will be his Queen. And the name MacDermott will ring down the centuries, when the great houses of Europe are long forgotten."

"Foul, unnatural—" Duggan spat, leaping towards her, his dagger in his hand. "Grainne requested an audience."

"Duggan, no!" Seamus shouted, jumping between them. "It won't help Grainne. We have to go."

The dagger remained poised. "But he accepted her request. By his honour, he cannot attack."

"But he has. How will killing an unarmed, defenceless woman help? Look, we can help Grainne, but we have to go. Now!"

Reluctantly, Duggan nodded, his face tense, and slowly lowered the dagger.

With no time for stealth, they ran for the main staircase, Brennan carrying Cormac as if he were a small child. There was another explosion, another blinding flash of light. Duggan reached the first step, Seamus right behind him. Coming up the second flight was Morain.

"He was too fast; I lost him outside," he said, breathing heavily. "He made it to far tower, to the men."

As if on cue, they heard shouting and the sound of rapid footsteps. Heads and arms appeared, racing up the first flight.

"Out the way," Seamus shouted, pushing Morain to one side and sending a pulse of Iomlan down the stairs.

Men fell, their bodies tumbling in a jangle of metal and startled cries.

They charged down the stairs. Jasmine's heart pounded, her feet stumbling and catching, threatening to pitch her forwards, but somehow she kept her balance. At the bottom, Seamus was stepping over the fallen bodies, using Iomlan on any that stirred or tried to get up. Morain and Duggan had reached the main door. Duggan stretched out his hand, then stopped. Swinging round, he ran over to a flame torch.

"Duggan?!" Seamus yelled as Morain threw open the door.

Duggan took down the torch.

"Get to the boat," Seamus ordered as the rest filed past him. "We'll follow. Duggan, what the hell are you doing?"

Ignoring him, Duggan thrust the torch into a tapestry. It ignited with a loud whoosh, the flames instantly catching.

"Duggan!" Seamus roared, the incredulous look changing to one of thunder.

"Helping Grainne," he replied, thrusting again.

Outside, flames, reflected in the glass, climbed high as the fire quickly devoured wood and tapestries.

"Seamus!" Jasmine shouted, turning around to go back in.

"Jasmine, no, come on." Grabbing her, Malachy pushed her towards the water.

Morain and Brennan were at the boat. Brennan lowered Cormac inside, then he and Morain began to drag it across the beach and back towards the lake. A bell pierced the night, the peal shrill, urgent, calling MacDermott and his men back from across the water.

Two more men appeared around the side of the castle. Seeing

Jasmine and Malachy, they drew their swords and charged. Iomlan caught them, knocking one sideways, but the other kept going. Without thinking, Malachy leapt to meet him, his sword swinging. The blade caught the enemy across the shoulders, bounced off bone and sliced into his neck. He fell, twitching.

"Come on," Malachy cried, taking her hand and pulling, unaware of the blood splattered down one side of his face.

*

Back on the water, with Brennan and Morain inside, the boat was already being taken by the tide. Slowly, but gathering pace, it drifted. At the edge of the beach, Jasmine and Malachy plunged into the lake and began to struggle towards it. There was still no sign of Seamus and Duggan. The water up to mid-thigh, they reached the boat, and with the men's help slid inside. Behind them, the castle burned, the flames curling and licking across the battlements and into the night sky. Seamus and Duggan appeared, their figures dark against the flames, running across the grass. Brennan and Morain grabbed the oars and, thrusting them into the water and down into the sediment below, tried to use them to stop the boat drifting.

"Look!" Morain pointed, not towards the castle, but the other way, towards the shore, where two large boats, alight with torches, moved steadily in their direction, the oarsmen rowing furiously. MacDermott.

Jasmine turned back. "Seamus, come on!"

They were already in the water, their arms swinging wildly as they waded out to meet them. But MacDermott's boats were coming closer, and Seamus was slowing. A voice shouted, someone on MacDermott's boat giving orders. They'd seen them. Two metres; Seamus and Duggan were almost there. One. Seamus' teeth were clenched, his face drawn with pain, and then Duggan was there, and Seamus, and one by one they clambered awkwardly aboard, the boat tilting crazily.

With Seamus and Duggan lying panting in the bottom of the boat, Jasmine focussed, letting Iomlan build.

"Hold on," she shouted and let fly

The boat surged, slipping easily across the water. But MacDermott's boats were still coming; it wasn't fast enough. She pushed harder, imagined Iomlan as an engine, propelling the boat, speeding it across the miles. She looked back; it was working. Flying, skimming the surface, they were leaving MacDermott's boats behind. For a moment, she thought she saw them turn to follow them, but it was just the light. The boats continued on, towards the castle.

*

They approached the shoreline. Pulling back on Iomlan, Jasmine allowed the boat to slow. No one spoke as the boat slipped gently into the shadow of the trees and followed the curve of the shore.

"The shore," whispered Duggan, pointing.

It was the beach they'd left from. Jasmine turned the boat and eased it carefully forward until it touched ground. Duggan and Morain jumped out and held the boat while Jasmine and Malachy helped a wincing Seamus out. His feet sank, his right knee giving way beneath him. He would've fallen but for the hands holding him. Slowly, his face creased with pain, he limped across the beach and over to the grass.

"I'm OK," he told them, leaning against a tree. Reluctantly, they let go.

Cormac, still unconscious, was again slung over Brennan's shoulder. Then, with the night sky behind them glowing crimson, slowly, wearily, they made their way back to the horses.

*

Still tied to the tree, the horses were where they left them. Behind them, the foliage rustled and a horse stepped out of the shadow, revealing its rider. Jasmine froze, but Duggan went over up to him.

"Grady! How fares Grainne?" he asked anxiously.

"M'lady is well. She sends word to meet her in the place ye parted."

"Is it possible? We heard cannons."

Grady grinned. "Aye, but it was not us that felt them. MacDermott will think again before he devises such a treacherous plan."

"We will meet her there, at dawn."

"At dawn." With a nod, Grady turned his horse and, kicking the flanks hard, sprang off through the trees.

"We must ride. MacDermott will send men to scour the lakeside," Duggan decided quickly. "Brennan, I will take Cormac."

Untying his horse, he led it away from the tree. Together, he and Brennan placed Cormac over its neck, his arms and legs dangling. Waiting for the others to join him, he led them away from the lake.

It took them almost two hours to find their way back to the clearing. Duggan would not permit the use of torches for fear of alerting MacDermott's men. Pulling her horse behind her, Jasmine stumbled along the path, her feet catching on the uneven ground and the exposed tree roots that twisted treacherously. She was getting tired, her body becoming increasingly reluctant to move. They seemed to have been walking for ever. In front of her, Seamus was still limping, his head bobbing as he stepped awkwardly. He was too old for this, she thought bleakly; if she felt rough, she couldn't begin to imagine how he must be feeling.

They reached the clearing. It was empty; Grainne and her men hadn't arrived yet. Brennan and Duggan pulled Cormac off the horse and lowered him gently to the ground, as Seamus limped to a tree stump. He sat and immediately began to massage his right knee.

"Can I help?" Jasmine asked him quickly.

He shook his head. "No, it's just the arthritis. It'll ease off with some rest." He glanced up at the sky. "You and Malachy should try and get some sleep. Dawn's not far off, and Grainne will want to get as much distance between us and MacDermott."

Too tired to do anything else, Jasmine lay down next to Malachy and, using her cloak like a blanket, pulled it up to her chin. Brennan was already asleep; she could hear him snoring. Duggan had insisted on keeping watch. Sitting opposite her with the unconscious Cormac lying next to him, he lifted one hand and lightly pressed his shoulder. Jasmine's eyes pricked. She turned over to look at Malachy. Laid on his back, he was still awake, his eyes fixed on the stars. She'd forgotten about the blood, the patches that looked almost black against the whiteness of his skin.

"Are you OK?" she whispered.

He wiped at his eyes. "I'm fine. Get some sleep." He rolled over, away from her. "Night, Jas."

Chapter Ten

Jasmine woke, shifting uncomfortably. The morning was bright, dawn already long passed, and noisy from the sounds of people starting their day. She opened her eyes. Grainne had arrived while they slept and the camp was full. Some men milled about while others were sat eating, or laid down trying to get even the smallest nap. Yawning, she sat up. Seamus was back on his tree stump, Grainne knelt in front of him. Brennan and Morain were talking to some men, but of Malachy and Duggan there was no sign. Cormac still slept, his body curled in on itself. Pulling back her cloak, she scrambled up and went to join Seamus and Grainne.

"Yer awake, finally," he greeted her. "Ouch."

"My apologies," Grainne said quickly.

She was dressing his knee, applying a grey-greenish looking paste to his skin with her fingers.

"What's that?"

"It's a poultice, made from herbs and the fat of a pig. We use it to ease the pain of age."

"Arthritis," Seamus explained unnecessarily.

Finishing, Grainne wiped her fingers on her leggings and closed the lid of the small clay pot. "I asked if he could not heal himself, but he tells me he cannot." She glanced up at Jasmine. "So we must use this."

Across her left cheek was a long, thin cut, the area around it bruised and swollen. The bruising had moved up into her eye, blackening the bottom of the socket. Noticing Jasmine's look, she lifted her fingers to it.

"It will heal." She shrugged. "Many men lost their lives last night."

She pulled out a long strip of cloth. It reminded Jasmine of gauze, only thicker, heavier, and began wrapping it around Seamus' knee. "This will help keep the poultice in place."

She sat back, as if admiring her handiwork. There was, Jasmine had to admit, far more to her than she'd thought.

"Thank you," Seamus said seriously.

He leant forward, and she lifted up, onto her knees. They kissed.

"I owe you thanks for bringing Cormac home."

"Oh, we're not there yet. He still believes in Ellyllon, but I have an idea."

Avoiding his knee, Grainne began to stroke his leg. "As do I." She grinned.

Inwardly cringing, Jasmine turned away and saw Malachy sitting next to her cloak, eating and drinking with Duggan. He'd washed his face, she noticed.

"You were up early," she said, slipping down beside him.

"I couldn't sleep." He passed her a bottle, and she took a gulp.

Water. She threw back her head and drank.

"Where'd you go?" She passed the bottle back.

"Practice," he said shortly, with a look at Duggan.

"You have the instinct, but lack the skill." Duggan tore off a piece of bread. "It will come, in time."

Jasmine looked across at Cormac. "I can't believe he's still asleep."

Sleeping, his face did look very young. More like the face of the spoilt, indulged child Grainne had described than someone near her own age.

"Seamus had to knock him out a couple of times." Malachy passed her a loaf of bread and small piece of hard cheese.

"He's an O'Malley, like his aunt," Duggan said proudly. "Only she has the guile to turn MacDermott's trap onto himself."

"What — what happened?" Jasmine asked, curious despite herself.

Duggan sat back and stretched out his legs. "On the south shore, at the agreed meeting place, Grainne's speech was met with defiance and disdain. He rejected her plea, bade her leave and he fired on her retreating back. Or so he thought." He laughed, the sound harsh, guttural. "MacDermott's a fool; he hasn't half Grainne's wit. She sent men out and discovered his cannons. When they fired, they fired not on Grainne, but on MacDermott! They could have destroyed him, but Grainne did not wish it. She let him escape, allowed his men back to try and save their castle. The English tolerate her; she plunders their ships, steals their wealth, and they puff and they bluster, but do nothing." He leant forward, his face dark. "But it will not always be so, and a war between chieftains serves only them."

"But won't he want revenge?" she asked.

"And reveal he fell into his own trap?" He paused, and his face reddened. "But I fear you are right. In my anger, I set his castle alight. I was too hasty. This is an insult few could ignore." He shook his head. "MacDermott will not forget, and would, I think, make a deal with the very devil to avenge himself."

Maybe he already had, thought Jasmine soberly, and one he was probably already regretting.

*

Her breakfast finished, Jasmine yawned. She could easily fall asleep again, but they'd be leaving soon. She wasn't the only one; Malachy looked wrecked, Duggan too. She closed eyes, her head nodding.

Someone yelled, an earsplitting yell that echoed around the forest. Jasmine jumped and opened her eyes in time to see the others go running. Scrambling to her feet, she followed them.

It was Cormac. Unnoticed, he had woken and, using the chaos of the camp had tried to creep away. Caught on the camp's edge, he was surrounded by a circle of men, watching him warily. Iomlan spilled out of him like sparks from a fire, catching anyone that came too close. Roaring, swearing, he cursed them, their wives, their children, threatening them with disembowelment and worse. Grainne tried to reason with him, to soothe him, but he was like a thing possessed. Jasmine watched, horrified.

"Seamus," Grainne pleaded, holding her hand to him.

The last of Cormac's control snapped. Flinging out his arms, he sent his Iomlan hurtling towards her. Instantly, Seamus was there, deflecting it, sending it harmlessly down into the ground. He refocused, and Jasmine could feel his Iomlan shifting and changing, until it was a mass of throbbing energy. It fell on Cormac, literally flopped on top of him, squeezing the life out of his Iomlan. Sinking to his knees, Cormac's eyes bulged as he fought to move, but Seamus' power overwhelmed him. His body sagged and he bowed his head, defeated.

"Jasmine, quick, I need yer help," Seamus cried, beckoning.

Morain and another man parted, letting her through. Cormac lifted his head and, seeing her coming, watched her suspiciously.

"We haven't had chance to talk about this, so I need you to trust me. Cormac's too far gone to listen to reason, but maybe, if we show him — I want you to show him the truth about Ellyllon. How he lied, tricked and manipulated you." He paused. "I'd do it, but I don't just want him to see it. I want him know how it felt. I want him to know how you felt, to feel it with you. Can you do that?"

"I can try."

"Good girl. When I say, put your hand on his forehead and concentrate. Remember all you can, and don't hide your feelings. You want him to see them, feel them. But don't force him; let him come to you. Now, are you ready?"

She nodded, her heart in her mouth. Kneeling, she did as Seamus said. Cormac jerked his head, trying to pull away from her, but she simply moved with him.

"Cormac, I'm not going to hurt you. I just want to show you something," she explained gently, trying to ignore the look of hatred in his eyes.

Closing hers, she thought back to that final day at Killaspugbrone, starting at the airport. Willing Cormac to see it, she tried to follow Seamus' advice and rather than try to push him, to simply open herself up to him. At first, he couldn't take it. The things she was trying to show him were too strange, too alien. His mind baulked at them. He tried to look away, but it was happening too fast. Confused, he watched Ellyllon, listened to what he said and suddenly he had to know, to understand what was happening and what would happen next. . She hid nothing. He saw it all, every action, every thought, every feeling, and it was as if she were in two places at once; in one, reliving it, in the other watching herself with older, wiser eyes, with Cormac alongside her. Incredibly, he was feeling her emotions, her pain, and in her turn, she could feel his; his fear and disbelief at what he was seeing. His shock when her father was revealed as Ellyllon, his attempt at denial when he saw Ellyllon as he truly was. Connected in the strangest way, they were still themselves, still separate, distinct, and yet also fundamentally, intimately linked. Jasmine's body shuddered with the power flowing through them. It was becoming too much. She tried to pull away, but now it was Cormac who wouldn't let go. He wanted, demanded, to see it all. His grip tightened, refusing to let her go. She was attacking Ellyllon now, lifting him up until he was suspended against the sky, the golden light appearing around him. Cormac watched, transfixed, and she could feel his fascination and something else, something darker, but all she could think about was that she knew what was coming next and she didn't want to see it. Mustering all her strength, she tried again to pull away.

"Malachy!"

With her own scream ringing in her ears, Jasmine was flung violently backwards, her body hitting the ground hard.

"Jasmine, Jasmine."

Seamus was calling her name; she opened her eyes. He frowned down at her, Malachy stood next to him. Still back in Killaspugbrone, she was momentarily confused, but then she remembered. Both cheeks tickled, her lips tasting salt, and she wiped at them, realising that she'd been crying. Behind them, Cormac too was on the ground, his eyes closed and his face pale. Grainne knelt next to him, Duggan at her side.

"Are you OK?" Malachy asked.

She eased herself up, wiped at her face again. "I think so. What happened?"

Seamus reached out and, grabbing her hand, helped pull her to her feet. "I'm not sure. It looked like you were struggling with each other and then you shouted and the two of you were thrown apart. Don't you remember?"

"I know he was with me, seeing it. I could feel him react, but I don't know what went wrong."

"Maybe nothing; we won't know till he wakes. Now that was tough. Rest for a bit, have some water. I'll watch Cormac." He turned to Malachy. "Malachy, go with her."

Taking her by the arm, Malachy steered her to a quiet spot and eased her down on a fallen tree before sitting beside her.

"Why were they staring at me?" she asked, disliking the way Grainne's men had looked at her. As if she were some kind of freak.

Malachy looked away. "You shouted really loud."

"Oh, I thought it was in my head." She flushed.

"You really don't remember what happened?"

"Kinda. It's all a bit jumbled." She thought back. "I remember Ellyllon was telling me he'd killed my dad, how he'd planned for so long and, I — I remember thinking that I wanted to stop. No, I think I tried to stop, but I couldn't. Iomlan wouldn't let me. I think…" She shook her head helplessly. "Or Cormac. I'm not sure. But I know I couldn't stop it."

"Do you think it worked?"

"I dunno. He was with me, I know he was; he felt everything. I can still feel him there, inside." She touched her head and grimaced. "Mal, it's weird."

"Where is she?! No, I don't want to. Where is she?!" Shrill, Cormac's voice cut through the camp.

Instantly, Jasmine and Malachy were on their feet. Cormac charged through the watching men, his head twisting frantically.

"Cormac!" she called, knowing instantly he was looking for her.

The men fell back and Seamus, Grainne and Duggan appeared.

"I saw you." Cormac had stopped and was gazing at her with wide, unfocussed eyes. "You showed me."

"Yes. It was Ellyllon. He killed my father."

He frowned. "I felt it. How?"

She touched her stomach. "We call it Iomlan. Didn't Ellyllon tell you?"

"Iomlan." He mimicked her gesture. "No." His hand dropped. "You showed me a lie."

"No, I didn't." Stepping away from Malachy, she moved towards him. "But then you know that, don't you? You didn't just see it, you felt it. You felt me." He was wavering, she could feel it, and she pressed her advantage. "Ellyllon doesn't want you, he wants your power. He doesn't care about you; he doesn't care about anyone. He feels nothing; no love, no sympathy. All he wants is power. He needs it. And if he has to manipulate you and lie to you to get your Iomlan, he will."

Cormac shook his head. "He does care for me."

"If he cares for you, why does he hurt you? Why does he tell you that your aunt doesn't love you? Why does he tell you that your father rejected you, blamed you for your mother's death? Or say that she died because of the power you have?"

His head snapped up. "How do you——?"

"Because you showed me. When you saw me, I saw you. When you felt my feelings, I felt yours. Ellyllon lied to you, but that's what he does. He takes your deepest fears, the things you can never say to anyone and twists them until they're all you can see." She sighed. "I know; I believed his lies too. I wanted to believe them. My dad coming home was my dream. But your aunt, she risked war, her life, the lives of all these men, just for you."

"For me, or what I can do?"

"Cormac," Grainne interjected, coming forward. "You are the child of a most beloved sister, my flesh, my blood. I would have you with me, magic or no."

"Do not lie to me, for I saw your face as he swore his allegiance. I saw your heart."

"Then I will say it. I was a fool, and like others before me, seduced by the promise of power. But like the devil, for the little he gives, he takes much, much more. You talk of my heart." Her voice lifted, and she slapped once at her chest. "When Ellyllon took you, he took my heart. These men know me. I am their chieftain, their leader, and a leader does not speak of such things. But no more. I will speak. You are as a son to me. I would rather never ride the waves, feel the ship beneath my feet, than lose you."

"And I you." Cormac's face crumpled; he gave a cry, and threw himself into his aunt's arms. "Forgive me."

"No, it is I who should ask forgiveness," Grainne whispered, kissing him. "For not knowing what I had."

They hugged.

"That was very well done, Jasmine," Seamus said softly, beaming at her.

"Is that it then?" Malachy asked. "Is he really free of Ellyllon?"

"I think so. Luckily, Ellyllon's control was the same as for Jasmine; emotional manipulation. Once he saw Ellyllon's true nature, he saw through his lies."

Letting Cormac go, Grainne slipped her arm into his. Heads bent, they walked away, talking.

"So, what now?" Malachy asked.

"We go back to Clew Bay. I have questions for Cormac; I want to know why Ellyllon went to so much effort to take him from Grainne."

"Duggan thinks MacDermott will be looking for revenge," Jasmine offered.

"That might have something to do with Duggan burning down his castle! Of course, it won't help having Ellyllon whispering in his ear, encouraging him."

"But what if he doesn't?" Malachy asked. "What if he decides to move on, try and manipulate someone else?"

"Possibly," Seamus admitted. "But don't forget, if I'm right, he doesn't want to be here. He doesn't care about what's happening now; he wants to get back to the time of the druids. And *if* I'm right, then somehow Cormac is the key."

Chapter Eleven

They rode back towards Clew Bay, through the forest and back onto the wide, grassy plain. Although not yet midday, without the cooling shelter of the trees it was very hot. Malachy, riding next to Jasmine, was quiet, deep in thought. He was probably thinking about Cormac, wondering, like her, why he was so important to Ellyllon and what he had that Ellyllon so desperately wanted. Riding alongside his aunt and Seamus, the object of her thoughts abruptly wheeled his horse around and joined her and Malachy.

"May I ride with you?" he asked formally.

"Of course." She smiled, wanting to him to know there was no hard feelings.

She moved her horse sideways, and he slipped into the gap between them. They rode in silence for a few moments.

"It is strange. I know ye, and yet, I do not." He shook his head, as if perplexed. "You are Jasmine, and you, Malachy."

"Yes." She didn't know what else to say.

"I am in your debt." He smiled and his face lit up.

And for the first time she saw his aunt in him, in the same dazzling smile.

"No, no." Her face reddened. "I'm just glad you're OK, I mean, I'm glad you're free from Ellyllon."

"As am I!" He glanced at Malachy. "Do you too, have, magic?"

"Iomlan? No, I'm just a friend."

"A friend." Cormac studied him for a moment, then turned back to Jasmine. "Your magic, your Iomlan. Will you tell me of it?"

She grinned. "Of course; what do you want to know?"

*

Grainne stopped the company for another break, water and rest for the horses and food for the men. Off their horses, and with a low bow and another dazzling smile, Cormac was gone, back to his aunt's side. Jasmine watched him go. He was nothing like she'd been expecting. He was funny, self-deprecating and not at all spoilt, given the way his aunt seemed to idolise him. At some point, she wasn't exactly sure when, Malachy had got bored and ridden over to join Duggan. He was there with Duggan now, the two of them preparing for another lesson. She hoped he hadn't felt excluded with the two of them chattering away, but it had been just so good to talk to someone with Iomlan who was around her own age. There were so many similarities between them, so many things he too had tussled with. It made her feel less alone, even though she hadn't actually realised she'd been feeling alone. But she couldn't expect Malachy to understand, and Seamus had had Iomlan so long he'd probably forgotten what it was like. How much worse had it been for Cormac? He'd had no one, no Seamus to guide him or to talk to. No wonder he'd believed Ellyllon's lies.

*

"Jasmine." Cormac was back, carrying a small cloth sack and a jar of beer. "Please, eat with me."

She glanced at Malachy; oblivious, he took the stance Duggan had taught him. "Yeah, OK."

Leading her away from the camp to a small hillock, Cormac waited for her to sit, then, taking out the food, placed it on top of the cloth.

"It's good to have someone to talk to about Iomlan," she said as Cormac flung himself down next to her.

"It is," he agreed. "But you have Malachy."

"Yes, but, er, it's not the same. He doesn't understand; he can't, not really." Cormac passed her the beer and she took a swig. "But you must have had friends."

He smiled, his lips tight. "Grainne's nephew and a sorcerer?"

She took his point. "So, Ellyllon?"

His smile slipped. "Was as the sun. I thought him my kith, and if not of my blood, then something close. He listened to me, knew my thoughts, my heart, even before I did." He shook his head. "I was a fool. He cared nothing for me. Sought only what he accused my aunt of seeking, and more, for I was a gift for MacDermott, the nephew of the woman he hated."

Breaking off a piece of bread, he chewed it for a moment. "When my aunt was young, MacDermott made advances to her. When she refused, he tried to force himself on her. He has a scar on his forearm where her knife cut. A chieftain, the leader of his tribe, his will thwarted by a mere girl. Now I see I was to be part of his revenge."

He paused, his eyes unfocussed as he stared into space. Guessing

99

that there was more to come, Jasmine waited.

"There was much MacDermott would have me tell him, but I would not. I fear there was hatred in my heart for my aunt, but I would not help him to destroy her, or harm the men, women and children of my clan."

He looked at her then, willing her to understand. And she did, all too well. No matter how small, there was some consolation in knowing that you hadn't meant to hurt anybody. In that moment, they seemed so alike, but maybe that was just how it was, Jasmine thought gloomily, when you had Iomlan and the power to hurt, maim and kill.

"I cannot undo what I have done, but Grainne has made a pledge to you. Let me help fulfil that pledge, if I can. But maybe, what I have to tell, it isn't important?"

A thrill of excitement raced through her, but she ignored it. "Why don't you tell me, and we might find out?" she suggested, trying to keep her voice even.

He nodded.

"Late one night, when the castle was quiet, I could not sleep for the darkness of my thoughts. I went for ale and, passing the Upper Hall, I heard voices talking. Curious, I stopped to look. It was Ellyllon and MacDermott. They were speaking of a legend of an ancient oak tree, from the time of the Celts. Ellyllon told MacDermott the world's riches would be his if he would help him discover this tree. It was then MacDermott told him of the library at Ballintubber Abbey. O'Connor patronises the Order, protects them from thieves and raiders and those that seek to destroy the faith. There is tell of a monk in the abbey, who had brought together all the knowledge of the Celts, their pagan beliefs, so that nothing would be lost. Surely, he asked, would not the location of the tree be written there? I never saw Ellyllon so excited; he rose to his feet and paced and paced. When at last he stopped, he told MacDermott that this was a place which he could not enter, and that he would send me in his stead." Cormac sighed heavily. "I left then, unwilling for Ellyllon to find me listening, but my heart was thick with pride."

Jasmine turned it in her mind. "And you think Ellyllon's gone to this abbey to try and find out where this tree is without you?"

"I do not know, but how can it be that only I can enter?"

"It wouldn't make sense. It's just an abbey. Unless there's something stopping him, maybe from the druids, like in the tombs—" She stopped, conscious that Cormac was staring blankly at her. "But then why you?

Why not just anyone?"

She frowned, trying to figure it out.

"We should go tell Seamus," She decided, scrambling to her feet. "You were right; this is important."

*

Malachy lunged. Duggan parried easily, but already Malachy was moving, trying to slip sideways, under his guard.

"Good." Duggan beamed as he caught Malachy's sword, the blades clanging. "Much better."

Grainne turned to Seamus. "He learns quickly."

"Yes." Seamus looked away, and saw Jasmine weaving hurriedly through the men, Cormac behind her. "Jasmine, what is it?"

"It's Cormac; he has something to tell you, about Ellyllon."

Reluctantly, Cormac sat, and with Duggan and Malachy joining them, the group closed in around him. Glancing from one to the other, Cormac coughed, to clear his throat, and began.

*

"This legend, has anyone ever heard of it?" Duggan asked a few minutes after Cormac had finished, the first one to break the silence.

No one answered.

"In Celtic mythology, the oak tree is the gateway to another world, a portal," Seamus said suddenly. "A potent symbol of life. It still is."

"A gateway to another world?!" Grainne repeated, her eyes wide. "The fairy world?"

"Not exactly." He glanced at Malachy. "This confirms it. When you fought with him, you knocked him off course. We——"

"You fought Ellyllon?" Cormac interrupted loudly.

Malachy flushed. "It wasn't really like that."

"Why Cormac? Why not seek the book himself?" Duggan asked Seamus.

Cormac was still staring at Malachy, as if seeing him for the first time.

"If the abbey was built on a place sacred to the druids, it would most likely be protected from Ellyllon and his kind."

"His kind?" Cormac switched his attention to Seamus.

"You saw what he does. No man could do that, not even with Iomlan, with magic." He shook his head. "A book on Celtic lore could run into volumes, but Cormac, using Iomlan with Ellyllon's guidance, could've found it relatively quickly."

"So why can't Ellyllon just sense this tree? Like he does you, or

Jasmine?" Malachy asked.

"As with the abbey, it must be protected. The druids took their magic, their beliefs, their responsibility very seriously. They would've kept it hidden, out of the grasp of those who would misuse it. But nothing can be completely eradicated; there's always a trace, no matter how small." He looked at Grainne. "This changes everything. We must go to Ballintubber abbey, find the book and discover the location of the tree. Ellyllon knows we have Cormac and knows it's only a matter of time before we learnt the truth. He may already be there."

"But he can't do anything without Cormac," Jasmine interjected.

"Oh yes he can. Cormac would've made his search quicker and easier, but there are other ways, and he'll be desperate now." He placed his hand on top of Grainne's. "You have fulfilled your promise, your vow, and I thank you for it. We must go."

Twisting her hand, she slipped it into his. "You may still have need of me. I will go with you."

"But what about MacDermott?"

She smiled. "MacDermott's a coward. Without Ellyllon he will not attack. Duggan can defend as well as I, if we have need of it." She looked over at him. "Cormac will go with you, and together you will prepare for MacDermott."

"No, aunt," Cormac interrupted quickly. "You may have need of me at Ballintubber. I would aid Seamus."

"Very well." Grainne nodded, looking pleased. She let go of Seamus' hand and gave him an impish look. "It is decided."

*

Continuing west, the group separated just as the Nephin Beg range came into view, the mountaintops a distant, hazy blue-grey in the sunshine. With Brennan and Morain joining them, five became seven. Stood in a row, they watched as Duggan and the men moved off, and then, swinging their horses around, headed south.

The afternoon lengthened into evening and dusk. Ahead, the faint outline of a long, narrow escarpment began slowly to take shape. Following Grainne's lead, they headed straight for it. Higher than the land around it, it grew steadily until it dominated the landscape. Grassy, its top smooth, rounded, it was empty but for the odd bush, patch of gorse and the scattered white rocks and stones, strewn by nature like confetti.

"Far behind the hills lies Ballintubber Abbey," Grainne declared, stopping her horse and pointing. "To go around would take at least another half day. And it is a good place to make camp, for no one will go there."

"Why not?" Malachy asked no one in particular.

"It is said to be haunted by the fairy folk," Brennan, replied, his face serious.

Fairy folk: the Sidhe. "*Shee*".

"Said by the ignorant, the superstitious," Morain scoffed.

Brennan shook his head, his eyes fixed on the slopes. "Those that go up never come down, or worse, come down without their wits."

Chapter Twelve

Urging her horse forward, Grainne led them up the escarpment. Following a horizontal line through the bush and bracken on the lower slopes, the ascent was gentle at first but it steepened quickly. To keep her balance, Jasmine leant forward, over the neck of her horse. They were almost halfway up when Grainne gave the order to dismount and they continued on foot, leading the horses behind them. Couch grass grew in tall, high clumps that caught at their feet and threatened to send them tumbling. Panting, her legs aching with the effort, Jasmine trudged upwards. Above her, the top loomed. They were almost there. Reaching the top, Grainne climbed over the ridge and disappeared. Seamus followed next, then Cormac. It was Jasmine's turn. Her heart pounding, she gave herself one last push and scrambled over the top, pulling her horse after. She stopped and, breathing heavily, gazed at the view. It was stunning. Along the furthest edge of the plateau lay a second, slightly higher ridge with three jagged peaks behind it. Short, coarse grass was interspersed with swathes of rock and stones, as bleak and as beautiful as any mountaintop. Malachy was coming up behind her; she was in his way. Moving quickly, she joined Cormac, waited with him for the rest to join them, and then they were remounting and again following Grainne, as she led them in single file, along the edge of the escarpment.

*

Keeping to the grass, they weaved their way through the rocks and stone. Jasmine, riding between Malachy and Cormac, looked out across the plain, and saw the ground dizzyingly far below. And it was cold; she wished she was wearing her cloak, but there was no time to stop and put it on. The plateau began to widen and, nudging her horse into a faster walk, Grainne led them away from the edge and into the middle. The ground dipped, lowered into a gentle slope, then slowly evened out. Over Grainne's shoulder, and slightly to the right, lay a small lake; its water, black and motionless, looked as thick and endless as a pool of oil, reaching up from the depths of the earth.

"Here," Grainne said, pointing to the far end of lake where a group of low trees were sat huddled in a rough semicircle, the only cover in sight.

They dismounted. No one spoke; there was an emptiness here, a stillness that put everyone on edge. There was no wind, despite the high, cold air, as if it too was reluctant to visit. Shifting his reins to his left hand, Malachy edged in close beside Jasmine. They were almost to the lake. The trees behind it were still leafless, even though winter had long gone, and their limbs, twisted into unnatural shapes, were stark against the evening sky. Jasmine's horse stopped. She pulled on the reins, but it refused to move. As if catching its mood, the other horses stopped and bowed their heads, their bodies tense, trembling.

"Grainne," Brennan said warningly.

"We'll camp here until dawn," she ordered, ignoring him.

She tugged at her horse and, reluctantly, it followed. Jasmine patted hers, whispered soothing words into his ear. After a moment, he too began to move.

They reached the edge of the lake. Between the water and the trees lay a small, sandy beach edged with rough white stones, almost as if a hand had placed them there. A horse neighed behind Jasmine, its voice sharp with alarm. She jumped, turning just in time to see Cormac's horse, his ears flat to his head, digging the heels of his hooves into the grass. He neighed again and, lifting his head, pulled away from the reins.

"Come!" Cormac cried, tugging as hard as he could.

The alarm was contagious; for a moment Jasmine thought hers was going to bolt, but then Seamus stepped forward, Iomlan working within him, reassuring, soothing, hypnotic. The horses settled instantly, allowing themselves to be led and tethered to the trees.

"It's late; we must make camp," Grainne said, looking upwards, into the sky.

The last of the light was fading, late evening disappearing into the darkness of night. Leaving Brennan and Morain to tend the horses, Seamus helped Grainne to get the fire started while Malachy, Cormac and Jasmine gathered sticks. There were plenty of them, especially around the trees, the bark worn away by the elements, giving them a white, bleached look. Holding a pile in the crook of her arm, Jasmine cradled them to her, and thought unnervingly of an old battlefield, where the bodies had been left to rot and litter the ground with bones.

*

When they had a pile of sticks the same height as the fire, Grainne called to them to stop, and they joined the others around the fire. They talked as they ate, in the quiet, hushed tones of people afraid to disturb. The fire roared, the flames rising as the wood cracked and spat red, glowing ash spittle. Jasmine yawned, and yet, she'd had the most sleep of any of them. Another time, another place, she would've found a quiet spot, curled into her cloak and blanket and slept, but not here, in this bleak, lifeless place. Behind them, the horses shifted nervously.

"Come, Malachy. I promised Duggan," Morain said suddenly, jumping up, as if desperate for something to do. "Take your sword."

Moving away from the fire, they unsheathed their swords. Brennan joined them, sitting down on a nearby rock so he could watch more closely. Seamus and Grainne were talking, their heads bent low together. Jasmine heard Seamus exclaim and Grainne laugh softly as he reached up and wiped something from her face. Jasmine looked away, trying not to smile. They looked so intimate, so natural, Malachy was right; it was impossible not to be happy for him.

"Jasmine?" Cormac was watching her with unreadable eyes.

"Yes?"

He got to his feet. "Will you walk with me?"

"What, in the dark?"

"To the other side of the lake." He pointed.

"Yeah, alright."

Reaching out, he gave her his hand and helped pull her to her feet.

*

They walked around the lake, skirting the water's edge, the light of the fire reflecting on the smooth, dark surface. At the far side, under a low, overhanging ridge, was a second beach. Without either needing to say, they walked towards it. Jasmine looked into the black depths and wondered how far down it went. She'd read somewhere that these small lakes were called tarns, and born of time long before Man, they went deep, very deep. Behind them, Morain and Malachy's swords clashed. Cormac looked back and sighed.

"Did you want to join the others?"

"No. Duggan taught me, but I've no skill, no instinct. Not like Malachy."

"But you don't really need it, not with Iomlan."

"No, but I think Duggan wished me to."

"Oh." She gave him a sympathetic smile.

They reached the second beach. A stone, or rather a boulder, lay next to the water. Flat, smooth, it looked almost like someone had deliberately left it there for people to use, to sit and gaze into the water. It was an invitation, impossible to refuse. They sat close together, their legs almost touching.

"Cormac, do you believe in the Sidhe?"

"I did once, as a child. Brennan does; my aunt too, although she does not say it." His eyes searched hers. "Why do you ask?"

"Just curious."

It wasn't what she wanted to say, but then, she didn't quite know what she wanted to say, or why she'd asked.

Cormac smiled. "And does the Sidhe believe in herself?"

It took her a minute.

"You think I'm a fairy?!"

He laughed softly, a laugh that reminded her again of his aunt. He was very good-looking.

"You speak so strangely. I hear the words, I know what you say, but not the way you say it. And I saw you in my head. I saw your home. I thought at first it must be England, but the people were dressed so strangely, talked so strangely, like you. I saw the hall, and the long, thin — with wings like a bird — they climbed inside." He shook his head. "It is so strange, and yet I know their names. I heard them in my head. You called it a-e-r-oplane. What is an a-e-r-oplane?"

"I can't say; it wouldn't make much sense to you even if I could. But I'm not Sidhe any more than you are."

"No." He stared at the water, as if trying to see into its depths. "Ellyllon told me we are descended from druids. He told me he was once a druid." He turned towards her. "How can that be? Can we live so long? Centuries?"

Jasmine hesitated. Reason told to her to lie, to prevaricate, but he looked so amazed, so earnest, his eyes bright with wonderment, that she couldn't do it. "I don't think we can, but Ellyllon's not like us. He was once, but Seamus told me his need to feed changed that."

"His power is our power. We are as he once was. We can, if we choose, to become as he." He sighed heavily, his eyes slipping away and back. "It is a thing of darkness."

"It won't happen," Jasmine reassured him quickly. "It can't happen. Not without the other druids. It was his punishment that made him like this."

There was a pause. On the other side of the lake, Malachy and Morain had finished their practice and were putting their swords away.

Brennan was checking the horses as Grainne and Seamus prepared for bed.

"Jasmine." Reaching out, Cormac took her hand. "Forgive me, but there is one more thing I must ask. You did not mean to show it, but I saw a storm. Faint, like a ghost. I saw sand, people choking, and a wind like no other. Is this possible?"

"I — I —" Shocked, she didn't know what to say. She hadn't realised he'd seen so much.

"Forgive me, I have given you pain."

She swallowed and looked down at her feet, "No, no, it's OK. It's just, er, I caused the wind. I didn't mean to, but I did, and in the sandstorm thirty-eight people died."

"You did that!"

His voice throbbed. Thinking she heard excitement, she looked up, but saw only sadness in his face.

"I was very young when I first knew Iomlan. Some children teased me, and in my anger, I hurt them very badly." He smiled regretfully at her. "We share more than we know."

She nodded. "Sometimes it can feel like a curse."

"Yes, it holds a high price. But Jasmine…" Straightening, he held his head up and his eyes gleamed. "How can the power to do this, to move the world as only God can, be a curse?"

He gestured with his hand and sent his Iomlan out, across the lake. It skipped lightly over the water, skimming like a stone, and the water close to the shore opposite stirred and plopped, sending up a small spray and small ripples outwards.

Cormac grinned, his eyes dancing. "Come, Jasmine, how far can you go?"

His mischievousness was infectious and a balm to her heavy heart.

"I can't go much further than that, but—" She focussed, curved hers to the left and sent it out in a wide arc. The water to their far right stirred and plopped.

"Impressive," he murmured. "But watch." He raised his hand, and stopped, then nudged her with his elbow. "Look."

Unnoticed, Brennan had finished the horses and was standing between the camp and the lake, staring at the water.

"He must've seen. We'd better stop." She made to stand up, but Cormac put his hand on her arm.

"A moment. Brennan is a superstitious man; he believes in the fairy folk, the water sprite. I shall give him one."

He focussed, and this time he sent Iomlan down, under the water. She could sense it powering through the water and then, a few feet from Brennan, bubbles began to appear, as if something was coming up from the depths. Seeing them, Brennan moved towards them, but they'd gone by the time he'd reached them, leaving behind the smallest of ripples. Cormac focussed again, and more bubbles appeared a few feet away, and again, he followed them.

"Cormac, I'm not sure...?"

"Once more, and we will confess all." Cormac smiled.

The bubbles reappeared, much stronger this time. Reaching them, Brennan leant forward for a closer look just as Cormac jabbed his hand. Water spurted upwards in a wide arc, but quick as a cat, Brennan jumped back and just missed getting soaked. Cormac laughed, too loudly for Jasmine as she smothered her laughter behind a guilty hand. His head cocked, Brennan strode over to them.

"Cormac, Jasmine, come, rest." He glanced nervously at the water. "It is safer by the fire."

"Safer?!" Cormac laughed, "Brennan, forgive me, it was I. A jest."

"A jest?"

Cormac nodded, grinning. "I did not think you would believe it."

"We were just being silly," Jasmine confessed.

Inwardly, she winced; it sounded so childish, felt so childish, especially as Brennan was taking it all so seriously.

He shook his head. "There are creatures inside; white, thin. I saw them."

"No, only bubbles. Maybe, it was an eel, a white eel." Cormac smirked.

"Or maybe you imagined it," Jasmine offered. "In the dark, the water playing tricks on you."

Brennan looked hard at her, as if he'd suddenly realised.

"I would not sit so close," he said abruptly, walking away.

They watched him go.

"I did not think it would work nearly so well," Cormac laughed again, delighted.

"No," she agreed, her own, answering smile half-hearted.

*

Jasmine woke with a shudder. One moment she was asleep, dreaming the dream of screaming wind and children and sand and choking, with a white eel winding slowly up her leg, past her knee, her thigh, and up to her waist before swelling and widening, its head sharpening into the pointed mouth of a snake, and the next she was awake. It was still dark, dawn just a few hours away. The fire had almost completely died; all that was left were a few, glowing embers. Something moved, a stone, the sound as someone had stepped on it making it rock. Jasmine looked, her eyes readjusting in the dark. It was Grainne, stepping lightly, her hands to her leggings, as if she'd just finished doing them up. What a time to be caught short, Jasmine thought, putting her head back down and closing her eyes.

*

She blinked in the first of the morning's light. On one side, Malachy slept with his face buried in his blanket, his body turned away from her and curled in on itself in an effort to be warm. He'd barely spoken to her when she and Cormac had come back to the camp. She guessed he'd seen the joke they'd played on Brennan and didn't approve. Even when she'd said goodnight, he hadn't answered, pretending to be asleep when she knew he wasn't. On the other side, Cormac lay on his back, his sleeping face uncovered, one arm turned towards her. She sat up. Everyone else was sleeping — even Morain, who was supposed to be on watch, was asleep, sat upright, his head leaning forward almost to his chest. Moving as quietly as she could, she scrambled out from beneath her cloak and blanket and tiptoed to the edge of the lake. It looked better in the morning quietness, more inviting, its colour paled to the dark blue of a moonlit sky. Seeing it and feeling the crisp, light air made the unease of last night seem ridiculous, like the nighttime fears of a nervous child

Jasmine scratched at her head, her nails clawing at the skin above her ears that was suddenly unbearably itchy. It was her hair; it needed washing, and now she was thinking of it, she could feel how lank it was, how greasy. And her body, coated in dust and dried sweat, needed a good wash too. She hadn't thought about washing for almost a day; with all she'd done, the riding and running, her body must stink. Slipping quietly over to the horses, she began to rummage through her pack. There, at the very bottom, was the bar of soap she'd taken from her room at Grainne's castle. It was hard and didn't smell too good, but it was all she had. Keeping a careful eye on the sleepers, she walked to the beach she and Cormac had sat on the night before and began to strip off. Down to her underwear, she thought of taking them off, but immediately decided against it. What if one of them woke up and saw her naked? There was nowhere to hide or to shelter, and besides, her bra and knickers could do with a wash. Leaving her underwear on, she grabbed the soap and made a dash for the water.

The water was freezing. Swearing softly, she lowered first one foot and then the other. Disturbed, the water lapped at her ankles and caressed her toes. She shivered, but it was too late to turn back now. Ha-ha-ing to herself, slowly, tentatively, she began to move further in.

The water up to her knees, she took another step and the ground fell away from her, plunging her full into the water. Gasping in shock, her feet scrambling, she found the lakebed and righted herself. Up now to her waist, water dripped from her arms and chest, chilling her skin into goosebumps. It was so cold. There was nothing for it. Holding her breath, she thrust her body forward and plunged her head into the water. Almost immediately, she was up again, gasping hard against the cold. A quick glance at the camp showed the others still asleep and, going as fast as she could, she began to wash, furiously scrubbing her body and then her hair.

When she'd finished cleaning every inch of herself, Jasmine threw the soap lightly onto the beach and dropped back into the water. Crouching, she bobbed up and down, keeping her body moving in order to stay warm, luxuriating in the feel of cold, fresh water sliding across her arms and shoulders. A couple more minutes then she'd get out, she told herself, closing her eyes. It was so peaceful in here, so relaxing, with the water gently lapping. Like being in the sea, floating as the tide imperceptibly took you. She opened her eyes. The edge of the lake was further away. Shit. She lowered her feet, toes scrambling for the bottom, but there was nothing but water. Something touched her foot, soft, silky, a piece of a plant, a water reed maybe. But this far out? She peered into the water. Dark, it was hard to see; she caught a movement, the flash of something thin, white. It twisted in the water, then darted away. Her stomach lurched. Something touched her leg, pressed into her lower thigh. With a cry, she began to swim, as fast as she could, back towards the shore, feeling Iomlan swirl. There it was again, harder this time, against the side of her calf. She bit back a sob. The lake churned with her movement, the water splashing her face and into her mouth. She was almost there. Her right knee hit the lakebed; instinctively she reached out, trying to put her hands down and lever herself up. But too late; she felt it again its touch cold against her foot, and suddenly it was pressing, separating and twisting, like fingers grasping her ankle. She caught a glimpse of one of the men sitting up, had time to open her mouth to try and shout, before she was pulled violently under.

Chapter Thirteen

Instinct made Jasmine hold her breath as she was pulled down into the depths of the lake. She twisted, kicked, tried to get free, but the hand was like a vice, the strength of the arm she could only just see impossible. The light from above was already beginning to fade, her world disappearing, leaving her here in this place of no fish, no life; just dark, dark water. Suddenly the hand let her go and she flexed her body, preparing to kick, desperate for impetus that would take her back, into the air and light, but a face appeared just in front of her, slipping out of the darkness. It was a woman, her face young and incredibly beautiful; her features almost too perfect to be real. The white of her naked body was indistinct, lost in the depths, but her long black hair floated free, drifting towards Jasmine, sliding over her arms, waist and legs, wrapping itself around her face, pulling her close. She felt hands on her back and then a body pressed into hers, moulding itself perfectly to hers. Green eyes gleamed, growing larger, boring into hers until they were the only thing Jasmine could see. She felt a mouth, the lips cold, tickling like trickling water, press over hers, and in her head, she heard her speak, just one word: *Rogha.*

The voice was high and its pitch hurt her ears, but there was something familiar in it, something that reminded Jasmine of cold, hard stone and the softness of moss and she knew then that the woman meant her no harm. She formed a question in her mind and the voice begun to speak again, answering her, when a roar sounded far above them. Immediately the voice stopped, and the trickling water began to tease across her teeth and tongue and drip down into her throat. There was a pause, then the whoosh of rapidly moving water and the mouth left hers abruptly, the face already receding as the air disappeared from Jasmine's lungs. She breathed deeply, her body desperate for the air it needed, swallowing the lake water that was now pouring into her. Choking, she was dragged upwards, her body angled as if tied to a rope hauled across and through the depths. Her head broke the surface near the water's edge and she saw Seamus standing on the beach, Cormac beside him, as Malachy, Brennan and Morain hurled themselves through the water towards her. She tried to breathe, but her lungs, already full, wouldn't move, and for a moment she thought she was going back under, but first Brennan, then Malachy and Morain, reached out and grabbed her, pulling her back into her depth. Her feet hit the ground and she tried to stand, but her legs refused to work. She wanted to tell them to stop, give her a minute, but they wouldn't wait. They continued to pull on her, dragging her up onto the beach before lowering her gently to the ground. Brennan rolled her over and began to press hard on her back, forcing the water up and out of her. It didn't take long; she coughed once, twice, felt air hit the back of her throat and closed her eyes in relief.

*

The feel of someone placing a blanket over her shoulder made her open her eyes. Grainne's face pressed close, her hands touching her hair and face, as if to soothe her like a child. "Shhh."

I'm OK, she tried to say, but nothing came out. She began slowly to raise herself up onto her arms, and then, with Grainne's help, sat up, her body trembling. Malachy, his clothes and hair soaking, knelt beside her. He watched as Grainne tugged the blanket further around her, gathering, folding the ends together to cover her body, then wrapped one arm around her. Jasmine rested her head on Grainne's shoulder and gave him a small smile, but he didn't smile back.

"Jasmine?!" It was Seamus, his face red.

She lifted her head. Grainne's arm tightened.

"I'm OK," she answered, her voice hoarse.

"I can see that! I just want to know why the feck you went swimming in that lake!"

"I wanted to wash."

"Wash?!" Seamus roared. "Washing is something you do at the side. Ya don't dive down into the centre of a deep bloody lake!"

"Seamus," Grainne interrupted, mildly.

"Grainne, don't." He dismissed her with a wave of his hand. "Do you have any idea of how dangerous these inland lakes are? Do you really think we have time for this? If it's not Malachy, it's you."

"What did I do?!"

"Don't get me started, Malachy. Waking up to find Jasmine half-drowning herself has not left me in good form." He sighed, "We'll leave ya to get dressed."

He stomped away. With a final squeeze and a sympathetic smile, Grainne let Jasmine go and, getting to her feet, followed him. Morain and Brennan had moved off and were checking the horses, the fire, anything to keep busy and out of the way. That left Malachy and Cormac.

The latter was watching her anxiously.

"I'm alright." She gave him a lopsided smile. "I just feel silly."

"He feared for you, as did I." He touched her arm. "He did not mean his anger."

Beside him, Malachy bristled, but he didn't seem to notice. "I thought he would empty the lake—"

"Oh, he's got more control than that!" Malachy interrupted, his eyes hard.

Jasmine looked at him, surprised by the vehemence in his voice, then over at Cormac.

"Yes, of course," he said mildly, with a smile as false as Malachy's, then got to his feet. "I will give the men my aid."

She watched him go, then turned on Malachy, "What's the matter with you? He didn't mean anything by it."

"No, of course he didn't. Like he didn't mean it when he played that joke on Brennan. I saw it and it was gas; I couldn't stop laughing."

Jasmine flushed. "That was as much me as it was him."

"Really? Whose idea was it then?"

"You don't understand. It's been so hard for him. He's been all alone with Iomlan. He's had no help, no guidance, no one to talk to. He's had no chance to learn the right way to use it."

"Must've been terrible." He snorted. "All alone with an aunt who dotes on him. Gives him everything he asks for."

"I don't think that's fair. You don't know him. You haven't even tried to talk him."

"It's hard to when every time I turn around you two have yer heads together."

"Yeah, well, it's nice to be finally able to talk about Iomlan to someone who really knows what I'm talking about, how it feels, what it's like." She sighed, knowing it wasn't coming out right "What I mean is, it's just something we have in common. It's weird; hundreds of years apart, but there's a bond there, like we're the same."

"The same," he repeated, almost as if trying the words on for size. "You mean he's not ordinary, like me."

"Mal, I didn't mean it like that. Mal, Mal!"

But it was too late, he'd already gone.

Climbing to her feet, Jasmine rewrapped the blanket awkwardly around her and made her way back to her clothes. With no shelter, she was going to have to take her bra and knickers off on the beach, peeling them down under the blanket. Reaching down, she found the wet edge of her knickers and began to pull.

"Jasmine." It was Grainne. "Allow me."

"Oh, thanks."

She slipped out of the blanket as Grainne grabbed the corners and held it, like a sheet or a screen. Working quickly, she peeled off her underwear and threw on her clothes.

"Thank you," she repeated, finishing.

"You're welcome." Grainne nodded, folding the blanket.

She glanced at the bra left on the ground.

"Do you want to have a look?" Picking it up, Jasmine held it out to her.

Grainne dropped the blanket and, taking it, began rubbing her fingers across the soft material, the line of the cups and the straps.

"The cloth is very fine," she mused, examining it closely. "You wear it as a bodice?"

"Yes."

She pulled at it, elongating it like a concertina. "Light and strong. It would be good for battle." She looked up at Jasmine. "Seamus told me."

"Told you what?"

"Everything."

"Everything?!"

She handed back the bra. "Will you walk with me?"

What was it with these walks? It was like a play, with the characters taking each other aside at the far end of the stage. And yet she was dying to know exactly what Seamus had told her, and why Grainne was telling her. Settling her feet, Grainne put her hand on her hip, and waited.

"OK," Jasmine nodded.

Grainne led her away from the lake and towards the edge of the escarpment. The sky was clear, promising another bright, sunny day. The ground sloped towards an outcrop; they climbed up one, two, flat slabs of rock and straightening up, looked out.

"Wow!" Jasmine's breath caught.

Clew Bay lay to the west, ringed by mountains to the north and Croagh Patrick to the south. The ocean glistened and shrouded in early morning mist, and Jasmine could just make out the high, rugged outlines of two islands. Further south, more peaks rose up; the start of the Connemara mountains.

"This is my land, the land of my ancestors. It is my blood. Would you not fight for it?"

"Yeah, if it were mine."

Grainne nodded. "And yet, for all its beauty, it is a harsh, barren place and perhaps, it makes its people so."

There was a pause.

"You do not trust me."

"I wouldn't — I don't know," Jasmine spluttered.

Grainne smiled. "You were wise not to trust me. Seamus was a fool."

"What?!"

Her smile widened, like a cat. "Or so I thought. Jasmine, the time for doubt is passed. We must trust one another, you and I, or Ellyllon will prevail. It is his way."

It was. Grainne was right. Mistrusting each other only played into Ellyllon's hands; she knew that better than anyone.

"But trust must be earned, so I will tell you. I felt Seamus' power and I longed for it, as I longed for Ellyllon's. As a girl, I wanted nothing but to be aboard ship, standing on deck and feeling the power of the ocean beneath me, the wind in the sails and in my hair. You cannot know the thrill of the chase. It is my name men fear, my ship that closes onto another, my men waiting, hearts pounding, for the order to board,"

Her eyes were shining, her face flushed with exhilaration. Inside Jasmine, something stirred. It was just the sensation of using Iomlan, she told herself quickly, but it wasn't, it was something more, something darker, like the ghost of a memory she'd forgotten. Her own thrill of the chase.

Grainne's smile faded. "But I am the fool. Seamus has shown me a world beyond mere earthly power. I have known men and it is not enough to be by my side, to share my bed, my riches and treasures. They must own me and take the title that is rightfully mine: King of Clew Bay, Chieftain of the O'Malley's. But not Seamus. He has no wish, no need, for titles, for wealth." She lifted up her hand. "What need for jewels, when you can touch the stars. Or ride the centuries?"

She looked at Jasmine, her face luminous. "I would know your world, know the wonders it contains. I would sit beside this man who commands the very elements, and yet takes my hand and listens to me so attentively. I would die far away from this, if he willed it, for he has become to me as my land, my blood."

They stared at one another in silence. Jasmine didn't know what to say. Malachy's legend had fallen for Seamus. It seemed almost comical, despite his power, he'd become so ordinary to her, like the grandfather (even down to the grumpiness) he'd first pretended to Grainne to be. And yet, he was also the man Grainne saw. The man who could do the most incredible things, who had taught her so much, but still had so much more.

"I saw your power," Grainne continued. "You gave Cormac back to me. I am in your debt and although I have not the right, I will seek another."

"What? What is it?"

"For all his power and wisdom, I fear Seamus has a weakness. You; you are his weakness, as Cormac is mine. Ellyllon will know this and he will use it."

"But he tried to use me once before. It didn't work; he failed."

"Perhaps." Grainne shrugged. "But he has the cunning of the wolf, and how does a wolf hunt?"

By going for the weakest, the smallest, separating them from the herd.

"Have you told Seamus?"

Grainne shook her head. "He will guard you as I would guard Cormac, with his life. I cannot change that, and I would not seek to. I only ask that you too guard him, and guard him well."

"I wouldn't, I won't, let anything happen to him. Not that I need to; usually it's him looking after me, protecting me." She stopped, seeing the look on Grainne's face, and realised she was only confirming what she was saying. "I won't let anything happen to him."

"Your vow, say it."

"I promise."

Grainne held out her hand, and Jasmine took it. Arms upright, fingers clasped, they gazed seriously at one another, for the moment, at least, united.

The others, when they returned, were sat in a wide, rough circle having breakfast. Seamus gave them a suspicious look but made no comment.

"Jasmine." Grainne passed her some bread, and turning her head, gave her a slow, meaningful wink. *This is our secret.*

Chapter Fourteen

With breakfast over, they returned to the horses. Having retrieved her now damp underwear, Jasmine began stuffing them into her pack.

"Jasmine."

Brennan held out a sock. Black, the top, toe and heel were coloured a bright, vibrant purple. In her haste to open the pack, she'd dropped it out.

"Oh, thank you." She flushed, taking it from him.

Bowing slightly, he turned away, seemingly unconcerned about such a curious piece of clothing.

"Brennan," She called and he turned back. "I'm very sorry about last night, er, the joke, it, er, was — silly, er—"

He held up a hand. "You are young."

"No, but…" She took a step forward, stared earnestly into his brown eyes. "I am, truly, sorry."

He gazed back at her and then, with one quick nod, turned away. She returned to her pack and stuffed her sock down into the bottom. Someone placed a hand on her head, the fingers pressing lightly, gently. She looked up. It was Brennan, but already he'd let her go and was moving away, back to his own horse. Slightly dazed, but feeling strangely comforted, Jasmine continued with her pack.

*

Remounting, they continued along the hilltop. The sun, still climbing in yet another beautiful, pale blue sky, was already hot, and there was no shelter from it on the wide grass plateau. Jasmine squinted against the glare and found herself wishing for sunglasses. Far to their right, clouds were beginning to roll in off the sea, large, fluffy cumulus moving ponderously in from the west on a light, fresh breeze. Malachy still hadn't spoken to her; he was riding just behind Seamus, with Cormac in between him and her. Another time, she would have confronted him, demanded to know what was going on in that tiny little mind of his, but now she had too many other things to think about. Forgetting about

Grainne for a moment, and Ellyllon, there was the woman in the lake. What she was, she had no idea, but she couldn't believe in Brennan's myth of the water sprite. But what did she want? Not to do her any harm, obviously, she'd known that, felt it from the moment the woman's lips had touched hers. No, like the woman in Jasmine's dream, which obviously wasn't a dream, what she wanted, what they both wanted, was to give her a message. Exactly the same word; it couldn't be a coincidence. There was an urgency in them both, as if they wanted, no needed, desperately for her to know. Rogha. Choice. What choice? Her choice? And what, what was she to choose? Inwardly, Jasmine shook her head. This speculation was getting her nowhere. None of it made any sense. Yet, if the women were right, surely when the moment came, she'd know it. Maybe. Her horse was getting behind, had probably slowed without her realising. Pressing her knees, she urged him on, faster.

Maybe she should talk to Seamus, she mused, tell him about the women and what Grainne had said. Almost immediately, she rejected it. What good would that do, a voice inside her reasoned; it would only confuse things, take away Seamus' focus from the book at Ballintubber Abbey and Ellyllon's search for the portal. No, it was better to wait and see. It just wasn't the right time.

After about half an hour later, Grainne swerved sideways across to the far side of the escarpment and stopped. Below them lay the plain. Directly south, sandwiched between two swathes of forest, a huge lake shone silver in the sunlight. Just ahead, on the northern edge of the forest, the pale grey stone of Ballintubber Abbey gleamed. A river meandered past on its way to the lake, framing the abbey in the wide curve of an ox bend.

*

Dismounted, the sun hot on their backs, they picked their way down. If the lumpy, uneven ground, the thick tufts of grass and scattered rock and boulders had made the ascent difficult, it made the descent doubly so. Jasmine skidded, her feet slipping away from her on a patch of loose rock and shale, and if it hadn't been for the horse's reins clutched in her right hand she would have tumbled helplessly down. A few minutes later, Cormac swore. She glanced back. He'd stopped and was rubbing at his ankle.

"It twisted," he explained, straightening up and standing on it.

"Can you walk?"

He nodded. "It will ease."

Finally, they reached the bottom. Jasmine's back was bathed in sweat, the sleeves of her shirt rolled up as far as they'd go. They stopped for a badly needed drink, gulping thirstily; Cormac, Jasmine noticed, was still favouring his left ankle. Morain passed the bottle again, another quick drink, and the riders set off across the plain.

*

They rode at a steady pace, somewhere between a walk and a trot. To Jasmine's surprise, Malachy steered his horse in next to her.

"You and Grainne friends now?" he asked casually.

"Yeah, sort of."

They continued, their bottoms bouncing.

"Mal, look—"

"Forget it," he interrupted her quickly. "I know what you meant."

Another silence, but this one felt a lot better.

"Do you really believe all this?" He looked sideways at her. "That a tree could be a portal, a gateway to another world?"

"I guess so. If a tomb can be a portal, why not a tree? The Celts believed it, and so does Ellyllon."

"But does he?"

It was her turn to look at him. "You don't think he does?"

He shrugged. "Well, we only have Cormac's word for it. What if he's lying?"

"God, Mal, why would he do that? He feels terrible about what he did and it wasn't even his fault. I thought you understood. It's what Ellyllon does; he twists everything, and it gets you so that you can't think straight. Afterwards it's so easy and you feel stupid and angry for letting him doing it, but, at the time, you just don't see it."

"I know all that."

"Yeah, but do you? I can't believe you still don't trust him. Ellyllon didn't just kill me dad, he was there watching me for years. He was people I knew, friends, people I trusted, shared things with. He knows me, not just about me, but the real me." She pressed a hand to her chest. "In here. When I look back, sometimes it seems like there was nothing I said or did that he hadn't meant for me to. I know now he was trying to shape me, groom me, but looking back I can see it all so clearly. D'you know, the scariest thing is that I think it was working. If John hadn't intervened, brought us to Ireland, to Seamus, who knows what I'd be."

"You wouldn't be any different."

"You don't know that." She sighed. "OK, maybe I wouldn't be any different, maybe not. It doesn't really matter, all I'm saying is

Cormac—"

"It's OK," Malachy interrupted her. "I'm not an eejit. I get it. Ellyllon manipulated him, just like he manipulated you."

"And he's trying to make up for it, he really is." She threw him a grin. "Are you sure?"

"What?"

"You're not an idiot."

"Very funny," he retorted, rolling his eyes. He paused, studying her. "But you do like him?"

"Yeah, of course. He's nice, when you get to know him. You should try."

"Yeah," he agreed, gloomily.

*

Ahead, the river sparkled in the sunlight, the cool water enticing in the heat. The abbey sat next to it, making Jasmine think of an oasis in the desert. Built as a cruciform, with a low tower rising out of the centre of the cross, and high, narrow windows, soft grey stone mirrored the slate roof above it. Behind the church, cloisters led to the great hall, the chapter house and refectory. A walled garden lay off to the right. Through the arched gateway, they could see two monks, dressed in long brown robes, milling about, among the vegetables and fruit bushes. They slowed to a walk, following the track that led up to the door of the church. Around them the grass had been carefully tended and trees planted to create the impression of a wide, sweeping garden. It looked an idyll, the trees lush with leaves, the grass patches of light and shade; quiet, peaceful, it seemed the perfect place for reflection and contemplation.

"Jasmine," Seamus said, swinging around and breaking the spell. "Inside, you'll be expected to cover your head and behave in a virtuous and demure fashion. Remember, these monks can get a bit twitchy around women." He glanced at Grainne. "Although, it's probably too late for you."

Reaching the church, they dismounted and almost immediately a figure appeared, dressed in a long brown robe, stepping silently through the open door. He stopped on the doorstep and waited with an expression of unearthly, divine patience for them to approach.

"Wait here," Seamus murmured as he and Grainne joined the monk.

"Welcome to Ballintubber Abbey," The monk intoned loudly, his arms outstretched, and his smile warm. "I am Brother Liam."

Seamus and Grainne dipped their heads and then, in a low voice,

Grainne began to talk, gesturing to herself and Seamus. As he listened, the monk's arms lowered and his smile faded. He frowned.

"I cannot say," he replied loudly. "But Father Abbot is within; I will take ye to him and he will hear thy plea." He glanced at their horses. "Your horses are tired. Take them to the stables and Brother Paul will tend to them, give them food and water."

"Thank you, brother." Grainne dipped her head again. "You are most generous." She looked over her shoulder. "Brennan, Morain, take the horses and wait for us."

"Perhaps they too would like some sustenance? Ask Brother Paul and he will show ye."

"Can I go too?" asked Cormac. "Forgive me, aunt, but my ankle still pains, and I would rest it."

"I will send Brother Luke to thee. He was once a physician."

"Thank you, brother." Grainne smiled.

Nodding his thanks, a limping Cormac followed Brennan and Morain as they led the horses away.

"Come," Brother Liam said.

Lifting up her hood, Jasmine followed the others inside the church. It was surprisingly plain, the stone walls painted a rough white and the floor made of brown clay tiles. She looked up. High above her head, thick, dark wooden beams held up the roof, the vaulted ceiling, the design surprisingly intricate. Pews lined the floor, made from the same dark wood, two rows of six. They walked through them, up towards the altar, their feet echoing. There was little decoration, a few marble plaques on the wall, a wall hanging and, in the corners, tall iron candelabrums. The only gold was on the altar, a cross and a large, round bowl. Beside them, in a plain earthenware vase, were sat a bunch of flowers, their petals small, delicate and wild looking. Jasmine thought of the brutality of life outside, all the possible ways to die, and could understand why men would want to come here.

"Wait here," Brother Liam ordered, as they reached the altar.

With a duck of his head, he walked swiftly around the altar and over to a small wooden door in the end wall, half-concealed by a tapestry. It opened with a creak. With a last look at them, Brother Liam was gone, shutting the door firmly behind him. They waited, no one speaking.

After a few minutes, the door opened again.

"Come, Father Abbot will see you now," Brother Liam called, beckoning.

Stepping back across the threshold, he held the door and beckoned again. Grainne went first, followed by Seamus, Malachy and Jasmine. Without a word, Brother Liam closed the door and stood in front of it.

An old man was stood in front of a large, rectangular wooden desk. Once tall, his body had shrunk with age, his spine bending as the vertebrae collapsed and sunk, giving him the faint look of a half-closed switchblade. His face was wide, his nose thin and his eyes a very pale blue. They squinted as the abbot slowly scanned their faces, trying to get a sense of them. Behind his desk and high, intricately carved chair, a tiny, narrow window was set in the furthest recess of the deep thick back wall, letting in so little light as to be hardly worth the bother it must have taken to build it. Behind the desk, a large candle in an iron holder burned brightly, creating most of the light in the room. Beside the wall, a second, smaller chair sat at an angle.

"Brother Liam tells me you have a request," the abbot said, retreating into his chair behind the desk.

His manner was mild, genial almost, but Jasmine sensed this was a carefully constructed guise; this was a man confidant in the ways of the world, a man not to be crossed, his mind too certain that he was right. As if to confirm Jasmine's thoughts, the abbot settled comfortably into his chair, but didn't offer anyone the second, spare one.

"Yes, Father Abbot—" Grainne began

"You are Grainne Mhaol?" the abbot interrupted her, his pale eyes piercing.

She lifted her head. "I am."

"The pirate? The godless, lawless woman who it is said would lie with any beast, man or demon and consorts with the devil himself?"

Grainne smiled, but her eyes narrowed dangerously. "Pirate, yes, warrior, queen and plunderer, but godless, a consort of demons and the devil?" She shook her head. "No."

"Father Abbot," Seamus interjected quickly. "There is a knowledge we seek. I have heard it lies here, in your library, your writings and parchments. We ask only that we can look at it."

The abbot frowned. "The permission ye seek, why would I give it? This is a sacred place, a place of peace and contemplation. It is a house of God; we serve God, we teach the word of God, and live the life of simple piety. Is it a place for such as her, and those that ride with her?" He stood up. "Her very presence taints us. Brother Liam, our guests are leaving."

"Father Abbot." Seamus took a step forward, his face tight. "The knowledge we seek, there is another who seeks it also. He does not consort with devils; he is a devil. And with the knowledge he seeks, all your prayers, your piety, will be for nothing. He will burn, rape and lay waste to the very land, and only I can stop him." He ducked his head. "But you are right; we would not wish to disturb your peace, your most holy of tranquillity. As Christ himself said, who among ye that is without sin will cast the first stone."

There was a silence. His face bright red, the abbot glared at Seamus, and Jasmine was sure he was going to demand they leave, when suddenly the air seemed to go out of his lungs and he sat.

"Brother Liam, will you show him the library?"

"Thank you, Father Abbot. You are wise indeed." Seamus smiled, showing his teeth.

"Ye will need Father Anthony. He rests in the garden. He has not been well."

"I will show them to the hall," Brother Liam suggested, quickly. "And go fetch Father Anthony."

The abbot nodded.

"And Father, it is long since I had the confessional," Grainne said. "Will you give it me?"

The abbot leant forward. "You wish to confess your sins? To purge your soul?"

Grainne lowered her eyes. "I do, Father."

The abbot sighed, caught between duty and a suspicion that she was mocking him. "I will."

*

Leaving Grainne behind, Brother Liam led them back into the nave of the church and through a second door that led down two steps to the cloisters. Stone pillars held up Gothic arches etched with symbols and tiny stone faces. Open to the elements, a single tree lay in the centre of the courtyard. Small, dark, Jasmine had no idea what it was. And then they were through the other side and into a narrow, dark corridor and on into a vaulted, sparsely furnished hall. Six rows of rough benches and tables spanned the width of the far corner. Three monks busied themselves, preparing the hall for the next meal. Cormac was the only person sat; of Brennan and Morain there was no sign.

"You join Cormac," Seamus said, stopping. "I'll go with Brother Liam. I want to see this Brother Anthony."

Jasmine sat down on a bench and, using her bottom, slipped along it until she was opposite Cormac. Malachy nudged in beside her.

"I think we're causing a bit of a stir," Malachy murmured in her ear.

The three monks had stopped work and were staring openly at them. Or at Jasmine, to be precise.

"Maybe they don't get many visitors," she offered uncomfortably.

"Definitely not many women."

Jasmine turned to Cormac. "How's your ankle? Is it any better?"

"Yes. Brother Luke is a skilled physician. And what of Father Abbot?"

"He gave his permission; we just have to wait for this Brother Anthony."

"Yeah, but what happened? One minute I thought the abbot was going to throw us all out and the next… Was it Seamus? Did he do something? Y'know, with…" Malachy made a vaguely magical looking sign.

"Influence? No, I don't think so. I would've felt it."

Cormac's ears pricked. "Influence?"

"Influence. It's when you use Iomlan to make someone do what you want them to do. Or see. Have you ever tried it?"

"Once, but I failed."

"Maybe you don't have the power?" Malachy suggested.

"I don't think it's that." Jasmine gave him a hard look, a look that asked how on earth he thought that was making an effort.

"Perhaps Malachy is right. I fear I do not possess the same power as you."

"No, it's not that. It's just learning how, getting the right knack. Seamus had to show me."

"With a power so great, I cannot believe there is anything you cannot do."

Malachy laughed, the sound carrying across the hall. The monks looked up again, and he leant in, sheepishly.

"I dunno, this great one took half a day to learn how to open a door."

Cormac looked shocked. "But it is not difficult."

Malachy was grinning widely now. "And if it hadn't been for Seamus, she'd've dropped me on me arse."

"I wish I had done!"

Footsteps, moving quickly, sounded across the hall. It was Seamus, with Brother Liam trailing behind him.

"Jasmine, I want ya," he called loudly, ignoring the looks of the other monks.

Again following Brother Liam, they stepped through another door and out in to a corridor that led away from the church.

"Brother Anthony wasn't there. He's probably already in the library.

But Brother Liam told me something very interesting."

He paused to let her go through a narrow doorway first. "Someone's been here before us."

She stopped. "Ellyllon?!"

"Keep going, or we'll lose him." He gave her a gentle push. "I don't think so, not by the way he described him. There were four of them, but according to the brother, they didn't get in. The abbot took a dislike to them, which of course is hardly surprising, but it's good news for us. They didn't want to leave, but O'Connor's nephew turned up with some men. He was here for a period of prayer. He's deeply religious, and he didn't really give them any choice. Trying to bully a bunch of defenceless monks wouldn't have gone down too well with him."

Ahead, Brother Liam turned into a narrow stone staircase. One hand traced the wall as he darted downwards, his legs, under his robe, going like pistons. Lacking his familiarity, Jasmine and Seamus followed more slowly.

Another corridor. There was no sign of Brother Liam, but there was only one way to go. Seamus slipped ahead. Underground, this corridor, cut out of stone, was dark, the only light coming from candles in iron holders attached to the wall. The light from the candles flickered as they passed, their motion creating the only breeze in the stillness. Jasmine glanced over her shoulder. Shadows cast by the candlelight shifted eerily. It was so quiet down here. The corridor seemed to be going on for ages, although it reality, she'd only gone a few metres. With the rough stone walls, it was more like the way to a crypt than a library. She could almost see the coffins that would line it, the bodies within, rotted down to the bone. Another quick look over her shoulder. Shadows merged, making shapes like moving figures caught out of the corner of the eye. She turned back. Seamus had gone. She was on her own. Resisting the urge to run, she sped up. Immediately, she saw an arch, an empty doorway, and dashing through it, she entered the library.

Chapter Fifteen

Jasmine stopped. Stood waiting, Seamus and Brother Liam regarded her with barely disguised amusement. She ignored them and looked nonchalantly around, trying to pretend to herself, at least, that she'd been racing to catch up with them, not running away from the shadows and the dark like some frightened little girl.

The library was made up of two rooms. The first, a small reading room, contained nothing but a high, narrow desk and stool in one corner, with a huge iron candelabrum sat behind it, a source of badly needed light. The second room lay through another archway. Dark, Jasmine could only just make out the books lining the first row of wood shelves. It was impossible to tell from here exactly how big it was. There was a small sound from inside the second room and a man appeared, coming through the arch.

"Brother Anthony," Brother Liam said, darting forward. "Guests, from Father Abbot."

Hairless, his face and tall body gaunt and thin, round eyes regarded them thoughtfully. Long bony fingers, and hands way too big for the wrists they were sat on, curled around a large, heavy looking book. Jasmine looked at the book and Brother Anthony's wrist, and wondered how the latter didn't shatter under all that weight. In fact, the whole of Brother Anthony looked as if it might shatter, his skin and bone weathered by time and the elements, like old sticks, bits of branches broken off diseased or half-dead trees.

"Brother Anthony." It was Seamus' turn to step forward. "My name is Seamus, and this is Jasmine. I am sorry to disturb you, but our time is short. We are looking—"

"Jasmine? Jasmine?" Brother Anthony tilted his head. "As the flower?"

"Yes, but—"

"The flower." He smiled. "What do you seek?"

"The legends and lore of the Celts. I am told there is such a book here."

His smile faded. "Yes, the book is here. It was the lifework of Brother Sebastian."

"May we see it?"

"Of course." With a dip of his head, he disappeared back into the bowels of the library.

"I will leave ye." Brother Liam bowed and quickly left.

"Thank you," Seamus called after him.

He and Jasmine looked at one another.

"Would ya like some help?" Seamus called again, after a moment.

No answer. They waited. Jasmine shifted, lifting her feet and resettling them, and then Brother Anthony was back, awkwardly carrying three large books in a stack. He took them to his desk, his wrists creaking audibly in the quiet, but staying thankfully intact, and placed them carefully, reverently down.

"There are two more."

He disappeared again, but this time only for a few moments.

"The abbot does not approve." He placed the final two books on top of the others. "They hold the knowledge, the beliefs of pagans. Brother Sebastian believed all knowledge should be treasured, that God had placed his truth in all things, no matter how deeply hidden."

"Brother Sebastian is a wise man."

Brother Anthony looked up at him, surprised, then smiled gently, gratefully. "There are few who would think so."

"There are few wise enough to. Brother Anthony, forgive me. It is best we seek this thing alone."

The brother nodded slowly, as if he'd been expecting it, and rested his fingers lightly on the top book. "Brother Sebastian died two winters ago. Ours is a simple life, but rich in our devotion to God. Brother Sebastian, in his goodness, sits with him now in the kingdom of Heaven, yet I cannot feel joy."

Unconsciously, his fingers traced the book's cover, so softly, so lovingly, it was as if the brother were trying to stroke its author back to life.

"The pain of loss will ease, given time," Seamus said softly, his eyes sad.

Jasmine looked away, not wanting to intrude on the brother's inconsolable grief.

"Brother Liam told me others came seeking."

"Yes." He gave Seamus a curious look, then nodded. "The abbot refused their plea, but they did not heed him. They came here, to the library, but God was kind to us, for O'Connor's cousin was here for a blessing, with many men."

"Did they see the book?"

"No. We called and when O'Connor's cousin came, they left. The abbey lies under the patronage of O'Connor; few would risk his wrath."

Brother Anthony looked as if he wanted to ask something more, but in the end simply nodded. Without another word, he slipped silently from the room.

"For the first time we're ahead of Ellyllon." Seamus darted around the desk and onto the stool.

"I can't believe he'd give up so easily."

"Oh, he hasn't. MacDermott might not want O'Connor's wrath, but Ellyllon won't care. He'll be back."

He opened the top book very carefully. Pulling her hood back, Jasmine crowded in behind him, eager for a look.

The pages were thick, the writing intricately beautiful in thick black ink. Typically, the first letter was huge and decorated with pictures in colours as rich and luxurious as a stained glass window, but in the half-light of the candle it was hard to read. Seamus tutted impatiently, and the flames of the candles swelled to an impossible height, light flooding every corner of the room. He peered at the first page.

"Just as I expected, bloody Latin! I hate it." He sighed. "We're going to have to use Iomlan, but what choice do we have? It'll take far too long to do this the old-fashioned way. I'll try these four and I want you to try this one."

He began pulling the second book out of the pile.

"But I can't speak Latin."

"It doesn't matter, not with Iomlan. Just focus on what yer looking for, like in the tomb, when we looked for Malachy."

"Yeah, but I knew then what I was looking for."

"And you do now. The portal. The legend of the oak tree, a special oak tree, one that's around here somewhere." He lifted the book towards her. "Here."

"OK." Still dubious, she took it from him. "So, I think of a tree."

The book was even heavier than she was expecting. Clutching it to her, she lowered it gently to the floor, then sat cross-legged in front of it. What now?

"Hmm." She glanced up at Seamus, but his eyes were closed.

Suddenly, without warning, a page in the book in front of him lifted. It hovered for a second, then slowly lowered. Almost immediately, a second page lifted, and then, that too, lowered. It was followed by a third, a fourth, a fifth, the pages turning faster and faster as he got into the rhythm of it. Understanding now, Jasmine closed her eyes and imagined herself searching the book, looking for the ancient oak tree, the portal of Celtic lore. She saw the book in her mind's eye, felt the dry parchment between her fingers, heard the crackle of the turning page. Iomlan moved inside her, searching, questioning; matching her mood, her intent perfectly, but she felt, saw nothing but endless indecipherable writing. She opened her eyes. The book was still closed; the pages hadn't moved. At the desk, Seamus' eyes were still closed. He'd finished one book and was halfway through the second.

She sighed, her stomach twisting irritably. She knew it wouldn't work. It was impossible to find something she couldn't recognise.

"Seamus?"

"Yes?" Stopping in mid-turn, the page hovered, but he didn't open his eyes.

"What if we don't find it? The portal, I mean?"

"We've no choice. We have to find it." The page finished its turn. "Because Ellyllon won't rest until he does."

We have to find it. Steeling herself, she focussed again. There, again, were the pages, the beautiful, intricate writing, the feeling of Iomlan with her. For a moment, nothing happened, and then Iomlan slipped in front of her. Tentative, but eager, like a dog caught in the dilemma of following a scent and waiting for its master, it made her whole body throb. She couldn't hold it; she let it go and it sprang away. The book flew open; she sensed the first page turn, the second, third, and then Iomlan was flying through her, it took all her concentration to keep up with it as it sped through the pages, fanning them like an invisible hand. Iomlan was reaching the end of the book, she could feel it, and then, abruptly, the pages slowed and stopped. Jasmine opened her eyes. The book was open and halfway down the page the writing glowed.

"Seamus, I think I've got it!"

He looked up. "Where?"

"Here."

Getting awkwardly to her feet, she picked up the book and took it over to him.

"Let me see." Waving her away, he bent over it.

Jasmine watched, her heart in her mouth, as he slowly read through it, using his finger to trace each word. Silence. Abruptly, the stool creaked and Seamus sat back.

"That's it! You found it. That's the legend. It says here that the belief in the oak tree being a portal between worlds goes back to a time before the Celts. From what Brother Sebastian said, the power of the portal, like the tombs, is the same power as Iomlan, or rather has the same source. And this oak tree was believed to be particularly powerful. According to the legend, it lies in Sligo, in what has become the garden of Sligo Abbey."

"In an abbey? That's a bit strange."

"Not really. Throughout history man has built his new religion on the sacred sites of the old ones. What better way to eradicate the old and indoctrinate its followers into the new?" He leant back over the book, reading further down. "Now that is strange."

"What?"

"Those words, they don't make sense. It's Latin, but it's nonsensical." He glanced up at her. "Why would Brother Sebastian write something like that? Brother Anthony told us this was his life's work; he would've taken it very seriously."

There was a pause.

"I have an idea."

She felt his Iomlan and then he was speaking, using words that seemed to resonate deep inside her, almost as if they were known by part of her, part of her DNA, although she had no idea what he was saying. The words on the page began to glow again, the colour getting brighter and brighter until it looked almost as if they were burning. A strange odour began to permeate the room, a mix of musk and what Jasmine could only describe as spicy sausages. She coughed as it caught her throat, and abruptly the light on the words went out.

"And… Voila!" Seamus bent over the page again, his eyes darting as he read swiftly.

"What did you do?"

"I don't know how, but somehow Brother Sebastian found the actual words that the druids used for opening the portal. But they'd hidden them, I think, as protection. It's hard to explain, but they work like a chameleon. When Brother Sebastian read them, he saw Latin and that's what he wrote. Without Iomlan you'd see English, and it's only with the power of Iomlan that you see through the illusion."

"But you saw Latin."

"Yeah, I guess the nonsensical gives it an extra layer of protection. Who'd bother with gibberish, except maybe someone obsessed with pagan traditions like Brother Sebastian? Oh, I see what ya mean. The book should've shown me Irish, or English." He shook his head. "Maybe because I understand Latin, and a few other languages, it got confused." He laughed. "A confused chameleon. But anyway, only someone with Iomlan can find them. Which meant, to the druids, that only one of their own could use the portal."

Jasmine frowned. "So, what language are they written in?"

"It's Gaelic Celtic — so a form of Irish, but it's changed so much over the centuries, much of it would be unrecognisable. The Celts rarely used the written form; what was written down came later and was coloured by the writer's own language, namely Latin. These words would not have been spoken for over a thousand years."

"That's why Ellyllon wanted Cormac."

"Yes. He couldn't just use anyone to get inside the abbey. He needed someone with Iomlan."

"But how did he know he'd need him to read the words?"

"Ellyllon was once a druid, don't forget. He'd've known their ways of protection."

"So, even if Ellyllon managed to find the portal, he can't actually open it?"

Seamus grinned. "No, not without the true words, and now he has no way of getting them. Well, not unless he finds another person with Iomlan, but think how long that could take, especially in this time, when anyone openly doing magic would be accused of all sorts."

"Can I see them?"

"Of course, take a look."

Turning the book towards her, he pointed at two lines near to the bottom of the page.

"It's English, but it's rubbish. But they haven't changed. I thought you'd changed them?"

"No, that would take the protection from them. I merely saw through them. Take my hand."

He held it out and she took it. "Now look again."

She did as he said, reading the first word, seeing it begin as English and end as something quite different. She couldn't even begin to think how to pronounce them, but still, they were in her head. Like a voice from the ancient past, whispering.

"Oh, I see!"

"And now?" He let her hand go.

She looked back. "English again. It's you, you're doing it."

Seamus nodded. "Of course, I'm using Iomlan. But you've seen them, you've heard them in your head. Now, can you remember them?"

Jasmine concentrated. She's seen the words, read them, knew their shape but they were too unlike any she'd ever seen or heard; they'd refused to stick. She tried again, but it was like trying to pluck the finest of threads from the air with just your thumb and finger.

"I can't. I can see them, but when I try to form them, say them in my head, they just slip away."

He nodded. "That's as it should be. Now try with Iomlan."

She focussed. Almost immediately the words formed in her mind, and she heard their sound, the flow of every syllable. She let Iomlan fade.

"You'll have to use Iomlan to say them," Seamus said seriously. "In this way, yer have the knowledge, but the knowledge is protected. It must always be protected."

"I understand."

Seamus, she realised, was trusting her with something very few people had ever known.

"Grand." He smiled. "Come on, let's get the others and get out of this place."

*

Brennan and Morain had joined Malachy and were enjoying the simple food of the priests' midday meal. Malachy and Morain sat on one side of the long table, with Brennan opposite them.

"What happened?" Malachy asked straightaway.

"We found it," Seamus replied, sitting down next to Brennan.

Jasmine slipped in next to Malachy.

"So?"

"We know where it is and how to open it." He looked from one to the other. "You don't seem too happy about it."

"It's not that," Malachy replied with a shake of his head. "Brennan has some news. Tell them."

"I—" He stopped as a brother approached the table, carrying two small plates of food.

Without a word, he placed one in front of Seamus and the other in front of Jasmine.

"Thank you," they said in unison.

The brother smiled and, with a nod, moved off.

"He's taken a vow of silence," Morain explained. "I only wish others did the same. The brother who tends the horses would talk the hind legs off a donkey."

"Well?" Seamus asked impatiently.

"Whilst with the horses, we talked with pilgrims as they readied for their pilgrimage to Croagh Patrick."

"Yes?"

Brennan rubbed his hand across his face. "MacDermott rides on Grainne's. They passed them only yesterday. They swore it."

"Oh. But Duggan is there with Grainne's men."

"She has another castle, to the south of Clew Bay. Few live there, enough men to guard it, women to serve and children. But there is a village nearby. They will have no warning. It is a petty act of vengeance, no more."

Seamus pushed his plate away. "Where's Grainne? Have you told her?"

"No." It was Morain who answered. "She is with the abbot."

"I'll find her. Go ready the horses and we'll meet you there."

Thanking the brothers, they dashed to the stables. Cormac was already there, stood under a tree and looking out across the plain, in the direction of the sea, his thoughts clearly elsewhere.

"Cormac?" Jasmine came over to him.

He turned and, seeing her, smiled. "Jasmine. The book?"

"Yeah, we found it. We know exactly where the portal is and how to open it."

"Open it? Is it possible?"

"Yeah, if you know the right words."

"And you know these words?"

Jasmine nodded. "Kind of." She paused, remembering Seamus' words. "It's hard to explain."

"Of course." He glanced up into the branches above his head. "And Ellyllon?"

"He doesn't know them. We're ahead of him, thanks to you. Without you, we'd never have known about the portal. Thank you."

"My honour." He bowed and then, stepping forward, took hold of her hand and, lifting it up, pressed it to his lips.

Embarrassed, she giggled. His fingers tightened and then, gently, he pulled her towards him.

"No, Cormac, wait, there's something else, I must tell you. It's important."

He dropped her hand, "What? What is it?"

*

They joined the others. Busy with his horse, Malachy didn't look up.

Jasmine's horse was next to his.

"I told Cormac," she said, grabbing her saddle.

He didn't answer.

"Mal, I said—"

"I know what yer said, I heard yer!" he snapped, picking up his pack.

Morain and Brennan looked over, their necks swivelling. Malachy opened his pack and peered inside.

"Damn! I've forgotten—" Without finishing, he dropped his pack and stomped away, back towards the hall.

Behind him, Morain and Brennan shared a look. Her face red, Jasmine placed her saddle on top of her horse's back.

She'd just finished saddling her horse when Malachy returned, carrying something tightly in one hand. Looking sideways, she watched surreptitiously as he carefully placed it in his pack, only letting go when it was safely inside and out of view. Curious, but still smarting, she knew better than to ask and risk another angry outburst.

"Grainne," Morain murmured, nudging Brennan.

The rest turned just in time to see Grainne and Seamus hurrying towards them.

"Your horse is saddled," Morain said as soon as Grainne was within hearing.

"Thank you. We must ride; our people need us."

"We're going too," Seamus said, with a look at Jasmine and Malachy.

"No." Grainne faced him. "You must go to Sligo."

"I told you, we're coming with you. You cannot face MacDermott alone."

"Morain will ride to Duggan, and he will come to our aid."

"It'll be too late by then. Brennan's pilgrims said they passed him on the road."

"Seamus." Grainne took his face in her hands. "Your fight is with Ellyllon."

He pulled away. "I will not allow innocent men, women and children to be murdered." His voice softened. "And I cannot allow you to risk it."

"I have faced much worse."

"Perhaps, but Ellyllon doesn't even know where the tree is. We have time."

"If it is as you believe, but if not?"

"Then… humph." He snorted in frustration.

Jasmine stepped forward. "Seamus, do you need me to come?"

His eyes narrowed. "Why?"

"Well, why don't I go to Sligo? I can watch the abbey. If anything happens, or Ellyllon comes, I can use Iomlan to let you know."

"But he'll sense you."

She shook her head. "Not if you teach me how to hide Iomlan."

"And I'll go with her," Malachy offered quickly.

"And I," Cormac agreed. "If my aunt wishes it."

"And I, to watch them." Brennan grinned. "If my lady wishes it."

*

It was decided. Seamus still wasn't happy about it; Jasmine could see the worry in his eyes, see it deepening the lines, the creases in his face, but what choice did he have? And it made sense, especially as Brennan had a brother in Sligo. They could wait with him; as guests, they'd be more unobtrusive.

"Jasmine, my thanks." Taking her arm, Grainne drew her to one side and lowered her voice. "Brennan spoke to me of what happened, in the village."

It took her a moment. "He — wasn't supposed to."

"Would you have him lie?" She shook her head. "I will not punish her because you do not wish it, although I doubt it's wisdom. But there is honour in your wish. Seamus is right; it matters not your country, your kith or your kin, only the honour in your heart and in your deeds. And if I can count one Englishwoman among my friends, then why not, one day, her queen and all her courtiers?!"

She laughed loudly, the idea obviously tickling her. Jasmine stared at her, wondering what she'd say if she told her that she and Queen Elizabeth would meet and, if not actually become friends, would, at the very least, part in mutual respect.

"Jasmine." Seamus touched her shoulder. "I must show you what to do."

Without a word, Grainne moved over to Cormac.

"Now, Jasmine," Seamus said gravely. "You have to focus, not on Iomlan, but on there being an absence of Iomlan. Think of it like camouflage, or a guard waving yer on, 'nothing to see', 'nothing to see'. Now, give it a try."

She did as he said and, light as a butterfly, Iomlan circled in on itself, covering its trace with a film as thin and delicate as gossamer.

"Good," Seamus said approvingly. "But you have to keep it like that. It'll take some practice holding it while you do everything else. Do you think you can do it?"

She nodded. "I think so." *I hope so.*

They said their goodbyes. Seamus giving first Jasmine, and then Malachy, a fierce hug, as Grainne hugged and kissed Cormac and Morain and Brennan clasped hands. Standing between Malachy and Cormac, Jasmine watched with the others as the three climbed onto their horses. Springing away, they galloped out onto the plain.

Chapter Sixteen

They watched the horse and riders disappear.

"Shit," Malachy breathed finally, voicing the feelings of everybody else. "What do we do now?"

Instinctively they looked at Brennan, the oldest, the most experienced among them, and he looked back at them and sighed. "We go to Sligo."

Brennan led them across the plain, going north, but veering to the east instead of the west. They avoided the roads, Brennan preferring to stay hidden, just in case MacDermott had men straggling. Around them, the land was changing. The soft green grass and forest gave way to the harsher, rougher wet of gorse, sedge grass and reed. Riding alongside Brennan, Malachy was quiet, but at least he didn't seem angry any more. He answered when she called to him and, if anything, he was more withdrawn than angry, as if he were just too busy with his thoughts. Cormac was the opposite; he seemed more gregarious than ever. With his blond hair in the sunlight, he shone, bright and confident, as Malachy's dark hair faded. She thought of how he'd kissed her hand and pulled her body towards him, and wondered if it were finally time to give up on Malachy and accept the attentions of somebody else.

*

The afternoon wore on, headed towards evening. One brief stop, to drink and rest the horses by a river and they were moving again. Brennan pushed them on, as if determined to get to his brother's house as soon as possible. His brother was rich, he had his own men, influence; they'd be safe there, he told them. Jasmine rubbed her forehead. She was getting tired. It didn't take much effort to hide and cover Iomlan, but it was hard to keep doing it. She kept losing her focus, distracted by other things; her horse and the act of riding, Cormac talking or even her own thoughts. She didn't know how Seamus did it, but she guessed it was practice. Time and lots and lots of practice. Time she didn't have. She straightened. There, she had done it again; even thinking about losing her focus had made her lose her focus. Sighing, she refocussed.

Without warning, Brennan shouted for them to stop and, pulling at the reins, urged his horse back.

"What is it?" Malachy asked.

"Bog." He pointed to the ground just ahead of him, where his horse's hoofprint was already beginning to disappear.

Jasmine looked at it, at the ground further ahead, then glanced back, the way they'd come. It all looked the same.

"We must ride around it. A wrong foot could injure a horse or unseat a rider." Brennan stared at the ground, trying to trace exactly where the bog started. "We ride single file. I will lead."

Turning his horse, he moved to the right and, keeping to a slow walk, checked the ground carefully.

"It doesn't look that bad," Jasmine muttered to Malachy, as Cormac followed Brennan.

"No, it doesn't, but that's the problem with bog. You don't know where it's safe to step, sometimes the firmest looking patch is the worse."

Malachy moved in after Cormac, leaving Jasmine to follow, and the four of them made their way around the bog, skirting the edges.

Lifting his head, finally Brennan sped up. They must have passed the bog. In the distance, the tops of trees heralded a return to forest, and the road. Jasmine yawned, realising suddenly how tired she was, how bone achingly weary. Around them, the light was changing, the tall tufts of grass glimmering gold in the last of the day's sun. It had been a long day, feeling like a lifetime since this morning, when the woman in the lake had kissed her with lips like trickling water. Brennan looked back over one shoulder. "We must stop, rest for the night. In the trees." He pointed to where a few scraggly trees had grown up higher than the gorse around them. "There."

They had almost reached the trees when Cormac's horse stumbled over a root. For one sickening moment, Jasmine thought it was going to fall, but somehow it stayed upright, Cormac clinging tightly to its back. Malachy's horse, close behind, tried to sidestep, but its momentum was too great and it half reared in an effort to avoid a collision. Jasmine watched, horrified, as Malachy tumbled helplessly off its back. He hit a thick, high tuft of sedge grass and bounced, his body crumpling, his left leg bent ominously under the other.

"Malachy!" she cried.

Brennan leapt off his horse and over to him, Jasmine a heartbeat behind. Cormac stayed where he was, motionless with shock.

"I'm OK," Malachy breathed, lifting up his arm. "I just need a hand up."

Shaking his head, Brennan took his hand and pulled. Malachy gave a cry of pain and clutched his left thigh with his free hand.

"Mal?"

"It's OK." Letting go of Brennan's hand, he waved her away and began rubbing at his thigh. "I've pulled something, but I don't think it's serious."

Slowly, gently, he lifted his right foot and placed it back down again. He winced.

"I think it's starting to ease." He did it again, and again.

They watched as he walked round in a little circle, testing his leg, still wincing.

"I'm OK," he said, finally stopping.

Brennan waved one hand. "We'll walk the rest."

They did as he said; it wasn't far. Malachy seemed better; he'd stopped wincing but he was favouring his leg, Jasmine noticed, stepping carefully, gingerly, as if fearful of jarring it on the uneven ground.

They reached the trees. Jasmine glanced around her; it was a good spot, the trees giving them natural shelter and seclusion. Letting go of his reins, Brennan was already looking around for firewood.

"Cormac, see to the horses. Jasmine, get wood. Malachy, sit, rest."

Cormac took their reins; Jasmine moved to help Malachy but he waved her away. She was tempted to insist, but knew she'd only get another blast. He was too proud, too stubborn. Brennan had found a few sticks; kneeling down, he began to arrange them into the base of a fire. Malachy joined him, wincing as he sank thankfully onto a large rock. Brennan said something and Malachy laughed, as if nothing was wrong, as if his hand, even now, wasn't massaging the top of his thigh. Jasmine rolled her eyes at Cormac and he grinned, and it was her turn to shake her head before wandering away in search of more firewood.

*

Back with an armful of firewood, Cormac had finished the horses. He and Brennan had collected the blankets and food from the packs and were sat with Malachy next to the fire. The fire was already burning brightly. Jasmine dropped her armful, added more wood to the flames, then joined them, sitting opposite.

*

The meal finished, Jasmine's head nodded. With her back against a tree and the warmth of the fire, the food and beer in her belly, it was hard to stay awake. Malachy, Cormac and Brennan were talking, their voices a deep murmur against the night, her own impending sleep.

"You should rest. I'll take first watch."

Brennan's voice jerked her into wakefulness. She opened her eyes and sat up, blinking against the feeling of unreality, disjointedness.

"Let me," Malachy offered. "I won't get much sleep with this leg." Brennan cocked his head, his eyes narrowed. "I'll wake you," Malachy continued quickly. "Let me. I've not done much else."

After a moment, Brennan nodded and, getting awkwardly to his feet, Malachy moved off to a small hillock at the edge of their camp. Jasmine watched as he sat down, trying to get his leg into a good position, then pulled her blanket over her. She closed her eyes. All was quiet apart from the odd crackle of the fire. She shifted, trying to get comfortable, and settled again. Someone gave a snore. She opened her eyes again. It was Brennan, laid on his back, his mouth open to the stars. He was asleep already. She rolled over, snuggled down. More snores; they were becoming regular, as if the sleeper was just getting into his stride.

Sighing quietly to herself, she threw back her blanket and got up to join Malachy.

"Jas, you need your sleep," he whispered as she sat down next to him, his eyes fixed on the darkness ahead.

"I can't." Another snore. "Not with that."

Malachy laughed softly. "I bet you wish I'd let him take the first watch."

He rubbed his leg absently.

"Your leg's still hurting."

"It's alright." Conscious suddenly of his hand, he moved it.

She looked at his face half framed in the fire light, his features as familiar to her as her own, "Why were you so cross with me earlier? Is it Cormac, because I thought you two were getting on now."

It took him a moment. "No, it wasn't Cormac, well sort of, it was —— it doesn't matter."

"But it does. If I've done something wrong…" she stopped, not quite sure what to say.

"It's just I have this feeling like something bad's going to happen. Look, forget it, it's just me, I'm in bad form." Malachy pulled at his pack lying beside him; she hadn't realised he had it. Cormac must've untied it from his horse and given it to him. He found what he was looking for, his fingers closed; she watched as he began pulling it out. "I got this in the abbey — for you."

His fist appeared. He lifted it out towards her, palm up, and unfolded his fingers to reveal a small cloth bundle loosely tied with a string bow.

"Go on, undo it," Malachy nodded. "It's for your birthday. The one you missed."

"Oh, Mal." Grinning stupidly, she reached out, and very carefully undid the bow.

The cloth fell back. Inside was a small, wooden comb and a long, thin string. Beads had been attached to it, brightly coloured pieces of ceramic, and what might have been jewels but were probably glass. She picked it up, ran it lightly through her fingers. It wasn't string; it was too thin, pieces of strands, like hair, carefully plaited into a delicate braid.

"It's made of horsehair. It's for your hair. To tie it back, instead of that shite bit of string."

"Oh, Mal, it's beautiful."

She picked up the comb. Only just a rectangle, dark wood had been cut from two sides to create two rows of teeth, giving the comb a strange 'H' shape.

"Thank you." She wiped at her eyes. "But I didn't get you anything."

He shrugged. "It doesn't matter."

"There is one thing. Hold on." She dropped the comb and braid into the cloth and, taking it from Malachy, carefully placed it on a patch of grass beside her.

"Give me your leg." Kneeling down in front of him, she took hold of his knee.

"No, Jas. I told you, I'm OK."

It was too late; Iomlan was already moving.

"Jas..."

Very gently, she began to rub, feeling the warmth tingling her hands transfer to his leg.

"Ow!"

"Sorry. But if it hurts, I think it means it's working."

"You think?!" Malachy gasped.

She moved above the knee, to the spot she'd seen him rub. He winced.

"Try to relax."

"That's easier said than done. Ow!"

"Shhh, you'll wake the others," she told him, trying not to laugh.

She worked in silence for a few minutes.

"Hey, that's really starting to help."

"That's good," Instinctively following the line of pain, she began to move inwards into the inner thigh.

Malachy, his face tilted backwards and his eyes closed, looked to be in bliss. Even in the loose peasant clothes she could see the lines of his body, his chest, waist, hip and upper thigh.

"Who'd have thought it, you on watch with a sword?" she said quickly, focussing on her hands.

"Yeah, and you tending my wound. Like some old Hollywood film." He laughed softly; then grunted.

"Sorry, did I hurt you?"

"No." He opened his eyes. "It feels good, like a proper massage."

"You've had a few then?"

"Well, no, but it's how I imagine them to be."

"I'm glad it's working. Just a minute more." She paused. "There, that should do it."

She looked up. He was watching her, his face close. She could almost feel his heart beating.

"Thanks." He glanced down at her hands. "Healing hands."

"I wouldn't quite go that far."

"I would."

He looked so serious, so intense, with his deep, blue eyes and lips slightly open. They stared at one another; his face seemed to be coming closer, and for one heart pounding moment she thought he was going to reach in and kiss her.

"Jasmine?" It was Cormac.

Malachy turned his face away. Jasmine removed her hands and rocked backwards onto her heels.

"Yeah, just easing Malachy's leg. You couldn't you sleep either?" she asked, trying to keep her voice even.

Malachy was still turned away; she couldn't see his face.

"No."

Shifting sideways, Malachy moved away from her and scrambled to his feet. He pressed down with his left his leg, testing it. "Thanks Jas, that's much better. You two should go and get some sleep."

"Yeah, I suppose." *Bloody Cormac*. In that moment she could've killed him. Now she'd never know what'd just happened, if it was real or just her imagination.

Cormac was watching Malachy. "I will watch next. Malachy, wake me, not Brennan."

"Yeah, OK," he called softly over his shoulder.

Back at the fire, Jasmine added more wood before returning to her blanket. Cormac's eyes were already closed, his blanket pulled tight to his chin. Lying down, Jasmine covered herself. From here, she could see Malachy, sitting still, staring out at the darkness. He turned around, as if sensing her gaze. His face, lined and with shadow from the darkness and the faint light of the fire, looked suddenly old, as if the teenager had disappeared, melted away in weeks instead of years.

*

She woke the following morning to a cool grey day, the beautiful blue warmth of yesterday already a distant memory. Malachy's present lay next to her, carefully rewrapped in the grey cloth. She'd been in such a rush last night she'd forgotten it, and Malachy had seen it and left it there for her. *What if he thought she didn't like it? Or thought she didn't care?* Laid next to Brennan, he was still asleep; they were both still asleep. She sat up. Cormac's blanket was empty. She looked across to the hillock. It too was empty. Alarmed, she scrambled to her feet and ran over to it.

There was no sign of him. The land around them was quiet, the gorse and ground untouched.

She opened her mouth to shout, to call for him, but the thought of those still sleeping stopped her. Something rustled; she spun, seeing a large, tall gorse shake and then Cormac appeared, coming out from behind it.

"Shit, Cormac, where were you?"

"I was..." He fluttered his hand.

"Oh, yeah, right." She sat on the hillock, waiting for her heart to stop thumping. "Sorry."

He joined her. "Did I scare you?"

"No. Yeah, just a little." She shivered.

"Here." Untying his cloak, Cormac wrapped it first around her shoulders and then his, pulling the ends together so that it covered both of them. "The morning is cold."

"Thanks." She shivered again. "You didn't wake me."

"There was little time. Malachy watched much of the night."

"They're both still asleep."

"Yes."

There was a pause.

"Jasmine, I must speak, although I fear you will not like it."

"What, what is it?"

"Last night, after food, when you slept, we talked." His voice lowered. "In MacDermott's castle, I heard Ellyllon speak of a spy, a traitor to my aunt and the O'Malley tribe. Among my aunt's most trusted, Ellyllon boasted the spy had her ear. I told my aunt this, and she dismissed it. I confess, I thought it was Duggan."

"But you don't now?"

"Brennan spoke of his wife. She's a MacDermott."

"You think Brennan is the spy?!" She glanced at the sleeping figures.

"I pray not."

Brennan was always there, alongside them, but in the background. She thought of how he'd followed her in the village, how he'd told Grainne when he had said he wouldn't, and they only had his word about the pilgrims. But then there was his kindness to her after the woman had spat, and at the lake, his concern for them despite their childish joke, the incredibly gentle touch on her head. It couldn't be Brennan, it just couldn't.

"It could be anyone. And if it was, why would he offer to come with us? It doesn't make sense. He'd want to stay close to Seamus and Grainne."

What was it Grainne had said? *It matters not your country, your kith or your kin, only the honour in your heart and in your deeds.*

"I don't believe it. It's not him. It must be somebody else."

Cormac gave her a sad smile. "I hope it is so. But if it is not? I beg you, ride beside me; do not leave my side, for together our power must surely be as great as Seamus'."

He looked so worried, although she was sure he had no reason to, she had to reassure him.

"I will, I promise."

A cough made them turn. Sitting up, Brennan rubbed the top of his head sleepily. At the sound Malachy stirred, unbending himself and pulling the blanket from his face. He glanced over to where Jasmine and Cormac were sitting.

"Thank you for — this," she said quickly, shifting.

Without a word, Cormac let go of his cloak, and she sprang to her feet, and back towards the fire.

Putting the last of the firewood on the fire, Jasmine dived into the sack and began pulling out food. Malachy sat up and, using his bottom, inched closer to the dying embers. She could feel him watching her, his gaze intent. After a few moments, Cormac joined them.

"Malachy, how fares your leg?"

"Fine. It's fine now, thanks." He was still looking at her, but she ignored it, focussing on the food as if it were the most important thing in the world.

"Ye should have woken me," Brennan admonished, stretching.

Malachy's neck swivelled, "The way you slept, you must've needed it. We were fine."

There was no answer to that. Looking sheepish, Brennan moved over to the horses, as Jasmine went to get her comb.

*

Her hair combed and tied into a rough, loose bun with Malachy's braid, Jasmine returned to the fire. They ate a terrible breakfast quickly, reminding Jasmine of the worst of times with her mum and John, the air thick with the tension of unsaid things, Brennan's woeful attempts at small talk and her own brittle answers. Malachy didn't even bother, just sat staring at the ground as he chewed, as if deep in thought. *Like a cow*, she thought to herself angrily, knowing she was being unfair but not really caring.

"It is time to leave," Brennan said finally. "Come, Cormac, you and I will ready the horses."

He gave Cormac a meaningful look, and the two shot away. Jasmine could hear them talking, but they were keeping their voice down, as if not wanting to be overheard.

"We should sort here," Jasmine told Malachy. "Can you pass me the sack?"

There was a pause. And then, without looking, he picked up the sack and tossed it towards her, missing her outstretched hand by a couple of inches.

"Thanks!" Fuming, she picked it up and began placing the food inside.

"Here, yer missed one."

She looked up; Malachy was holding a package out to her.

"Thanks." She took it from him and he smiled faintly.

She placed it inside and, closing the sack, tied the end into a rough knot.

"I'll do the fire."

There wasn't much left, but Malachy killed the last of it, kicking apart the embers, the small pieces of wood still lit.

She watched him finish, opening her mouth to speak, but too late. "We'd better go," he said, glancing over his shoulder. "They're waiting for us."

*

They rode towards the trees. If possible, the grey closed in even further, the low clouds sapping out the light. It began to rain. A steady, heavy rain that Jasmine knew would be in for the day. She lifted up her hood, tucked the loose strands inside and pulled her cloak tightly around her.

*

They reached the trees. Soaked by the rain, her hood smelt of damp wool and something else faintly unpleasant. She pulled it back, preferring the cool drops that slipped through the leaves and branches than the smell. They found the road, the ground opening up ahead of them. Immediately Cormac moved in beside her. She knew what he was doing — hadn't she agreed to it? — and yet she found herself wishing he was Malachy. A quick stop at the crossroads, and they turned north taking the road to Sligo. They hadn't gone far when Cormac reined in his horse.

"Cormac?" Brennan asked as he dismounted.

"He is favouring his left foot." Cormac ran his hand up down the horse's leg, near the calf. "It must've been the tree root."

"Walk him," Brennan ordered, sliding of his horse.

Cormac did as he said.

"He looks well."

Cormac shrugged. "He does, but I can feel it."

"Stop him; let me feel his leg."

Brennan ran his fingers expertly over the horse's leg, pressing down, "There is a swelling." He glanced at Jasmine expectantly.

"I can try, but I wouldn't know what I was doing and could just make it worse. Seamus would've known."

Cormac nodded his agreement. They all looked at one another.

"Wait a minute," Malachy said suddenly, looking around. "Jasmine, aren't we close to the village Seamus helped?"

"I don't know, maybe."

"Brennan, when we travelled from Sligo we passed a village. It's just south of here. Seamus helped the villagers; do you think they would help us now?"

Brennan frowned. "Perhaps, or have a horse we could buy."

"MacDermott's lands lie south. Is that wise?" Cormac interjected.

"We cannot travel with only three horses. These villagers owe a debt. A debt, MacDermott or no, they are honour-bound to repay. We must risk it."

Brennan and Cormac remounted. Brennan turned his horse,

Malachy following. Cormac flashed Jasmine a look as they too turned. Going south, back into MacDermott territory.

The trees began to thin. The road narrowed, and then they were out of the forest and moving across a meadow. It was still raining. Jasmine lifted her hood again, feeling the wet cloth damp across her head, the back of her neck.

"Ride close," Cormac murmured, staring at the back of Brennan's head.

She nodded, feeling sick. Cormac's foreboding was catching. She wished they hadn't come, wished she'd told Malachy of Cormac's doubts. What if Brennan was leading them into a trap? But there was no choice; they needed another horse.

*

They were almost at the village. They crossed the bridge, the horses' hooves clopping across the wood, sounding way too loud. There was no sound, no sign of life, no people, children or animals. The houses and the main street looked empty. Deserted. Malachy looked back at Jasmine and she saw the fear in his eyes. *Oh God!* She took a deep breath, trying to keep control. With Iomlan, she had to stay calm, keep her focus.

"I will ride ahead," Brennan said firmly and, urging his horse forward, rode cautiously into the main circle of houses.

Malachy, Jasmine and Cormac followed, going more slowly. They reached the first house.

"What is that?" Jasmine asked, catching something in the air, a scent, strangely familiar.

Faint, but unnaturally so, it was as if it had been deliberately masked. Cormac gave her a quizzical look. They reached the second house.

"It's like a ghost town in a western," Malachy said over his shoulder. "Jas, you know what I said about a bad feeling..."

Her stomach dropped. Ahead of them Brennan yelled suddenly and, yanking hard at the rein, brought his horse to a shuddering stop.

"Go, go!" he screamed, whirling.

He kicked his horse viciously in the flanks and it sprang forward, a second too late; an arrow whistled through the air, catching him high on the shoulder and sending his body tumbling to the ground. Men appeared from everywhere, out from behind the houses, the barn, running with swords lifted, shouting ferociously and spooking their horses. Jasmine fought for control of the reins as the men surrounded them.

Inside her, Iomlan swirled in confusion, and then Malachy yelled, his voice carrying through the chaos. "Jas, this way!"

In a heartbeat, he was gone, his horse speeding into a gap, the one exit left. They tore after him, hooves thundering, Cormac slightly ahead. Behind them the men followed, pouring like a swarm, filling the space they'd left behind them. Ahead, open countryside beckoned, tantalisingly close. Malachy was almost there. His horse drew alongside the last house and, out of nowhere, a figure appeared. Ellyllon. Dressed in a long, black cloak, he was stood directly in Malachy's path. He raised one hand and instantly, without thinking, Jasmine responded, sending Iomlan streaking towards him. It caught him hard in the stomach, knocking him to the ground as Malachy's horse thundered past. Ellyllon leapt to his feet. Cormac's horse shied, pulling back and away, its front legs lifting with the effort as Jasmine struck again.

"Cormac, move it!" she shrieked alongside him.

But Ellyllon was already back on his feet. Panicking, Cormac clutched at her arm, catching her and bringing both of them hard to the ground. Winded, there was nothing she could do but watch as he scrambled desperately off her. The seconds slowed. In the distance, Malachy and his horse had stopped and were looking back at them helplessly. She willed him on and away, a voice inside her telling her that was all that mattered, but he couldn't hear and the two of them turned in a slow, undecided circle.

"Watch." Ellyllon smiled and, again lifting his hand, turned slowly and deliberately to face Malachy.

Power emanated from all around him. It washed over her, something new, more ferocious than any Iomlan she'd felt before. She could feel its rage and yet it was strangely off-key, disjointed, like light refracted by a prism. Dragging herself up onto her hands, she focussed and, pulling everything she had to her, let fly. It streaked towards Malachy, a second before Ellyllon's. There was a pause, the agonising wait of an explosion, and then whatever Ellyllon sent hurtled back, as if bouncing off an invisible barrier. He staggered with the force but kept his feet. Jasmine was flattened by it; she gasped, feeling Iomlan drain from her. But she'd done it. Malachy and his horse were disappearing into the distant trees, leaving them far behind. Spent, she lowered her head as Ellyllon stepped into view.

"Jasmine, it's been too long. What, almost four hundred years?" He smiled, leaning over to look at her.

She sensed movement from behind her, felt a sharp pain in the back of her head and then nothing.

Chapter Seventeen

Malachy's horse galloped away from the village, the ground beneath him disappearing at a dizzying speed. He was dying to look back, to see who was following, but he needed all his energy to keep his horse going and retain his seat. Up ahead lay the forest, but a different part, following the river back towards its source, away from the road. The village was obviously a trap. Once again, Ellyllon had been one step ahead of them, maybe even more. Jasmine filled his head, the image of her laid on the ground with Ellyllon standing over her, but he pushed it away. He didn't have time for it, didn't have time to think what might be happening to her. Ellyllon certainly hadn't meant for him to escape; he'd felt the force of his power when it had hit whatever it was protecting him, the two colliding like a pair of juggernauts. No, he'd have to use his whole energy and all his wits just to keep from getting caught.

Reaching the forest, Malachy slowed his horse to a stop, jumped down and, pulling it behind him, darted in amongst the trees. He risked a quick glance back. Some of Ellyllon's men were following, their horses spread out, filling the ground between forest and the village. He had to hide. Tightening his grip on the reins, he continued, moving as fast as he dared, weaving around trunks and clumps of bramble and going deeper into the forest. Already the undergrowth was beginning to thicken, the light dimming as the foliage grew over itself, blocking out the sun. Malachy paused, looking for a way through. He could push through, squeeze through the smaller gaps, but what about the horse? It was stood quietly behind him and he marvelled at its calmness. There was only one thing he could do. Taking out his sword, he used it like a machete, hacking at the bushes and brambles as if they were vines in the jungle. He stopped after a few minutes, breathing heavily. This was taking too long. Maybe he should go back, try and find another way through. His horse shifted nervously next to him and, sheathing his sword, he began to murmur to it, stroke its face and neck. Distant voices, subdued by the undergrowth sounded behind him. Malachy froze. They'd reached the forest. His horse shifted again and, pulling out of Malachy's grasp, began to back up, pushing into the bramble and bracken behind it.

"Whoa," Malachy whispered, trying to stop it.

The horse snorted, tossing his head in alarm and the reins swung wildly.

"It's OK, it's OK." Hands held out, Malachy stepped sideways, towards the reins.

He took another step, his left foot landing on earth that slipped and slid away from him. Overbalancing, his arms going wildly, he fell.

He crashed through branches, his right foot trailing, and then bounced on soft grass and ferns. He hit the bottom, his body rolling before coming to a complete stop. Dazed, he looked up at the canopy of leaves and branches, wondering idly how he'd got there. Vegetation rustled above him and, after a moment, his horse poked his head through the bramble, searching for him. He giggled, then, realising it was relief, he sobered and sat up. His body felt sore, tender in a few places and he knew he'd have some nasty bruises later, but amazingly there was no serious damage. With a groan, he got slowly to his feet and looked about him.

He was in a gully. Walls of earth rose high above his head, covered with long, green ferns. Underfoot, edges of stone peeked out from a thick carpet of soft, verdant moss. Hidden by the forest that had grown up around it, no one had set foot in it for a long time, perhaps not ever. Ellyllon's men were shouting, their voices echoing; he could hear them pushing through the undergrowth. They were coming closer. *Think*. His horse ducked his head, looking almost as if he were nodding. He had it. Ignoring the pain in his back and thighs, he scrambled back up the sides of the gully, using the stems of ferns to keep his balance. At the top, he found the reins and began pulling his horse down the sides with him. He protested with a loud neigh, his hooves slipping, but he kept his feet and the two of them made it safely to the bottom. The shouts were even closer, drawn by the sound they'd made. They needed more cover. Breathing heavily, his back bathed in sweat, he looked right. He was in a bend; he couldn't see around it. He looked left; the same. There was no time to dither. Pulling the horse after him, he went right, moving swiftly through the moss. The pressure of their feet and hooves left imprints behind them, but the moss was thick and springy and it closed over their marks, hiding their trail.

They turned the corner. Ahead, the gully narrowed, the walls changing to rock and stone that jutted out in huge round slabs, the gap just wide enough for Malachy and his horse to slip through. His horse was shivering, his ears flat to his head, and it took all Malachy's skill to coax him through the rock and out the other side. Malachy's heart sank. It was a dead end. Rock covered in thick green moss and ivy towered over him, curving round in a wide arc. At the bottom, just above the ground, was a hole. For one glorious moment, he thought it might be a cave, but it ended before it began in a wall of stone. Above him, leaves rustled; he could hear the noise of their bodies as they moved above them, near the edges of the gully. They were almost on top of him. A twig snapped, sounding unbearably close. Malachy pressed his body against the rock and waited, eyes straining against the green. Above him, on the left side of the gully, the branches of a bush began to shake. He held his breath. The branches parted and a man stepped out to the edge of the gully. The man looked around, his eyes narrowed, and then, with agonising slowness, he looked down. Malachy flinched, waiting for the shout that would bring his comrades. Nothing happened. The man looked away. Amazed, incredulous, Malachy waited, still not daring to breathe as the man took one last look around before disappearing back the way he'd come. Shit. He breathed out. He could still hear the voices, but already they seemed to be moving off, away from him. Unconcerned, his horse had found a tuft of grass, and was munching at it. Malachy smiled and, pulling his cloak tightly around him, sank down onto the nearest rock.

Sat amid the dark, dank moss, Malachy waited, too afraid to move in case the slightest sound brought the men back. He thought he could still hear them, crashing about in the distance, but he wasn't sure if it was just his imagination. How the man had missed him he had no idea. It was impossible. He'd looked straight at him, and at his horse. He couldn't've missed them, and yet he had. Malachy shook his head. Maybe it was the same thing that had protected him from Ellyllon. There was only one thing it could be: Jasmine's Iomlan. Somehow, even now, she was protecting him. He sighed heavily. He shouldn't think about it, shouldn't think about her; it only made him picture her, on the ground, Ellyllon towering over her… he had to stop, had to think instead about exactly what he was going to do. He shifted, uncomfortable, on the cold, hard stone.

Firstly, he couldn't believe how easily they'd fallen into a trap, how Ellyllon had known exactly where to find them. Or how he'd known Seamus wasn't with them, for surely he wouldn't've have faced the two of them together? Could he have been watching them, from somewhere unseen? No, Seamus would've felt him. Then what? A spy? But, who? Despite, his own misgiving, he knew it couldn't be Cormac. Jasmine was certain he was no longer under Ellyllon's influence, and she should know; she'd been inside his head. Malachy frowned. Maybe it was one of the brothers at the abbey. That made sense. When Ellyllon had sent men in to find the legend of the portal, they'd persuaded one of the brothers to act for them. Probably bribed them with money. Maybe it was even the abbot himself, and that was why he'd changed his mind so bizarrely.

Malachy looked at his horse. Secondly, what now? He had to get back to Seamus. Brennan was dead, Jasmine and Cormac captured by Ellyllon; he was the only one left. But why hadn't she used Iomlan against Ellyllon? Or Cormac? Surely their powers combined were more than enough to defeat him, or if not, enough to give them the chance to get away. His stomach tightened with frustration. What was happening back there? But there was only one way to know that. He had to go back, sneak inside the village, making sure he didn't get caught. Then he'd go to Seamus. He stood up, listening, preparing to go. The forest was silent; probably Ellyllon's men were long gone. But, a voice inside him warned, what if they were still there, waiting quietly on the edge of the forest, waiting for him to come out thinking the coast was clear? He sat back down. *A little longer. Just to be sure.*

Cold, he shivered, his mind wandering. He thought of the first time he'd met Jasmine, the air of cheekiness she had about her, the inner-city cockiness she didn't even realise she had. Ever since she'd arrived, he'd been doing the same thing, trying to keep her out of his head. She was different, not just because she came from someplace else; she'd've been different there too. Only then, he hadn't realised exactly how different she was. Niamh was the opposite. They'd known each other since they were kids. He'd been flattered by her, his ego stroked, and he'd enjoyed the reaction of people seeing him with her; their surprise that someone who looked like her would bother with someone like him. But it had worn off, her view of the world, of life, had first bored then irritated him and he'd been too cowardly to break it off. And then Jasmine had arrived, and all these things had started to happen to her, drawing him deeper and deeper into her world, until it felt as if she'd always been part of his.

It had taken those three months with Thady to realise exactly how he felt, and it had taken him until last night to finally accept that it was hopeless. She had such power; in MacDermott's castle she'd killed a man without even meaning to, a simple miscalculation of force. He didn't think she saw it, but Iomlan had changed her profoundly in his absence, had become not just part of her, but was her, like her eyes, or her smile. She could travel back in time; make a hole in reality, for Christ's sake. How ordinary, how helpless, he must seem in comparison to her and to Cormac. He frowned. Cormac. He always seemed to be there, next to her, chattering, laughing with her or bending his head to hers, low and conspiratorial. It was as if he was drawn irresistibly to her, and she to him, united in something that was so completely out of Malachy's grasp. And it blinded her to him, to his faults. She couldn't see what Malachy saw; the selfishness, a trace of meanness, spite that came out when Cormac thought people weren't looking. All she saw was those big, baby boy sad eyes, his angst, his internal suffering caused by Iomlan that made everything he did alright. Not that it mattered: at the lake Morain and Brennan had looked at one another knowingly and one of them had said something like birds of a feather, and Malachy had felt stupid and angry and hopeless all at the same time. Jasmine in her usual roundabout way had said the same thing. Even before he knew her, Cormac had shared her thoughts and feelings in a way someone like Malachy never could. How could an ordinary person compete with that?

*

Jasmine woke slowly, reluctantly, her head throbbing. She felt movement, as if she were being propelled forward, and a rocking from side to side. There was pain too, in her back, bottom and running down her legs. She swallowed awkwardly, her mouth dry.

"Here, here." It was Cormac's voice. "Drink this; it will help."

She drank greedily from the cup he pressed against her lips, drinking as much as she could before her breath gave out. She opened her eyes, wincing as the light turned the throb in her head to a stab. Cormac's face leant into hers.

"Cormac?"

"Yes. We're in a carriage. On the way to Sligo." He moved back and she saw the walls, roof of the carriage, black wood and black leather, ornate, opulent.

"Malachy?"

He shook his head. "I don't know."

"He got away." That simple fact gave her a glimmer of hope.

*

Malachy shivered. Apart of the rustle of a breeze through the trees, the forest was silent. Surely the men were long gone. His horse was stood at the other side of the gully, his eyes fixed on Malachy, as if to ask, "Are you ready yet?"

It was time.

"I'm coming," Malachy whispered.

*

Jasmine's mind drifted. It was hard to focus, to concentrate. A voice inside was telling her to use Iomlan, do something to stop the coach and escape, and yet she couldn't quite pull it together. She was so tired. Her head nodded, following the movement of the coach. Her body felt so heavy, her limbs weighed down. Frowning, Cormac reached over and began stroking her forehead. It soothed her, and she closed her eyes.

"Sleep, Jasmine," Cormac murmured. "And wake well."

She opened them again. There was something she wanted to say to him, to tell him to do, something important, but she couldn't remember what it was. She opened her mouth and then closed it again. Sleep was almost there, but still she fought it. She tried to lift her hand, but it wouldn't move. Something was wrong. Inside, the voice was screaming, but it was already faint, getting fainter, disappearing, like the lights of a train down a deep, dark tunnel. She closed her eyes.

*

Malachy led his horse back along the gully. He reached the spot where he'd fallen in and, following a hunch, continued on. A few metres on and he realised his hunch was right. The gully walls were getting smaller as the ground levelled out. He sped up, and a few minutes later he was out, back into the main body of the forest and stepping into a clearing. He stopped. Ahead, half-covered with moss and grass, the smooth flat, tops streaked with lichen, was a tiny stone circle. A fairy fort. He looked back. Sat where it was, at the entrance of the gully, made it look as if there was something special about the whole place, something sacred. As if those that built the stone circle had paid homage to something living inside the gully. It was a creepy thought. Stepping carefully around the circle, Malachy led his horse across the clearing and back into the trees.

Circling the gully and using it as a reference point, Malachy headed back to what he hoped was the same way. It was hard to tell; it all looked the same. They reached another patch of thick, dense vegetation, but this time, he saw a clear path through where Ellyllon's men had hacked and chopped. He was right. He continued, and again the forest was changing, the light increasing as the trees and vegetation thinned. He sped up, the two of them darting through the trees. They were almost at the forest edge; he could see the meadow through the gaps in the branches. Letting go of the horse's reins, he drew his sword and crept cautiously forward. A few more steps and he was out of the trees, back into the meadow and bright sunlight.

There was no one there. Ellyllon's men had gone. He lowered his sword. Behind him, something moved. He whirled just in time to see his horse walking towards him. With a smile, he put his sword away. He wasn't sure how, but something had changed between them, and it was the horse that had decided they belonged to one another. The horse stopped just in front of him and, lowering his head, nuzzled gently against Malachy's shoulder.

"Better think of a name for you," Malachy said, reaching up to stroke his nose.

*

The afternoon sun high in a now cloudless sky, Malachy rode back to the village. It looked quiet; he could see no sign of Ellyllon or his men, but then again, they hadn't seen them the last time either. He slowed his horse to a walk, resting one hand on his sword. From a distance he might look convincing, but Duggan hadn't had time to teach more than just the basics. He'd be useless in a fight with a skilled opponent, like in MacDermott's castle. *Then why are you doing this*, he asked himself crossly. *You should be riding as hard as you can towards Seamus.* But he couldn't; he had to know what had happened to Jasmine. He reached the first house. With a sharp peal of laughter, two young children ran out from behind it, one chasing the other. They stopped when they saw him, and then, with a wild yell, ran over to the second house. Almost immediately, two men appeared from inside, one holding an axe, the other a pitchfork. Stepping out into the street, they stopped and, with weapons casually laid across one arm, waited for him to approach. More appeared, each one carrying a tool or a weapon. He stopped his horse a few feet in front of them.

"You." The man with the axe took a step forward. "What do you want here? They went that way." He pointed north, towards Sligo.

Malachy squared his shoulders. "And the man they killed? He needs a decent burial."

The man hefted the axe. "No need; we buried him." He pointed again. "That way."

"Wait!" a husky voice called and slowly the villagers parted.

It was the man Seamus had helped.

"Come, come with me," he beckoned to Malachy, admonishing the other man with a stern look. "You forget there is a debt to be paid."

He waved his hand and, as Malachy dismounted, a young boy came out from nowhere and held his hand out for the reins.

"Yer horse needs attention," the man explained quietly.

Malachy stared at him for a moment, then handed the reins to the boy. "Thank you."

The man nodded his approval and, with a slight inclination of his head, indicated that Malachy should walk with him.

"I am called Walsh. I am the elder of this village."

"I've met you before, I think."

"Yes." Walsh nodded placidly. "We owe Seamus a great debt." He paused, and his eyes wouldn't meet Malachy's, "The black eyed one serves MacDermott. MacDermott is our lord, our chieftain, we are farmers, with women and—"

"There was nothing you could do. You had no choice. As you said, MacDermott is your lord."

"I am humbled." With a small bow of gratitude, Walsh stopped outside a house. "I wish I could offer ye more, but we have food and drink, and will show you where your friend lies." He cocked his head. "Come."

"In here? But I thought you'd buried him."

"Come." Walsh smiled and waved his hand, gentle but insistent.

Malachy stepped inside and the first thing that hit him was the smell; it was a strange, heady mixture of flowers and something acrid, bitter. Bare, with little furniture, the room contained two women; one small with white hair and a round, wrinkled face, stood by the fire, stirring a metal pot, the other sitting on a stool by a rough wooden bed. She was leaning forward, across a body, her raised arm obscuring its face. The body spoke, its voice low and murmuring. Malachy's heart leap, the woman moved back and, seeing the face, he rushed over.

"Brennan!" He couldn't believe it; he was sure he was dead.

Brennan tried to raise himself up. "Malachy."

"Lie still," the woman tutted and, getting to her feet, made as if to push him back down.

"Mary." It was the woman at the fire who spoke, her low, calm tone containing the faintest hint of steel. Immediately the younger woman fell back.

Wooden spoon raised aloft, the old woman gave Malachy a steady look. Her skin was darker than the usual white suffused with pink, making Malachy think of the Mediterranean, Spain maybe, or even further south. Most of her teeth were gone; there were three, no four, at the front of her mouth.

"Mary is right. He needs rest. We will give you a moment, no more."

"Thank you." Bowing his head, Malachy waited for them to leave before dashing over to the bed and throwing himself onto the stool. "I thought you were dead."

"As did I!" Brennan smiled grimly. "The arrow pierced the flesh to the bone, but the old woman says I will live. They tell me she is a healer." His smile faded. "And what of ye?"

"We were riding out, the only way left, and Ellyllon appeared out of nowhere in front of us. Jasmine knocked him to the ground and I got by, but something happened and when I looked back she and Cormac were on the ground. I wanted to go back, but I could feel her, willing me on." He looked away.

Reaching out, Brennan awkwardly took his hand. "It takes great courage, great strength, to do not as you would wish, but what is right."

Malachy flushed, but immediately felt better. Letting him go, Brennan shifted, then gasped in pain, the blood draining from his already pale face.

"Brennan! I'll get the old woman." Malachy leapt to his feet, but he put out his hand.

"No," he panted. "Sit. I am well."

Reluctantly, Malachy did as he said. They waited for the spasm to pass.

"Now," Brennan said eventually. "Ask me."

"Do you know what happened to Cormac, to..." He took a deep breath. "Jasmine?"

"I saw only Jasmine. Walsh and two others hid me in the barn, under the hay. Why they gave me such aid I cannot say. But I could see. MacDermott's man carried her and placed her in a carriage."

"Carried her?"

It was Brennan's turn to look away. "She lay still."

Malachy's stomach dropped.

"But, Malachy, she lives. Else, why take her?"

Malachy's head spun; he leant over and pushed his fingers into his hair, trying to calm himself, to ignore the whirl in his head and the fear in the pit of his stomach.

"Give me a minute," he breathed.

There was a silence. Sitting was suddenly unbearable; Malachy leapt up and began to pace.

"Whatever we do, Ellyllon's always two steps ahead of us! But why did he take her? What does he want her for? It's not that he can use her, manipulate her, not like he did before. Not like Cormac."

"Be thankful they did not find you."

"But he has Cormac; he can just use him to get to her."

Brennan gave him a puzzled look. "But he does not hold her heart."

Malachy stopped. "What?! What did you say?"

"Is it possible you do not know? Have ya not seen her looks?" Brennan snorted, incredulity laced with disgust. "You and Morain. He was married before he saw his lady's interest in him. Are the two of ye related?" He laughed then coughed, hard. "The camp would speak of naught else," he continued, his voice rasping. "There were wagers."

"Wagers? Bets?"

"Of course. I wagered you'd be married by Lughnasa."

"Married!" Malachy's jaw dropped. It took him a moment. "Who else, Duggan?"

Brennan nodded.

"Grainne?"

He nodded again.

"Seamus?" That thought disturbed him more than he could say.

"Of course."

"Who else?"

"Everyone."

"Morain?"

"Everyone!" Brennan's eyes shone with suppressed laughter.

"Shit." Malachy sat down. "I thought…" He stopped, tried again. "I thought I'd hid it."

Brennan smiled. "The heart cannot so easily be hidden. You need only the eyes to see."

Malachy nodded, but he wasn't really listening. He was too busy, wondering how he'd missed it, how he hadn't seen. He thought of the night in Grainne's castle. Lying next to her, feeling her warm body next to his, the softness of her thighs, her breasts, but after Grainne's manipulation she'd seemed so vulnerable, so innocent and trusting of him.

"Malachy, you must ride to Seamus." Sharp, Brennan's voice brought him back to reality.

He was right; to get to Seamus had been Malachy's first instinct too, but that meant leaving Jasmine to Ellyllon's mercies. He stopped.

Why Sligo? Why take her to Sligo and not back to MacDermott's castle?

"Malachy?"

He went cold.

"Malachy?" With a gasp of pain, Brennan leant forward, one gripping the side of the bed.

"The portal! He wants Jasmine to open the portal. Don't you see? She knows the words as well as Seamus. He knew they'd seen the book, must've had a spy at the abbey, and Seamus and Grainne leaving played right into his hands." He looked Brennan straight in the eye. "Or did they? What if, that man you spoke to, it wasn't an accident? What if Ellyllon set it up?"

"To—?"

"Separate Seamus and Jasmine. To get her on her own. He must have found a way to stop her using Iomlan against him. He was going to use me, but now he must be using Cormac."

"Then we must ride on Sligo."

"But what about Seamus? We have to tell him."

Brennan frowned. "The castle lies two days from here."

"And Ellyllon will already be in Sligo by then and have opened the portal."

"Then we must send a message. Ask Walsh for a rider."

"Yes," Malachy agreed, nodding. "It's the best we can do." A thought occurred to him. "You said we. You can't come; you're not well enough."

"You cannot ride alone, and without me, my brother will not give his aid." Brennan grinned suddenly. "The old woman, she is a canny one. I would not play cards with her, for fear of the tricks she may have up her sleeve. I wager she has some art, some potion, that can heal me."

*

Jasmine woke for a second time. She opened her eyes; for a moment everything looked distorted, blurred around the edges, and then, slowly, it cleared. She was in a room, big, like the hall in MacDermott's castle, but more ornate, with tall high windows. Voices, coming from another room, talked over one another, and then one, strangely familiar, rose above the others, its tone abrupt, commanding. She heard it say a name; it sounded like Brennan. Brennan. Why was that name important? The question was too much. Already her mind was drifting, the effort of staying awake too much. She closed her eyes again.

*

To Malachy's surprise, the old woman raised no complaint to Brennan's plan to travel with him. She merely nodded, resigned or experienced to the determination of men. The younger woman made no effort to hide her disapproval, and only held her tongue, Malachy guessed, out of respect for the elder.

"Wait outside," she told him coldly.

The old woman moved over to a tall, wooden cabinet that looked as if it belonged to a richer, grander room, and opened one carved door.

"May we speak with Walsh?" Malachy asked neither of the women, or both.

Turning, the old woman regarded him for a moment. "Mary will take ya."

She turned back, dismissing him.

Without a word, Mary led him to the stables. Walsh was inside, talking quietly to the boy who was tending Malachy's horse.

He saw them coming and turned to greet them. "You see, your friend is well."

"Yes, thank you." Malachy glanced at Mary who, with an incline of her head, had already turned away. "Thank you."

She didn't answer. Walsh gave Malachy a sympathetic smile. "Can I aid ye?"

Careful to avoid too much detail, Malachy explained what he wanted.

"The road is dangerous; if the messenger met MacDermott..." His eyes narrowed in thought. "I will ask. Wait here."

Malachy watched him go, then turned to the boy.

"Thank you for looking after my horse."

"He's here." The boy pointed to the last stall. "He's very clever."

"And brave."

Moving over to him, Malachy stroked his rump, his side, his hand sliding towards his head. The horse turned and nuzzled him in recognition.

Malachy rubbed his ear. "He looks grand; you did well." The boy swelled visibly. "What's ya name?"

"Eoin."

"A good name; he needs a good name. What d'you think?" he asked the horse. "Eoin it is."

*

Walsh was back. "You have yer messenger. Padraig, saddle the bay."

"I don't know how we can ever thank you. I'm sorry to ask, but we're desperate."

Walsh shook his head. "Come, you must return to your friend, and I, the messenger."

They walked back along the street towards the house.

"There was a sickness," Walsh said suddenly. "Six children died before you came, the sickness beyond even my mother's art. I thought to bury my two youngest, but Seamus healed them, as he did four others. He did it freely, without my asking and asked nothing in return. The sickness has not returned. Such is the debt that cannot be repaid."

"No, this repays it. It gives us our only chance to rescue Jasmine and stop Ellyllon."

Walsh stopped, Malachy stopping with him. "A letter can be read; tell me your message and I will give it to the messenger."

"But, how will he know Seamus?"

"What man could forget the healer of his daughter?"

"OK." Malachy thought. "Tell him Ellyllon has taken Jasmine and Cormac to Sligo. I'll be with Brennan's brother; he can meet me there."

*

They parted, Malachy continuing alone. He reached the house and saw Brennan stood in the doorway. Propped up by the wall, Malachy was amazed that he was even upright. The old woman, Walsh's mother, was stood next to him, a small sack in her right hand.

"He will need to rest after the journey." Walsh's mother passed him two sacks. "In one is the medicine he needs. Dress the wound with the balm and clean cloth each night. If the pain is bad, or he becomes hot, give him a handful of herbs in water."

"And the other?"

She smiled. "Food and fresh water."

"I don't know how to thank you."

Impatient, she waved his gratitude away. "I have my grandsons."

"I know, but thank you anyway."

She smiled again, the wrinkles in her face deepening. "He has a great magic."

It wasn't a question exactly, but Malachy nodded anyway.

"And the girl?"

He nodded again. "Yes, she has Iomlan too."

"Iomlan," she repeated, slowly, as if tasting, savouring the word's sound. "Iomlan."

She looked straight into his eyes, holding his gaze with her own deep brown. Huge in her tiny, wrinkled face, their colour the timbre of rich, melted chocolate, they threatened to pull him down into their soft, warm depths.

"I, too, have a small magic. The power to heal and to see past the light and into the shadows. The magic inside her is strong. Yet I sense it is still grows." Her eyes turned inwards. "I see darkness, the madness of ages." She blinked and, with a small shake of her head, her eyes refocussed. "The black eyed one is wise to fear it, and to use his potion to keep her sleeping."

"Of course!" Malachy said excitedly, with a quick glance at Brennan. "He drugged her. It's the only way he could've controlled her, stopped her using Iomlan on him."

Impulsively flinging his arms around her, he pulled her close. She was even smaller than she looked, her frame so thin, her bones lacking any meat, that he felt he could have encircled her twice over.

"Thank you," he whispered, letting her go.

Giving him an impish smile that took years off her, she lifted her hand to his face and rested it on his cheek. Her smile faded.

"You must heed my words. The other with Iomlan, his heart is bad, his mind twisted. Do not trust him."

"Ellyllon?" Malachy asked, momentarily confused.

"No, not Ellyllon; Cormac," Brennan interjected. He straightened, wincing. "She means Cormac."

Chapter Eighteen

"Jasmine, Jasmine."

She opened her eyes and Cormac's face, frowning with concern, hovered fuzzily above her.

"I feared you would not wake. The day has passed."

His face slipped into focus.

"Where are we?"

"A house," Cormac shrugged. "I know not where."

"Where's Ellyllon?"

"Close." He looked furtively behind him.

They were in the same hall as she'd seen earlier, but now shutters covered the window, shutting out the dark, the room illuminated by candles. Someone had placed her half sitting, half lying in a tall wooden chair, her arms and draped across the sides.

"We have to get out." She went to get up, to lever her body up out of the chair.

Nothing happened.

"Cormac?!"

Staring down at her hands, she tried again. Hanging, white, flaccid, her fingers didn't even twitch. She tried again, throwing everything into the effort, but still they lay there.

"Cormac, I can't move," she panted. "I can't feel anything."

From somewhere deep inside she sensed the panic that should've been welling up inside her, but it felt disconnected, as if it belonged to someone else.

He stared at her. "It must be Ellyllon, his magic."

She swallowed, her throat tight. Her mind was curiously clear, her thoughts, her breath too loud in her head, as if her ears were filled with water. Even worse, she realised suddenly, she couldn't even feel Iomlan.

"Cormac, what has he done to me? I can't feel Iomlan," she cried, feeling her panic grow, despite the strange, numbing calmness.

"He said only that it was sleeping."

"Help me up."

Standing over her, he grabbed hold of her waist and, with an effort, pulled her upright, her head flopping onto the chair back with an audible thud.

"You need to get out of here, find Malachy, find Seamus."

Another quick look back. "I will not leave you."

"You have to. I can't move, and you can't carry me."

He pressed his face close. "You must tell me the words to open the portal."

"No, I can't."

He frowned. "I do not have your power. What Ellyllon has done I cannot undo. But if you tell me, he will turn his gaze towards me, and you will be free. Free to aid us both."

"Cormac, you don't understand. I can't, and even if I could, I wouldn't, not here. You don't know who's listening."

A flicker of annoyance crossed his face, but it was gone almost as quickly as it had come.

"You do not trust me."

"It's not that; I promised Seamus." She stopped. Cormac didn't realise, but this was exactly the kind of manipulation Ellyllon excelled at. "This isn't you; it's Ellyllon. He's manipulating you. Trying to get me to reveal the words."

Someone laughed. Coming from behind her, she tried desperately to turn her head. And then, slowly, deliberately, Ellyllon stepped into view.

"I told you to wait."

It took her a moment to realise that his words were not meant for her. He was talking to Cormac.

"But I wanted to—"

"To what? Give yourself away? Sabotage your only chance to atone for your failure to deliver them both to me?"

Cormac got to his feet. "The fault was not mine. She does not trust me." His whine turned into a snarl. "If she will not say, cut it out of her. Or teach me, and I will cut it—"

"Enough!" Ellyllon snapped, swinging his arm and slapping Cormac hard across the face. Cormac's body rocked, the sound of the slap echoing across the hall. Inwardly, Jasmine flinched.

Ellyllon smiled. "Don't feel on his account. He's betrayed you, betrayed everyone who cares for him."

"But only because of you, because you turned his mind."

He laughed loudly, more theatrics than genuine mirth. "Believe that if you like. Do you really think I needed to do that to him?" Leaning forward, he placed his hands on the arms of her chair, and spoke slowly, deliberately. "He jumped at the chance. He needed no persuasion, no influence, no Tionchar as Seamus calls it. Nothing but his nature." He straightened. "Poor Jasmine, too trusting, too quick to see only the good in the lost, the feckless."

"But, I saw, I felt him, when I was in his head. He showed me."

"Exactly what he wanted to show you. Or rather, exactly what I wanted him to show you. Just enough, just enough of what was real for you to believe it."

"But, the way he feels, his mother's death, you, I felt it."

"Oh, he feels it. He feels everything you saw, you just didn't see far enough. He hates me. You think he serves me out of regard, admiration? Can you not see the way he looks at me? He hates me to the centre of his sick, rotten being, and if he had the chance he would kill me, slide a knife between my ribs into my heart, or poison me and watch me die, my body writhing in agony. But he needs me, needs the power that only I can give him."

"Then Malachy was right."

"Ah, yes, the faithful Malachy. Cormac?" Ellyllon lifted up his hand, held it palm upwards towards him.

Cormac dropped his hand, revealing the angry red weal across his face. Eyes burning, he gathered himself and focussed. Ellyllon's body stiffened and an expression of peace came over his face.

He sighed. "Thank you, Cormac."

Smiling, his eyes gleaming, he threw out his other hand and, with a loud screech, a dining chair slid across the room towards him. He lowered himself into it and, placing his elbows on the arms, clasped his hands together.

"Now, Jasmine. Malachy. I had MacDermott's men out looking for him, but they couldn't find him. I even tried myself, but he eluded me. He's surprisingly resourceful. Or maybe protected?" He rested his chin on his hands. "Of course, if we had him here, how long do you think it would've been before you told me what I want?"

"But he's not here, and there's nothing you can do to make me tell you."

It was an admission, but nothing he didn't already know. He'd taunted her with it on the sands at Killaspugbrone, but he'd known even before then. Had probably known before she had, before she'd been willing to admit it to herself.

"No, Iomlan protects you just as it protects him. It strengthens you. Even quiet as it is now, I would have to rip your mind apart to find the information I want." He dropped his hands. "I could do that, do as our friend wishes, and I think he could bear your death with surprising ease. But it might not work; I could lose the information and I would definitely lose you. And why would I take such a risk when Malachy and Seamus will be heading for Sligo, exactly where I want them to be. There was no spy, no duplicitous Brennan or Brother, only Cormac. Through him, I sent you into the Abbey for the book because I needed Seamus to find the words for me. And through him I sent Seamus and Grainne on a fool's errand. MacDermott's not even there!" He grinned. "As if I'd waste my time on him. I left him snivelling into the bosom of his wife. Now, she was worth my time."

Jasmine's heart sank, realising that by trusting Cormac, how easily they'd been outmanoeuvred. Her hand slipped down inside the chair and she stared at it, not understanding what it meant.

"You see, Jasmine, from the moment Seamus began to close the void I knew he'd follow me. He has a quaint loyalty to the ways of the druids; their need to give back or replenish the soil. And I knew that with no hope of overpowering me alone, he'd be forced to bring you with him."

Jasmine's body tingled; she could feel her toes, the tips of her fingers, and for the first time since she'd woken, she felt Iomlan. Ellyllon sighed, his eyes boring into hers, as if he could sense what she'd finally realised; the drug was wearing off and her body, her will and Iomlan were starting to return.

"If you followed me to my own time, there are others of my kind to help me, but thanks to Malachy, I was stuck here, with no way back that I could use. I thought at first that I could use this one to find the portal." He jerked his head at Cormac. "But once again, he failed me. The words he found were nothing, pure gibberish. A druid trick — I needed someone with a greater art. But he has his uses; he showed me a drug his aunt uses, made from a plant that grows here. As soon as I saw it, saw what it could do, I realised I could have everything I wanted. I would send Seamus to the book, he would decipher the words, and I would use the drug to incapacitate you and your power, leaving Seamus to face me all alone. And now I have a way to finish this, finish him, and take my rightful place in my own time. We will be in Sligo tomorrow. When Seamus is dead and Malachy is returned to us, I promise you, you will *tell* me how to open the portal."

Turning, he nodded to two men who had come in and were waiting in the shadows. "It's sooner than I was expecting, but it's already time for another dose."

The men stepped forward, one carrying a bottle and cup on a tray. He placed the tray on the dining table and picked up the cup. Dark liquid swirled. Desperate, Jasmine reached down and felt Iomlan flicker.

"I've used plants before, but nothing quite like this. It doesn't make you sleep; it does something much more interesting, much more special. It silences the body, silences the will. Not enough to stop Iomlan, but I made changes to it. Changes that took a great deal of time, I might add, a great deal of experimentation, which MacDermott was only too happy to volunteer his men for." He sighed. "Which was just as well; I made a lot of mistakes at the beginning. But now, it's perfect. See how easy it is to contain you."

The man with the cup stood in front of her, the other behind, the latter grabbing her head and roughly pulling it back. Knowing she had only seconds, she closed her eyes and focussed. For a moment nothing happened, and then Iomlan flashed, weakly, just enough to send both men reeling from her. Metal clattered, rolled across the floor, and Ellyllon swore. She opened her eyes. Ellyllon was on top of her, the bottle in his hand. One hand grabbed her face, its fingers pressing and pinching, forcing her mouth open as the other tipped the bottle. She tried to focus, but it was too late; liquid poured into her mouth and down her throat. She choked, coughed, lifted one hand feebly, trying to stop it, but he kept pouring and in the end all she could do was swallow.

Ellyllon stopped pouring, let go of her face and stepped back, breathing heavily. His eyes never left her face, as if he were afraid to miss a moment of her struggle. Iomlan was still strengthening inside her; the drug hadn't had time to work. She could feel the chair beneath her, her feet, her legs. There was still time. She could draw it out, like Seamus in Grainne's castle. She focussed, pulling Iomlan to her and imagined it washing through her body, purifying and cleansing. Incredibly, it was working. Pressing down with her hands, she pulled herself upright. Ellyllon's eyes glittered.

"Nice try," he murmured approvingly. "But you're out of time."

Like the turning of the tide, a new wave of the drug washed over her. She fell back, the little control she'd gained swept mercilessly away.

"Do you see, Cormac?" Ellyllon crowed. "Even that much should've been beyond her. What would you do, give, to have Iomlan as strong as that?" His black eyes bored into hers as he watched the lassitude slip back over her. "Didn't Seamus tell you? I can feel your power, taste it. It's stronger than I ever imagined, and still growing. You know, Jasmine, it shouldn't do that. By the time you've joined, Iomlan is fixed. But not with you. Do you know what I think? Seamus is scared. He's scared how strong you will become. Imagine what you could do, if only you realised it? What you could do for me? What we could do together?"

*

Riding side by side, Malachy and Brennan left the village. Thinking of Cormac, Malachy still found it hard to believe that someone could lie, could fool them all so completely, especially as Jasmine had seen inside his mind. Of course, he'd had his doubts about him, but after that conversation with Jasmine, he'd started to think he'd been blinded by jealousy. They followed the road through the meadow, walking the horses, trying to minimise the jar to Brennan's shoulder. Walsh's mother had given him something for the pain, but without morphine, Malachy couldn't imagine how agonising it must be, but Brennan didn't complain, not once.

They entered the forest. With hindsight, Ellyllon's plan seemed amazingly simple. It could have easily failed, if they hadn't believed so much in Cormac, in Ellyllon's ability to corrupt him. Jasmine had believed it, had believed that only circumstance had created the difference between her and Cormac, but that was exactly what Ellyllon had wanted her to believe. But maybe it was more than that. Malachy knew she blamed herself for the storm, the death of the villagers. Did part of her think she'd already been corrupted, tainted by what she'd thought she'd done? The road dipped sharply and Brennan gave a small, involuntary cry of pain.

"Are you OK?" Malachy asked. "Do you want to rest?"

Brennan shook his head, but his face was pale. "No."

Continuing, they passed a horse and cart going in the opposite direction, and unknowingly greeted the same driver Ellyllon's coach had passed hours before.

They rode until late evening. Brennan had wanted to go on, but Malachy had insisted. Riding with his head down, Brennan hadn't spoken for almost two hours, and Malachy guessed it was only his strength and his stubbornness keeping him going. He didn't so much dismount as slide off his horse and would've fallen if Malachy hadn't been there to catch him. Together, they staggered to a tree, Malachy almost buckling under the weight of all that muscle. Lowering Brennan to the ground, he covered him with a blanket, then went back to sort the horses and collect the packs of food and the medicines. He gave Brennan the bottle of fresh water and went in search of firewood.

*

Brennan was asleep when he returned, the bottle lying next to him. Working as quietly as he could, Malachy slowly built the fire. It took; Malachy added more sticks, and after a few minutes, it was burning brightly. He flopped down, exhausted suddenly.

"Here." Awake, Brennan held out the bottle.

"Thanks." Pulling out the cork, Malachy took a long drink, gulping thirstily.

"I'm slowing ya down."

"No, I'm glad you're here. I'm not sure I'd want to be on my own at the moment." Passing the bottle back and climbing onto his haunches, Malachy placed some of the thicker sticks onto the fire. "We must be almost halfway there, d'you think?"

Brennan nodded. He looked exhausted, his face covered in a thin sheen of sweat.

"I'd better take a look at your wound."

Brennan winced as slowly, carefully, Malachy undid his tunic just enough to get to the wound. Untying strips, he peeled back the cloth. The wound was bleeding, the skin around it flushed, although the wound itself looked clean. Malachy touched the redness lightly and Brennan hissed with the pain.

"It's getting infected." Malachy frowned, reaching for the bag of medicines. "You need rest."

"I can rest at my brother's."

"If this doesn't kill you first." He picked out what he needed, nodding unconsciously as he went through her instructions in his head. He looked up. "This is going to hurt."

"Do it."

Using herbs crushed into alcohol, he began, carefully, to wash the wound. Brennan roared, swearing loudly, cursing Ellyllon, Cormac, calling them every name under the sun, his body flinching. Finished, Malachy didn't wait before gently smearing the balm all over it.

"Done." He replaced the cloth, tied the strips as tight as he could without cutting off the circulation and lowered his tunic.

"Lord," Brennan breathed.

His head dropped back against the trunk of the tree and he closed his eyes.

"Brennan?"

He opened his eyes. "Promise me to never become a healer."

"I promise," Malachy replied with a laugh.

He needed to keep Brennan warm. Placing yet more sticks on the fire, Malachy turned to the food pack Walsh's mother had given him. Inside were more packs, the food carefully wrapped in cloth. He unfolded them, revealing three kinds of meat, bread and a pale, hard yellow cheese. Using his knife, he hacked at the bread and cheese, cutting rough slices.

"You must eat," he said, handing some to Brennan.

Brennan did as he was told, chewing slowly, as if even eating were hard work. "Walsh's father was a lucky man."

Malachy didn't answer, chewing on a piece of meat that was so strong he thought it might be rabbit; he was too busy rooting down into the bottom of the sack. He brought out a small bottle.

"Is that...?" Brennan asked, his eyes suddenly bright.

"I think so." Malachy pulled out the stopped and sniffed. "Jesus, that's strong."

He passed it over and Brennan took a quick drink, then another. He passed it back. After a moment's hesitation, Malachy did the same. The alcohol was rich and strong and it burnt going down, making him gasp, but almost immediately he could feel the warmth in his belly, feel it radiate outwards. He took another drink.

"Not too fast," Brennan warned him, holding his hand out. "Yer not used to it."

Reluctantly, he gave it back. Already Brennan was looking better; his face had lost its sheen and the colour had returned, but whether it was the rest, medicine or alcohol Malachy wasn't sure. Taking a longer drink, Brennan gave a heavy sigh of pleasure then passed the bottle for a second time. "You look tired."

Malachy glanced at the bottle, then quickly stoppered it. "I'm OK."

Brennan nodded and took a bite of his bread.

"How did you know it was Cormac that Walsh's mother was talking about?"

"From the first, he was, not liked. There was a strangeness in his eyes, and talk of his power, but I see now it was not that that made him so, else Jasmine and Seamus would have it and they do not. But he was kin to Grainne Mhaol, the favourite of Duggan, and no word was said against him." He paused, shifting uncomfortably against the tree. "As he grew, the strangeness faded, but still he was arrogant, superior, and there were stories."

"Stories?"

"Small cruelties, petty things. Told by the other children. We did not listen to them, for the village children did not like him either."

"What kind of things?"

"It is said, one day, he played with the village children and one hit him. Knocked him square on his arse. The children laughed, for who wouldn't? But Cormac became angry, and the children's taunts wilder. The morning after, the child's kitten was found dead in a corner of the courtyard, its belly sliced open and the innards taken out. The cut was clean, too clean for an animal." Brennan made a face. "It is a story. Cormac is no longer a boy."

"But can a leopard change its spots?"

"A leopard?"

"Nothing." Malachy couldn't help but smile, despite everything. "But you think Cormac hasn't really changed."

"If Ellyllon had never come?" Brennan shrugged. "He may, in time, have become a man worthy of Grainne Mhaol and the men that follow her."

But I doubt it, his face said. Malachy took this in. If this was true, then Jasmine was right after all; there was something very tragic about Cormac. But then, Jasmine wasn't like that, and, despite her fears, would never be. He had another thought, and this one chilled him.

"From what you're telling me about Cormac, how do you think he'd feel about Seamus, Jasmine?"

There was a pause. Brennan stared at him, as if deciding how much to say. "Seamus is a man. We are taught to respect men, our elders; it is our way. Jasmine is but a girl, yet her power is so much greater than his own." He grimaced. "I think he would hate her."

Malachy stared back at him. "That's just what I was thinking."

*

Ellyllon left her as soon as he saw the drug had taken, calling Cormac to follow him, like a dog to heel. Cormac obeyed, but slowly, so that Ellyllon was already through the door by the time he'd reached it. He paused, one hand on the door frame and, with a twisted smile, waved his free hand. A candle on the far side of the room went out. He waved his hand again and, with exaggerated slowness, one by one, each of the candles were snuffed out. Behind them, darkness crept across the room towards her. "Sleep well," Cormac whispered when they were all out.

He closed the door. In the darkness, she heard footsteps, wood creaking and then nothing. Silence. There was no light, no sliver around the shutters or the door; all was black, quiet, still. She could hear her heart beating, the sound loud in her ears. Helpless, unable to move, to even turn her head, it was like being buried, the blackness pressing onto her, like earth in a grave.

The house creaked. Unable to sleep, Jasmine's mind drifted, wandered in that place that if it wasn't actual sleep, neither was it fully awake. No clock ticked to mark the passing of time; it could have been four hours, maybe five, possibly not even one. She thought of Seamus, wondered if he and Grainne had realised MacDermott wasn't coming and were racing back to find them. And Malachy; as he'd been when she'd last seen him, his face turned towards hers, as his horse circled and circled. She hoped he was alright. She wished she could warn them both, tell them not to come, but without Iomlan there was no chance. The worst thing was they still didn't know about Cormac; whatever Ellyllon had planned, she was sure it would involve him somehow. He almost seemed to enjoy using him, as if by using him he was using what was good in them against them. Cormac. He was the pivot; if only she could copy Ellyllon and find a way to exploit him, exploit his weaknesses. Or like Seamus had the rich man. Influence, Tionchar. Like a salesman, Seamus had said. And how many salesmen had Iomlan to help them make a sale? Jasmine concentrated, thinking hard.

Another creak, louder this time, sounded above her head, as if someone were walking across the room above. Her eyes narrowed. Something about the room had changed; she couldn't put her finger on it, but something was different. The chair Ellyllon sat on was still there, its outline dark against… the room. It was lighter, black changing to a dark grey. Dawn was coming, the new day not far off. Her little finger in her right hand began to tingle, and her heart leapt. The drug was wearing off. Quickly she dug down for Iomlan, but it was too soon. She was too eager and nothing happened. The tingling moved to the next finger. She strained, tried hard to make it move, twitch, curl, anything, but it was useless. She almost cried with frustration. With the day dawning, they would all be up, and this moment, this chance of escape, would pass. She tried to move her head, to look at the door. *Calm down*, a voice inside of her warned, you can't force it. *You have to wait for the drug to wear off.* The voice was right; she needed it to wear off just enough and then she could use Iomlan to do the rest. It couldn't be long now. The tingling had moved to her feet. With an effort, she lifted her finger. *Please wake.* Inside, Iomlan stirred. She was almost there. The candles nearest her spluttered into life.

"It's that time again," Ellyllon said from the chair.

Her heart sank. Uncurling, he held up a cup, presenting it to her, his smile vicious.

Chapter Nineteen

Malachy slept badly that night. Brennan had fallen asleep as soon as they'd finished eating and, worried for him, Malachy had covered him with a second blanket before stoking the fire and heaping on more wood. There was no need to keep guard, but still, when he finally laid down, sleep wouldn't come. In the end, after hours of turning, of checking the fire, checking Brennan and thinking of Jasmine, dawn broke, the sun rose and Malachy rose with it. He left Brennan sleeping, checked the horses, then went for a short walk, trying to clear his head of the last of the night's dark thoughts. It was a beautiful morning, the air fresh, the colours of the trees and undergrowth vibrant with the slowly drying dew. Birds chirruped and tweeted above his head, singing with a gusto he'd never noticed before, as if their very lives depended on it. Their mood, their desire for life, was infectious, irrepressible, and as he made his way back to Brennan, his heart, though not actually lighter, was determined. Brennan was awake. He'd even got up and was trying to rekindle the fire.

"Let me do that."

"Aahh." Brennan waved him away, crossly, but Malachy saw the wince.

"Sit, rest. We have a long ride."

Reluctantly, Brennan did as he said.

*

Malachy helped Brennan onto the horse and the two of them set off. The road was quiet and surprisingly familiar, Malachy remembering more than he'd thought. He'd forgotten it was less than a week since they'd travelled down; it seemed like a lifetime ago. Riding under trees, Brennan chattered away, almost continuously, regaling Malachy with stories of life in Grainne's service, each story more grandiose, more improbable than the last. It should have reassured him. That's what it was supposed to do, but it didn't. Brennan wasn't normally so chatty, Morain the more loquacious out of the two, and there was a flush to

Brennan's face, a mania in his speech, that made him think of the fever Walsh's mother had. They passed a crossroads, glanced idly right, but couldn't see the house that lay four miles west of it, with Ellyllon's black coach standing outside, waiting to receive its passengers.

Stopping twice, they rode north, the road slowly growing busier, those on foot moving to the side of the road to give way to horses and carts. Finally, the forest opened up before them and they saw the turrets of Sligo castle, the square towers in the city wall, through the trees. A few hundred yards more, and they joined the slow uneven train of people heading for the city gates. Trying to look unobtrusive, Malachy watched the city walls, noting the guards stationed along it, the impenetrability of its stone. Brennan, he knew, was doing the same, despite his injury. Who knew what allies Ellyllon had made inside the city? They reached the bridge. It was full, streams of people moving in and out of the city, jostling one another, reluctantly making way for the horses, the thought of being trampled their only incentive. Below it, the moat looked deep, the water dark and still. Malachy followed Brennan through the gates, unable to resist looking up at the portcullis, the lethal metal spikes suspended high above his head. And then they were through, into the city beyond.

*

Malachy stared, disorientated by the sheer volume of sights, sounds and smells around him. Nothing had prepared him for such chaos; Grainne's castle had seemed quiet, serene in comparison. There were houses, buildings in all directions, separated by narrow main streets and interspersed with the tiniest lanes imaginable and full to overflowing with people. They walked or stood shoulder to shoulder, some sat or even lay down on cobbled stone, careless of dust or dirt. With Brennan leading, they made their way along the street, heading straight into the centre of the city. Into the main thoroughfare, they passed market stalls and saw people stood, impervious of those pushing past them, talking, shouting, haggling, poking at meat, vegetables and cloth and gesturing. Some gestures, the rudest ones, hadn't changed much in all the centuries. They turned again and the streets widened. The houses here were bigger, grander. Brennan led Malachy down a side street, then turned again, for the last time. He stopped in front of a house large enough to have a carriage beside it, but plainer, less ornate than some Malachy had seen.

"My brother's house. A prosperous merchant, but a man of simple taste."

Dismounting, Malachy helped Brennan off, and the two of them lurched up the steps to the front door.

*

Jasmine dozed. Back in the carriage, its movement lulled her almost to sleep. Cormac sat opposite, his eyes fixed on the woodland passing by the window. It was already midmorning by the time they'd left. Ellyllon's lack of hurry puzzled Jasmine and frustrated Cormac, who was eager to get to Sligo and see the tree and wondrous portal. At first, she'd tried to talk to him, tried to get under his skin, make him doubt Ellyllon, but it hadn't worked. Despite the looks he gave her, Cormac had refused to rise to the bait and had simply ignored her. In the end, she'd given up trying. The carriage lurched violently to the left, jogging Jasmine awake. She glanced at Cormac, who yawned the wide, loud yawn of boredom. Maybe it was time to try again?

"You know he's not taking you with him," she said, trying to sound casual. "He'll use you up and spit you out."

Cormac s eyes flicked over to her, then back to the trees.

For a moment he didn't say anything and then, to her surprise, he answered. "Your words will not sway me."

"I'm not trying to sway you," she lied. "I tried to make you see him for what he is, but there was no point."

Cormac smiled. "Ellyllon's heart called to me and I welcomed it. When I know his power, it is I that will use him, and 'spit him out'. As a chicken bone?" He cocked his head, as if the saying amused him. "It is me that will roast *his* skin, suck the flesh from *his* bones and 'spit him out'."

"You're a fool. Ellyllon is letting you think that, just as he let MacDermott. You've sold your soul for nothing."

"MacDermott is the fool." He leant forward. "As are you. Soul? You think I believe in God, the heavens? What is right, or wrong? There is only what yer can do and what yer can take."

"You can't believe that!"

He sat back, his silence her only answer.

"So," she tried again, "how you were with me was just a lie, an act. Everything I saw in you."

"I was he, once." For a moment, his face softened and then, almost immediately, it hardened again. "That Cormac is dead."

"But what about your aunt, Duggan?"

"My aunt? Duggan?" He laughed. "They are pirates. They take whatever pleases them, do whatever pleases them; plunder, rape, kill.

They speak of honour, but it is the honour of thieves, murderers. Who does not? MacDermott, O'Connor, the English? All speak of honour, of right, justice, but it is nothing, lies, to cover their crimes." He leant forward again. "Ellyllon spoke of your time. He spoke of machines that do the work of servants, carriages without horses that travel to the stars. And still those with power and wealth take whatever pleases them, only they live as gods. Ellyllon will take me there and I will do the same."

Overbright, his eyes gleamed manically, and in that moment, it looked as if the gap between his ambition and ability, coupled with Ellyllon's stories, had sent him spinning over the edge.

"But he's not going there; he's going back, to the time of the druids."

Cormac smirked. "Perhaps."

"You don't know anything. I told you, once that's portal's open, and he's got what he wants he'll dump — leave you behind."

"He cannot. He needs me."

"He likes your power, but he doesn't need you. Why would he?"

No answer. Cormac's eyes dulled.

"What does he need you for?"

"Naught," he replied sulkily, sitting back and resuming his watch out of the window.

Jasmine's mind raced, her thoughts tumbling. She'd get nothing more out of him; she'd been too eager and pushed too hard. But she was sure Ellyllon was lying to him, telling him what he wanted to hear and inflating his ego. But what if he wasn't?

*

As soon as Brennan's brother had seen him, he'd whisked him away. A doctor had been called, Walsh's mother's potions had been discarded and the lady of the house had taken control, moving smoothly up and down the stairs to the kitchen. Malachy had been left to doze by the fire, the sleepless night catching up with him.

He woke suddenly, feeling a hand on his shoulder. It was Brennan's brother. He sat up.

"How is he?"

"Sleeping." Older than Brennan by a good few years, his grey hair and beard were immaculately groomed, his clothes cut from a finer cloth, made with a finer hand. "With rest, he will be well."

There was a pause. Brennan's brother sat down opposite him.

"He would not rest until I gave my pledge. My home is yours. But how else can I aid ye?"

"Nothing else, thank you. You're doing more than enough. But, I must ask, where is the abbey?"

"I will have my man, Feeney, take you."

*

Weaving through the streets, Feeney led Malachy across the city. If they had seemed chaotic by horse, then they were doubly so on foot. People thronged, pressed up against them, some to squeeze past, others to see what they could pinch. Twice Malachy lost Feeney, only to have him double back and collect him, like an adult recovering a curious, errant child. They turned into a side street. A man swayed towards Malachy, lurching as if intoxicated, but he sidestepped him easily. Simultaneously, another came from the left, bundled into him, his right hand reaching. Quick as a flash, Feeney was there, one hand on the man's arm, his scarred rough face pressed in close. There was no need for words; Feeney let the man go and he and his friend melted back into the crowd, looking for an easier and less protected victim.

They turned a corner. At the far end of the street lay the abbey. Rebuilt after a fire, it was newer than the one in Ballintubber and more ornate, the arch over the main doorway and in the cloisters sharing the same intricate stonework of arches within arches. Surrounded by a thick wall, its tower was square and visible through a tall, wrought iron gate, deep stone steps led up to the door.

"Can anyone enter?" Malachy asked Feeney, gazing up at it.

"With the abbot's permission."

The sound of hooves made them turn. From the far end of the street, a procession appeared, men on horses, riding two abreast. Seeing them coming, people stepped instinctively back, moving as one. Malachy went very still. Behind them came a carriage, completely black, even to the wheels, followed by two more horsemen.

"Back!" Feeney hissed, reaching up and pulling Malachy behind him.

Fingers fumbling, Malachy covered his head with his hood. The procession stopped in front of the abbey and, almost immediately, the door to the abbey opened and a figure dressed in a long black cloak stepped out. Its face hidden by the hood, it slipped down the steps. Ellyllon. It had to be. At the gate, he paused and, lifting up his head, looked in Malachy's direction. He shrank back, his heart beating wildly, in behind Feeney, one hand pulling his hood even further forward over his face. Seconds felt like minutes. Still, Ellyllon looked; Malachy was sure he'd seen him, and then, abruptly, he turned towards the carriage. The door opened, a hand pushed the steps out and then Cormac's head appeared. He got out and, leaving the door open, went to join Ellyllon. Malachy watched them talk, or rather Ellyllon talk as Cormac listened, his head dipped submissively. Around him, people were moving again, jostling as they tried to get by, but he stayed firm, his eyes fixed on the pair on the other side of the road. And then, with a nod, Cormac was gone, racing through the iron gate, up the steps and into the abbey. Ellyllon walked over to the carriage. The door was still open. Two quick steps, and Ellyllon leant inside, his cloak spreading behind him. Lifting onto his toes, Malachy strained over Feeney's shoulder, hoping for a glimpse inside, but they were too far away. Ellyllon straightened and then, without pause, walked through the abbey's gate and up to the main door. It opened as he approached, and he moved swiftly inside, disappearing into the darkness. Without thinking, Malachy moved forward, his eyes fixed on the carriage, but Feeney grabbed his arm, holding him back effortlessly.

"They will cut yer down in a heartbeat," he growled, his voice low, his lips close to Malachy's ear.

He stopped, realising what he was doing, and Feeney's hand relaxed.

"I can't just stand here. I have to…"

Already Ellyllon was back, the abbot behind him. Stopping at the gate, the abbot waited, his eyes, small against his round, plump face, darting nervously. Ellyllon spoke, his voice low and harsh, and three men dismounted. The first reached inside the carriage and picked a bag up off the floor. Cradling it carefully in both hands, he took it inside the abbey as the second man stepped forward. Leaning into the carriage, he began to pull at something, his movement rough, like he was tugging on a sack of potatoes. A form appeared, solid and indistinct; then an arm, white against the black, appeared, flopping lifeless towards the ground. Malachy gritted his teeth, grabbing Feeney without realising. It was Jasmine. Holding her awkwardly under the arms, her body sagged, her feet trailing as he tried to pull her out and upright. The third moved in to help, taking her by the legs then lowering her feet to the ground. They turned her, and then the one holding her ducked, placed his left arm under Jasmine's legs and, with an effort, scooped her up. He staggered slightly, hefting her body to get a better hold and her head fell back, her face dropping. Malachy gasped. Her eyes were open. For one terrifying moment, he thought she was dead, then Ellyllon darted forward. Long white fingers caressed her head and then very gently he lifted it up and eased it into the man's shoulder. Jasmine said something, her voice too faint to catch and Ellyllon bent towards her, his lips close to hers, his fingers still shifting, still caressing. She said something else and, abruptly, he stopped. His hand dropped to his side, he took a step back and, with a nod of his head, moved back towards the abbey, the man carrying Jasmine following. They passed the abbot on the steps, Ellyllon not so much as giving him a second glance. Eyeing the waiting men dubiously, the abbot paused, and then, with a small shake of his head, followed them into the abbey and closed the door firmly behind him.

Chapter Twenty

Malachy and Feeney looked at one another. Realising he still had hold of Feeney's arm, Malachy let him go.

"Sorry," he whispered, flexing fingers stiff from the tightness of his grip.

Feeney nodded vaguely, as if he too hadn't noticed, the muscles on his arm too hard for Malachy's fingers to leave any impression. His eyes were wide, and there was an expression on his face that Malachy knew all too well. Disgust. For there was something obscene in the way Ellyllon had touched her, like a man touching something precious, something he owned.

"We'd best return," Feeney said eventually.

Malachy didn't answer. He knew it made sense, that there was nothing he could do, and maybe Seamus had already arrived and was waiting for him at Brennan's brother's house. Yet he found it hard to move, to take his eyes from the abbey door.

"Come, come." Feeney gently pressed his shoulder. "Alone, we cannot aid her."

Keeping the abbey in view, Malachy allowed himself to be led away. Behind them, MacDermott's men had all dismounted and were preparing for a long wait.

*

They made their way back. For Malachy, with every step the noise of the crowded streets became jarring, the push of the bodies around him more intrusive, more aggressive. With each knock and nudge he wanted to lash out, to pin the offender up against the wall and hit, hit, hit. He'd never felt so angry, or so helpless, and it was only the thought that this wouldn't, couldn't help Jasmine that stopped him from losing it completely.

*

They were almost at the house. They turned into a quieter side road. At the other end, coming their way, were Seamus, Grainne, and incredibly,

Duggan.

"Seamus!" Malachy shouted, breaking into a run, Feeney following.

They met in the middle of the street.

"Malachy, are ya alright?" Seamus asked, grabbing him.

He nodded, and the two of them hugged.

"Brennan told us what happened." Seamus let him go, and now it was Grainne's turn.

Her cheek pressed into his. "Malachy," she whispered softly.

He swallowed, but then she was gone and Duggan was there, clasping his hand, holding it upright, his smile grim. "Have ya practiced?"

Unable to speak, Malachy nodded.

"Good; we will have need of it." He looked as if he was going to say something more, but Seamus cut across him.

"We knew something was wrong when we got to the castle and MacDermott wasn't there and there was no sign of him on the road. We met Duggan and Morain coming back, riding with reinforcements, and he joined us while Morain and the men returned to the castle. As we rode, I searched for Jasmine, but I couldn't sense her properly, and she didn't respond." He sighed. "And then we met Walsh's man, and he gave me your message, and I knew. Is she here?"

Malachy nodded. "Yes. I saw her. She was awake; I heard her speak, but she didn't seem to be able to move, like she was paralysed."

"Where? At the abbey?"

"Yes." Malachy nodded again. "With Ellyllon. Cormac was there too." He glanced awkwardly at Grainne, but she didn't react. "Brennan was right, Cormac's still loyal to him. They took her inside."

"Paralysed? It would explain why I couldn't feel her or her Iomlan." He shook his head. "But how?"

"Seamus, my potion," Grainne exclaimed. "Could it do this?"

"I don't know. He could've stolen a sample from your castle, maybe altered it somehow. If that's the case, I can purge her of it. Malachy, go with—"

"Feeney," Malachy interjected.

"Feeney, back to Brennan, wait for me there. If Ellyllon sees you he'll try to use you." He began to move away.

"But—" Malachy began, but Grainne cut across him. "Seamus, wait, Ellyllon has set a trap," she said quickly, grabbing his arm. "He will kill you."

"No, he won't, for without me, he'll never be able to get the portal open. He needs me alive." He grinned suddenly. "He's a victim of his own cleverness. He can only control Jasmine by drugging her, but drugging her keeps Iomlan subdued, and without Iomlan she doesn't know the words to open the portal. But he doesn't know that. Doesn't know either that I can purge her of it, or that I know about Cormac, and that gives me the advantage."

"Us," Grainne quantified quickly. "Cormac is my kin. It is my right."

Seamus paused then nodded, and she let him go.

"Malachy, go back with Feeney."

"No, I'm coming too."

Feeney took a step forward. "The abbey door is guarded, but I know of another way inside."

Malachy lifted his chin. "And I can't find my way back to the house without him," He lied, conscious that the house was only a few streets away.

"What is it with you two?" Seamus growled, looking from one to the other. He sighed. "OK, but Feeney, this is not your fight; all I need is for you to show me the entrance. And Malachy, you wait outside with him. I want your word."

For a moment, Malachy hesitated, but going with Seamus was better than nothing. "I promise."

"OK then." He waved one hand impatiently. "Now come on."

*

The man carried Jasmine down the nave. Her head had fallen back again. White columns floated by, reaching up to the dark wooden beams. A candelabrum came close, missing her face by inches. She couldn't see Ellyllon, but Cormac was there, waiting for them in front of the altar. Without a word, he moved off, the man carrying Jasmine following. Sidestepping through a door, down three steps, and they were out into the cloisters. Sun flashed through the columns, flickering across Jasmine's eyes. A garden lay in the centre, the single tree carefully kept to miniature; below it was a rough, wooden seat. Opposite, three monks watched them pass by; one stepped forward, his mouth open, as to protest, but was quickly pulled back by his brothers. They turned a corner, away from the quadrant, into another corridor. Narrow, the walls rough as if it had been built in haste, it ended in a low wooden door. Cormac turned the iron handle, lifting the latch, and the door opened with a loud creak. Another sidestep; the man hefted, squeezing her shoulders and legs to get through. He turned, swinging her round, and her head rolled helplessly. The room swung with her; she glimpsed a round hole in the roof, the wide shaft of light falling from it, landing on Ellyllon and the branches of a tree behind him, and then she was back into shadow. Candlelight burned from a second candelabrum, illuminating a high-backed chair and small, round table with two small iron candlesticks sat on top of it.

"Here. Bring her here," Ellyllon's voice ordered.

The man did as he was told. Moving over to the chair, he placed her carefully into the seat. He grunted and, pulling roughly at her, sat her up as upright as her body would go.

"Leave," Ellyllon ordered. Without a word, the man turned and walked swiftly from the room.

His back to her, Ellyllon was gazing at the tree. Bathed in the light coming from above, the hole carefully designed and finished, Jasmine realised that the room had been deliberately built around it. The oak was ancient, the fork in the trunk unnaturally wide, as if the two main branches were sagging under their own weight, the bark scarred and discoloured with age.

"It's beautiful, isn't it?" Ellyllon glanced at her and she saw a look of reverence on his face.

It was beautiful, the marks, the signs of age only heightening its beauty. Jasmine found herself wondering all the things, the changes the tree had seen and what it would tell her if it could speak, the wisdom it would share.

"And such power, a power that could be for anyone. Should be for anyone." Ellyllon's voice throbbed with anger. "But the druids took it for themselves, harnessed it and kept it only for those they deemed worthy. As if it were their right to decide, to judge who is worthy."

He turned towards her, his eyes staring but unfocussed, as if he was looking inwards to his past and she knew he wasn't really seeing her.

"An act they will come to regret," Cormac sneered from just behind her.

Ellyllon's eyes refocused, and, although he smiled slightly at Cormac, he made no reply. He glanced at the table.

"Cormac, where are the vials? They should be here." He lifted his head. "I sense — Seamus, he's close."

Jasmine's heart leapt.

"Here?" Cormac asked.

"No, not quite. He's here in Sligo." His face lit up. "He's coming."

There was a pause, and then Ellyllon's smile twisted. "Cormac, I need those vials."

"I will find them."

He darted away. Ellyllon watched him go with the air of a person waiting for another to leave, then slowly turned towards her.

"Jasmine, I like it when we're alone," he purred, coming close. Placing his hands delicately on the arms of her chair, he leant in. "Can you feel its power? Like a pulse, only very faint, and yet it throbs through you, as if it were the heart of the universe, connecting all things."

Jasmine stared back at him in silence. He knew she couldn't feel it; without Iomlan her ability to sense was deadened. He was toying with her, enjoying her loss and total helplessness.

He smiled. "The universe unites us, brings us closer." Black eyes gazed into hers. "You and me, closer."

It was the same as before. He was deliberately manipulating her, building her up as if she were the most important thing in the world, then knocking her down. All the time he was circling closer and closer, ready to pull her in, to use those black, bottomless depths to suck her down, down, down. If she let him, she'd never get out. She closed her eyes. But it wasn't enough to reject him, if she wanted to defend herself, she had to attack.

"Does Cormac know that you'll never take him?"

The chair shook; he let go of the arms and she felt him withdraw. She opened her eyes.

"Cormac believes what I want him to believe."

"What, that you need him, need his power?"

His eyes flashed. "I need no one's power."

"Then, why all this? If you're so powerful, then why bother with me, or Cormac. Why don't you use it? Or is it that you can't? All this power, it's just another lie, another deception. You have no power; you have nothing, nothing but the scraps you take from us, like a dog grovelling, begging in the dirt. You have no Iomlan; you never did."

"No Iomlan?!" Hand raised, he leapt towards her, his eyes burning with fury. For a moment, she thought he was going to hit her, but somehow he controlled himself. "I had power. I had more power than you can imagine. In time, I would've become the most powerful druid in Britain, stronger even than the entire Druid Council. But my friends were weak; they lacked vision. They betrayed me and I was left to face my punishment alone." He lowered his hand and smiled bitterly. "They called it punishment, but it was, is, torment. I told you before, Ellyllon is not my name, it is my kind. The kind the druids create, when they take your power and leave you a hollow, empty thing. But even the Druid Council's power is limited. I was too strong, too powerful; they could not take everything from me. They left me remnants, remnants that only made the bite of loss worse, but they took enough." He thumped his chest. "They stole it from me, opened up my flesh and ripped it from me. Can you imagine it? The agony of it? The agony I feel every day, *every day*! But even that is not the worst of it, for there is the gnaw, the ache of what I have lost. They tore into the centre of me, took everything that I was, everything that I could've been, and made me — this."

He looked towards the tree. "You are right; for the moment, I need your power. I did need Cormac's, but it will not always be so. Cormac, at my request, flows his power through me. You saw it, and for the briefest of moments, I feel — bliss."

His shoulders dropped. For a moment, she thought he was going to cry, but then he turned back to her and she saw all that pain and loss and grief and that thwarted ambition had melted into a deep, dark rage. He stared at her, and if she could've done, she would've shrunk away. There was hate in his eyes, and worse. He would hurt, maim and kill, not just because he enjoyed it, but because he felt he had the right. The universe owed him for his pain, and to inflict the same on others was nothing but divine retribution.

"Seamus is a fool; so sentimental, soft, wasteful. If I were he, I would've burnt every last drop of power out of you. Oh, and I will, I promise you. But we must wait, for Seamus and, let's not forget, Malachy. When I take you home with me, he'll want to come and I have a lot to thank him for — will have a lot to thank him for, for when I start torturing him and you hear his cries, you'll agree to anything I say just to stop me."

Footsteps sounded, coming fast. Their owner slipped through the door.

"Cormac," Ellyllon greeted him.

She heard the door close and then Cormac stepped into her view, carrying the bag she'd seen in the carriage in one hand and a glass in the other. Giving Ellyllon the glass, he dropped on one knee and, reaching into the bag, brought out a small bottle.

"Pour it," Ellyllon ordered. "It's not yet time," he said to Jasmine, when Cormac had finished. "But better to be safe than to be sorry."

Grabbing her hair, he pulled back her head and began to pour. Too fast; liquid spilled down either side of her chin, tickling her skin before dripping onto her clothes. Unconcerned, Ellyllon stepped back and gave Cormac the glass. They looked at one another.

"Ellyllon." Cormac glanced towards the door.

"Yes Cormac. He's here, in the abbey," Ellyllon replied, his eyes gleaming. "And you're improving. You know what to do."

Cormac nodded. Focussing, he pushed with his hand, and slowly Jasmine's chair began to inch backwards, in towards the shadows. He followed it, only stopping when the back of the chair bumped gently into the wall.

"Shhh," he whispered, putting his hand across her mouth.

Silence. They waited, Jasmine and Cormac lost in the shadows of the far corner and Ellyllon in front of the oak tree, bathed in sunlight. No sound came from outside the door, no sign that anybody was there. Then, so gently that she wasn't sure she'd actually heard it, the door handle clicked. Her heart pounding, she sensed more than saw the door swing slowly open.

*

Outside, Feeney watched Malachy pace. The tomb's back panel had been forced open, revealing steep steps going down into darkness. The crypt lay fifty metres away from the abbey's outside wall. Built ostensibly as monument and final resting place to the man who'd ordered the building of the abbey, it hid a secret passage designed to help the monks escape from looters, marauders and religious persecution.

"We must wait," Feeney said, trying for reassurance.

"Yeah, I know."

A few minutes passed. Sighing to himself, Feeney looked down at his hands. Malachy whirled, and with one quick movement, threw himself over the side and down into the tomb.

"Malachy!" Feeney cried, leaping forward.

He was too late. Malachy's head disappeared. He tumbled down the steps, and as Feeney watched, his hands gripping the edge of the tomb, he vanished into the underground corridor.

Chapter Twenty-One

Light flooded the room, a second before they charged through the door. Jasmine closed her eyes against it, feeling Cormac's hand slip as he jumped in surprise. It was all she needed.

"Cormac's with Ellyllon!" she yelled as loud as she could.

Ellyllon swore and Cormac reacted instantly, using his Iomlan to throw the chair and send her sprawling across the floor. Flat on her back, she saw Seamus and Ellyllon circling each other as Grainne and Duggan charged Cormac. Cormac's Iomlan exploded, knocking Grainne to the floor and throwing Duggan hard into the wall, his sword clattering. Quick as a flash, they were on their feet. Reaching in under his tunic, Duggan pulled out his knife and threw it in one fluid movement, but Cormac deflected it with ease.

"Is that all?" he sneered.

Grainne stepped forward, her sword seeming to hang loose but for the tension in her wrist, "No, it is not. Have you forgotten your name, your blood? Where is your honour, aligning yourself with such as that?"

Cormac frowned. "Aunt, I've no wish to hurt you."

"Nor I you. But your taint on the name of O'Malley cannot be permitted. Defend yourself, nephew."

His face darkened. "Very well, aunt. Come."

He let his hands drop and, eyeing him closely, Grainne crept towards him.

"Grainne, don't," Jasmine warned.

Something shot through her, a jolt, like electricity, that sent her body arching. For the briefest of moments, she felt Iomlan, then her body flopped back.

"That won't work, old man," Ellyllon said loudly, stepping in between her and Seamus.

"You don't know that," Seamus disagreed.

Jasmine's heart swelled. The jolt was from Seamus, not Cormac; he was using his Iomlan like a cattle prod, trying to shock her body into life. All too briefly, it had worked. Grainne lunged at Cormac. He raised his hand and, inches from his stomach, the sword twisted away and down. Now Duggan leapt forward, but Cormac caught him with his other hand and, throwing him back against the wall, began to press. Smiling, Ellyllon bowed at Seamus with an exaggerated flourish and, without a word, vanished.

"Shite!" Seamus swore, spinning slowly.

His body squeezed against the wall, Duggan's face was twisted in pain. Cormac still had hold of Grainne's sword. With an effort, she forced it upwards, preparing herself for a final deadly lunge, but too late; with a flick of his wrist, Cormac wrenched it out of her hand and across the floor.

Jasmine's body arched as Seamus sent another jolt of Iomlan. For a second time, she felt Iomlan and then her body fell back, lifeless. *Wait, a minute*. She could feel Iomlan! Seamus had been trying to kickstart it, using his like a second engine, only without the jump leads. Now he had, she could use it to purge herself of Ellyllon's drug. It was very weak, but still she focussed. Behind Seamus, Ellyllon reappeared, his hand reaching.

"Seamus, look out!" she screamed.

He whirled and, pulling his Iomlan back, sent it into Ellyllon, knocking him to the ground.

Ellyllon disappeared again.

Cormac had forced Grainne to her knees. Still holding Duggan with his right hand, he flexed the fingers of his left and slowly began to squeeze. Grainne coughed, her hand going to her throat. He squeezed harder and she began to choke, her chest heaving as she tried desperately to breathe.

"Cormac," Duggan muttered through gritted teeth. "Stop."

Her gasps were becoming weaker, her body beginning to droop.

"No." Cormac's eyes glinted and, looking Duggan full in the face, he squeezed his hand into a fist.

Grainne's breath caught, she closed her eyes and her head fell forward, her red hair tumbling. Out of nowhere, Seamus' Iomlan struck Cormac high across the chest and he fell back, releasing Grainne and Duggan. They slipped to the floor, Grainne with an audible gasp. There was no time for anything else; Ellyllon reappeared, his hands flexing as he circled Seamus, trying to find a way through his defence. Then Duggan was back on his feet and he was again launching himself at Cormac.

"Duggan!"

It was Malachy, stood in the doorway, his eyes bulging with horror.

"Malachy, what the hell are you doing?" Seamus roared. "Get out!"

Ellyllon smiled, a wide, wolfish smile, full of teeth, and vanished.

Grainne's eyes fluttered. Behind her, Duggan fell slowly to his knees, his own knife protruding from his chest. Cormac followed him and, kneeling down, gazed into his face. He kissed his forehead and then, with a sharp jerk his hand, thrust the knife deeper into his flesh. With a sigh, Duggan's eyes closed and he toppled forward, his forehead coming to rest onto Cormac's shoulder.

"Cormac," Grainne whispered hoarsely, lifting her head. "What have you done?"

"Released myself," he answered, pushing Duggan's body off and standing up.

Watching helplessly, Jasmine's finger twitched. It was working. She was purging herself; already she could feel her whole body tingling, but it was too slow. Iomlan was still too weak; she needed more time. She looked at Duggan's body, at Grainne crawling towards it and Cormac walking away. Time they didn't have.

Across the room, Seamus darted towards Malachy just as Ellyllon appeared behind him. Jasmine tried to warn him, but her shout caught in her throat. Time seemed to freeze; she watched, horrified, as Ellyllon lifted his hand and spread his fingers, then, with a speed she'd never seen him use before, thrust his hand deep into Malachy's back. Malachy screamed and slowly, effortlessly, Ellyllon lifted him into the air, his feet centimetres from the ground, and Malachy's scream ended in a gurgle. Hearing it, Jasmine felt sick.

With an effort, Grainne flipped Duggan's body over. His eyes were open and she closed them, crossed herself then bowed her head in a short, silent prayer. Cormac moved to the table and rested one hand lightly on its surface.

"Don't try anything," Ellyllon said, glancing sideways at Seamus. "I have his heart in my hand. You couldn't possibly move fast enough."

Sidestepping him, he joined Cormac, Malachy's cries echoing up to the roof and out into the evening sky. Jasmine gritted her teeth.

"Tell me, Jasmine. Tell me the words to open the portal."

"I can't; I don't know them." She tried to move, managed to lift her head, her neck.

She dug down for Iomlan, trying to use it to remember the words. They were there, inside her head, she could almost see them…

Ellyllon's arm flexed and Malachy shouted with the agony of it, his lips tinged with blue.

"I'm squeezing his heart. Tell me!"

"Oh, God, I can't!" She was frantic, in her head pleading for Iomlan, what little focus she had scattering. "Not without Iomlan."

"Ellyllon, she can't tell you without Iomlan," Seamus shouted from across the room. "But I can."

Lifting Malachy up higher, Ellyllon watched his head droop, then looked down at her. "One more squeeze of his heart—"

"Please, stop it. I can't tell you. I would if I could, but I don't know!"

She wanted to scream. Already Ellyllon's promise was coming true; he was torturing Malachy and she'd do anything to stop him.

"Ellyllon, she can't tell you!"

"What?" Listening finally, Ellyllon cocked his head. "Why?"

"It's the druid trick. Without Iomlan you can't read the words; they're rubbish, nonsense."

"I know that. But Cormac said you'd told her, that you'd read them."

"I did, but she can't remember them without Iomlan. They make no sense. By subduing Iomlan you took away the only way to get if from her. So now it's only me that can open the portal."

"Then do it."

Seamus shook his head. "Not until you promise to let Malachy go."

"And who are you to give me orders?! Open it."

"Then you'll let Malachy go? You won't harm him?"

"You trust my word, old man?" Ellyllon smiled suddenly, as if tickled by the idea that anyone would be naïve enough to trust him, "It's been a while, but very well, I give it; I will not harm him."

"And you'll let him go?"

"Yes. If I said I will, I will! But do it now, old man; my arm, like my patience, is tiring."

"Right. OK then." Seamus faced the tree.

Cormac and Ellyllon were busy watching Seamus. Surreptitiously, Jasmine rolled onto her side, preparing to try and lever herself up, but then Grainne was there, grabbing her under the arms and pulling her up, first onto her bottom then onto her knees. They knelt together, Grainne's hands stopping her from swaying. Cormac and Ellyllon exchanged a look. Seeing it, Jasmine went cold. *What were they planning?*

Seamus had begun to chant. Deep and sonorous, the words echoed, reminding Jasmine of the soft, damp earth. Almost immediately a glow appeared in the centre of the tree, just below the fork. Deep dark green, pulsating like a heart, grew steadily, suffusing the room and giving their faces a strange green tinge. Jasmine gasped, one hand going to her stomach. Iomlan began to move inside her, pulsating like the light, following its rhythm. Throbbing, it spread through her, warming her flesh and bones, and now it was her holding Grainne. As her strength returned, the last of Ellyllon's drug melted away. Seamus too was getting stronger; she could sense the power coming from him, and it was immense, and Cormac, the three of them united, connected in a way she couldn't begin to understand. Still growing, the light obscured the trunk of the tree and made the smaller branches and leaves sparkle. Ellyllon took a step back, seemed unsure, as if this was a power beyond even his understanding. Seamus spoke the last word, the sound of it lingering, and Jasmine gathered herself, ready to let Iomlan fly. She was half a second too late. Cormac struck, throwing out his hand and sending the two candlesticks hurtling towards Seamus. In the middle of turning, he sensed them, even managed to deflect one, but the second caught him behind his left ear. He fell like a stone.

"Don't even think about it," Ellyllon warned Jasmine, turning and holding Malachy out to her like a trophy.

She stopped and, letting go of Grainne, got slowly to her feet.

"Cormac, that was very well done. You deserve your reward. I promised you more power, now's your chance. Take his. Do it. Do it like I showed you."

Cormac's eyes gleamed. Two steps, and slipping to his knees, he placed his fingertips lightly on Seamus' stomach.

"What's he doing?" Jasmine cried.

He focussed and his fingers spasmed and pushed inwards, through the cloth and into skin. Blood welled into tiny pools, blotting the shirt.

She looked wildly at Ellyllon. "But he can't do that; he'll kill him."

Ellyllon, smiled, his most silken. "He doesn't know that."

He backed towards the tree, holding Malachy between them, "This hasn't worked out quite as I planned, but still I gave my word." He glanced at Grainne, who was creeping towards Cormac, sword raised. "Unless… Grainne, I wouldn't if I were you."

She ignored him, took another step and raised her sword high, preparing to bring it crashing down on top of Cormac's neck. Nothing happened.

"No!" Her shoulders flexed and she pushed again, with her whole body, but her sword refused to move. She looked at Cormac, Ellyllon and finally Jasmine. "Jasmine, relcase me!"

"I can't. I'm sorry; he'll kill Malachy."

"I care not. Release me!" She tried again, and then, with a cry of rage that was almost a howl, let the sword go.

She fell on Cormac, grabbed him around the neck, trying to use the weight of her body to pull him off. He slid sideways, his hands slipping, revealing fingers streaked with blood up to the knuckles. Using Iomlan, he threw her from him, sending her flying into a jumbled heap.

Ellyllon was at the tree, his back already disappearing into the light. To Jasmine's amazement, he pulled back his arm and, with excruciating slowness, Malachy slipped off and onto the ground. His eyes were closed, but she thought she saw him breathing.

"Now Jasmine, your choice, who's it to be? Stop me or save Seamus. But you'd better decide quickly; Cormac's almost through."

There was only one choice. Knowing exactly what it was, Ellyllon turned his back on her and stepped into the light.

Quick as a flash, Jasmine focussed and sent Iomlan hurtling as Grainne leapt to her feet. Cormac yelled in pain, his back arching, but still he didn't stop. Another flash of Iomlan, another yell, and then Grainne was there, balancing on one foot, her right leg lifting. The full force of her body behind it, her foot caught Cormac square in the chest. With a cry, he fell back, his hands sliding out of Seamus. Ruthlessly, Jasmine focussed again and, lifting him off his feet, threw him sideways across the room. He tried to retaliate, but she blocked him, sending him crashing into the far wall. His body slid to the floor, motionless.

"Jasmine!"

Grainne was knelt next to Seamus, her hands already red where she's tried to stem the flow. There was blood everywhere.

"Oh God." She slipped down beside her.

Behind them, the light flickered and died as the portal closed behind Ellyllon. It didn't matter; all that mattered was Seamus.

"Heal him, before he dies," Grainne pleaded.

Blood was pouring from two rough, deep wounds, the skin torn, misshapen, where Cormac had used his Iomlan to claw his way into him. Taking a deep breath, she put her hands over the wounds and, closing her eyes, focussed.

Iomlan flowed down her arms and into her hands, warming her palms with a healing glow. The blood flow stopped, Jasmine broke off and opened her eyes. It started again.

"He still bleeds," Grainne said immediately. "How is he not healed?"

"It's not working. I don't — wait a minute." Jasmine closed her eyes again.

His wounds were too deep; she needed to heal the skin, not stop the flow. She refocused, imagined the sides of the torn skin pulling towards one another, coming slowly together. Iomlan responded, taking the edges. Inside she felt the texture of the open, raw skin and shuddered. They pressed together. She'd done it. Once more, she opened her eyes, just in time to see the edges of the skin fall back and the wounds reopen.

"The devil take me!" Grainne swore.

Something inside Jasmine broke. She was failing, just as she'd failed the villagers at Killaspugbrone and Duggan. She stared blankly at the wounds, the oozing blood.

"I don't understand; it was healed, Iomlan healed it. I saw it."

But Iomlan hadn't healed it, neither had she, and now Seamus was going to die.

"Jasmine." Grainne grabbed her face, and turned it towards her. "You must try. Only you can heal him."

She pulled away. "I can't. It should've worked. I don't know what else to do."

Grainne's voice sharpened. "But you promised to protect him. You gave your word, your solemn vow. You must save him."

"But don't you see?" Jasmine cried. "I can't save him, I don't know how!"

Chapter Twenty-Two

Grainne stared at her. Her mind was in a whirl; she couldn't seem to think straight, couldn't see beyond the fact that it was all her fault. She should've stopped him, stopped Ellyllon; she should've listened to the woman in the lake, in the tomb. It was her choice; in choosing Malachy, she'd killed Seamus.

"Jas?"

A hand touched her shoulder and Malachy flopped down beside her, breathing heavily. He looked at the wound in Seamus' stomach and their bloodied hands and his face, already pale, paled even further.

"Jesus, what happened?!"

"It was Cormac," Grainne explained.

"Can you heal him?"

Jasmine didn't answer.

He grabbed her shoulder. "Jas, can you heal him?!"

"I don't know. I don't what to do. It's my fault. She told me, she warned me, and I chose you. But I thought when Ellyllon left, I'd heal him, but I can't. I'm going to lose him, Mal!"

"No, you won't. It's OK." He tried to smile. "Use Iomlan, your instinct."

"But I tried, it didn't work. I don't know what I'm doing."

"So try again!" He caught her arms, hurting her without meaning to. "You can do this, I know you can. You opened up reality, didn't you? Think, remember what Seamus said; he trusts you, your instincts." He looked deep into her eyes, as if trying by sheer will to make her share his absolute belief in her.

Feeling calmer, she took a deep breath and nodded.

Her hands shaking, she placed them back over the wounds and, closing her eyes, focussed. Again, she saw the wounds, imagined the edges pulling and knitting together, the top layer of skin regrowing, creating a scar. Iomlan stopped. Confused, she pulled at it. Nothing happened and she pulled again. Still nothing. And then, out of nowhere,

Iomlan tugged sharply at her and began drawing her down into the wounds in Seamus' stomach. She felt his flesh, the layers of tissue. Revolted, she tried to pull back, but Iomlan was insistent, its grip on her total. It played it out in front of her and she saw what it wanted and finally, she understood. She hadn't to stitch the wound; she wasn't a doctor. She was to heal it, heal it completely, and the only way to do that was from the inside out. United now, they worked together, as one in thought, moving quickly, effortlessly through the layers. She finished the final layer of skin and opened her eyes; the holes had gone, the skin healed perfectly. She breathed out, unable to believe she'd done it, or rather that Iomlan had done it.

"Jas, you did it!" Malachy exclaimed excitedly.

He grabbed her and they hugged, holding each other tight in their relief.

"You're amazing." He grinned, kissing her lightly on the lips.

For a moment, she didn't know what to do, caught by the sheer unexpectedness of it all, and then she was kissing him back.

*

The sound of movement broke them apart. It was Grainne, shifting around so she could lift Seamus' shoulders and place his head in her lap. She stroked his hair, leant over and, kissing his lips, pressed her face to his, her red hair falling forward, as to cover them. Her body shook, as if she were repressing her sobs. Malachy and Jasmine looked at one another. Was she too late?

"He's still alive, isn't he?" Malachy asked, anxiously.

Grainne looked up; tears shone in her eyes, but her face was calm. "Yes, he lives."

"Thank God," Jasmine breathed. She looked at her hands covered with his blood. "But he has lost a lot of blood."

Malachy frowned. "Is there anything you can do?"

"I don't think so; no, wait a minute." Placing her hand on Seamus' stomach, she focussed again. His body rolled slightly to one side then back again.

Grainne's grip on him tightened. "What are you doing?"

"I'm giving him Iomlan. It won't hurt him."

She did it again, then removing her hands, sat back.

"Will it work?" Malachy asked.

She sighed. "I don't know. It worked when Seamus did it for me. I'm hoping it's like charging a battery, and with Iomlan and the body being connected— helping one should help the other. I think."

Inwardly, she shook her head at herself. She didn't know if it would work or not and felt as if she were making it up as she went along. But what else could she do?

Malachy gave her an encouraging smile. "I'm sure it'll help."

They looked at one another, each knowing that there was nothing else to be done but wait.

*

"What happened to Cormac?" Malachy asked after a few minutes.

"I don't know. I knocked him off, over to the wall, over there." Jasmine pointed.

The floor was empty; there was no sign of him.

She shook her head. "I was concentrating on Seamus."

"He'll be back," Malachy predicted grimly.

Grainne looked up. "He's no better."

"I'll try again." Jasmine replaced her hands.

She concentrated, staying with it for longer this time, wanting to get as much as she could into him.

"Jas!"

Her concentration broke. She opened her eyes, feeling her head swim.

"You were beginning to sway." Malachy explained, looking worried.

"I'm OK. It's just the weirdest feeling. How's he looking now?"

"Actually, he's looking better; he's got more colour."

Seamus groaned suddenly and moved his head. Grainne stroked his hair.

"Maybe some water'll help," Jasmine suggested.

"I'll get it," Malachy offered. "Help me up." Jasmine gave him her arm and he pulled himself up. "Thanks."

"Are you sure you're OK? Maybe I should get the water."

"Yer fine. You need to watch Seamus." Leaning down, his kissed her. "Better get that water." He grinned, straightening.

She watched him go, seeing the same soppy grin that she knew was plastered all over her face, but she couldn't help it; her heart glowed with a sudden, unexpected happiness. Grainne reached out her hand to her and she took it. They smiled at one another, two women sharing a moment of happiness. Seamus' eyes flickered. Their hands dropped, Grainne touched his face and called his name, but he didn't wake.

*

Footsteps. Jasmine turned just as Cormac appeared, creeping from the other side of the tree. His face was a mess, covered with dried blood and his nose red and swollen. He must have hit it when she'd thrown him against the wall.

"Don't come any closer," she warned, scrambling to her feet and standing between him and Seamus.

"He's gone, he left me." He hadn't heard the warning, or else he didn't care.

"What did you expect?"

"He gave his word."

"I told you not to believe him. He doesn't keep his word."

And yet, with Malachy he had. Why was that?

Cormac didn't answer. He looked broken. She should've felt sorry for him, but after what he'd done to Seamus, she just couldn't. "Your aunt's here; maybe you should ask her forgiveness."

He looked at Grainne, but still holding Seamus, she turned away. His eyes hardened.

"Why should I?"

"Because there's always a way back. You don't have to be like this. I can't forgive you, but if you really try, maybe othe—"

Cormac interrupted her, his face livid. "I killed Duggan and I would've killed Seamus. Whatever you saw in me is gone and I welcome it. I am what I am. I will beg to no one."

He took another step forward and she shifted, matching his direction. This time he saw it and smiled, bitterly. "I've no interest in him, I want only to go."

She opened her mouth to tell him he could go, that she wouldn't stop him, but a voice deep inside stopped her. Cormac was corrupt, his use of Iomlan tainted; to let him go would leave him free to inflict any horror that took his fancy. She couldn't let him go.

"What will you do?" she asked instead.

"What is it to ye?" Cormac sneered, his confidence returning. "There is much I can do with my power and many who would welcome me. And do my bidding."

The voice was right. He'd learnt too much from Ellyllon.

Jasmine stepped forward, feeling strangely calm. "I can't let you go, not after what you did to Seamus. You ripped into him, not just with Iomlan, but with your hand. You must have felt his flesh beneath your fingernails. It must still be there, but it didn't stop you. And if you can do that, you can do anything."

"To stop me, you must kill me, but I do not think you would do that." He made as if to go.

"You're right, I wouldn't. I won't kill unless I have to, but as you said, you took Duggan's life, would've taken Seamus', and now I'm going to take yours."

He hesitated, as if confused by her words, their meaning, and it was all she needed.

Leaping forward, she grabbed his arm and Iomlan burst out of her. It tore down her arm and into her hand, her fingers, then out into his arm. Cormac reacted instinctively, using his Iomlan to defend himself. For a few moments he stopped her, but she was too strong. She shattered his defences and Iomlan washed over him, penetrating his skin and flesh, as it searched for every cell his body, then slowly, steadily, began to change them. Cormac shouted in pain, his body spasming as his shoulders widened, his limbs and torso thickening.

"Stop!" He pulled away, trying to get free, but the force flowing between them was unstoppable.

He gave another shout as his face narrowed, losing the softness of youth, and a beard and moustache sprouted then lengthened. Long blond hair fell in waves and Cormac's eyes stared out of a man's face. Behind her, Grainne gasped, but she ignored her. Already Cormac's skin was beginning to lose its smoothness, fine lines appearing around his eyes and becoming deeper. With a wail of pain, he raised his free hand to his mouth, and pulled out first one tooth and then another. Flecks of grey appeared in his hair, around his temple, his earlobes, merging with then overrunning the blonde. His body began to contract, his waist disappearing and his limbs narrowing. His fingernails broke and regrew, then broke again before hardening into something like talons, thick and yellow. He stared at them, held them up to her for her to see.

"Please," he begged, his eyes shining with tears and his body exhausted by the agony of the transformation.

"What's going—?" It was Malachy, back with a cup of water.

He stared at Cormac in horror, at the face that was growing old in front of him, the body bending and stooping.

"Jasmine, what are you doing? Stop it!" he shouted.

Cormac half turned towards him, raising one hand up to him in supplication. "Please, Malachy."

Without thinking, Malachy reached out towards him.

"Malachy, don't!" It was Seamus, fully awake and back on his feet, Grainne stood next to him. His face was worn, tired, but his expression determined, "If you touch him, it'll affect you too."

Malachy shrank back, his face twisted with disgust. "This isn't right,

Seamus. Do something."

"I can't, and neither can Jasmine. Now she's started, it has to run its course."

But Jasmine had finished. Iomlan faded within her, she let Cormac go, and he fell, his body collapsing beneath him. Dropping the cup, Malachy jumped forward and grabbed him, stopping him from hitting the ground. Cormac shuddered once then lay still.

Malachy lowered him carefully to the ground. "Cormac."

Slowly, he lifted his head. He was old, ancient, his long hair completely white, his face lined and wrinkled and his skin paper-thin over bone. Without a word, he struggled out of Malachy's arms and clambered painfully to his feet. He looked at Jasmine, and she saw that his eyes were unchanged, untouched by time or experience. Inside, he was the young man he'd always been.

"Why?" his voice rasped.

"I told you, I wouldn't kill you. Instead, I've taken your life."

"Make me young again."

She shook her head. "Even if I knew how, I wouldn't."

"Please, Jasmine, you can do anything."

"No."

Malachy, still kneeling, was staring up at her like she was somebody new, somebody he didn't recognise. She knew she should feel concerned, that his opinion of her mattered above anyone else's, but she couldn't quite bring herself to. He was, the voice inside told her, irrelevant.

"But I still have my power; I will use it!"

Jasmine shook her head. "You don't have the power. As our bodies fade, so does Iomlan. It's as weak as your body, and you cannot harm anyone."

Cormac stared at her; she saw him focus and then his eyes widened and he lifted up his head and howled. The sound echoed across the room, heartbroken and endlessly pitiful, and yet she felt no pity. "You're free to go."

"Aunt?" He looked at Grainne.

Her eyes were sad, but she didn't move. "No one will stop ye."

He lowered his head, all his fight and defiance gone. Without another word, he shuffled slowly out through the door. In the silence, Seamus was the first to move.

"Are you alright?" He touched Jasmine's shoulder.

"Of course, why?"

"What you did — it doesn't seem like you."

"But it was just. Should I left him to do as he pleases?"

Seamus frowned, hearing only sarcasm in having his earlier words repeated back to him. She quickly backtracked. "I mean, he told me he was going to do the same as Ellyllon. All he thought of was power; he'd never have changed."

Malachy got to his feet. "Seamus, why don't you say something?!"

"What do you want me to say?" He rounded on him.

"That she shouldn't've done it. I didn't exactly like Cormac, but to do *that* to him? There must've been another way."

"Like what?" Jasmine protested. "Kill him? I was trying not to."

"Malachy, no one could've stopped what happened. The die was cast years ago," Seamus explained with a sigh. "Iomlan came to Cormac too young. He didn't understand how to deal with the power and there was no one there to teach him. It twisted him up inside. It's sad, but it happens. We need to go, follow Ellyllon through the portal, before it's too late."

"I'm not sure I want to, not if it's going to be like this," Malachy muttered, his eyes on Jasmine.

"It was your choice to come; no one forced you," Seamus replied evenly.

"I know, but—"

"What did you expect, Malachy? What did you think it was going to be like? That we'd ask Ellyllon to stop and he'd say 'oh dear, I'm ever so sorry, I didn't realise'? People have died and I'm sure more will die, but not as many as if we don't stop Ellyllon."

"That's not what I meant—"

"Malachy, neither me or Jasmine can make any promises. We don't know what we'll face. But I do know I'll do whatever it takes to stop Ellyllon and anyone who decides to help him. In fact, it's better if you don't come; you make us vulnerable." He paused, ignoring the hurt on Malachy's face. "We don't have time to take you home. Wait here with Grainne and we'll pick you up on the way back. *If* we come back."

Moving over to Grainne, the two of them embraced and then kissed.

"Good hunting," she told him, letting go. "I will await your return, for I am certain you will come back to me."

Jasmine and Malachy stared at one another.

"Seamus is right; Ellyllon will only try to use you if you come. It's safer for you to stay."

"But why don't you stay too? It's not too late; it doesn't have to be like this. You don't have to be like this."

"Like what?" She drew herself up. "Mal, I thought you understood.

None of this would have happened it weren't for me, if I hadn't helped Ellyllon to open the portal. I have to help Seamus finish it."

"But look at what you're becoming, what you did to Cormac. You don't seem to even care. That's not you." Moving in close, he took her hand. "The real Jasmine would care. You once asked me to stop you when you couldn't stop yourself. This is it, this is me stopping you: don't go with him." He touched her face with his other hand. "Now, after everything, I don't want to lose you, the real you."

Unconsciously, her body swayed towards him, his longed-for touch irresistible. There was something in what he was saying. What she'd done to Cormac was horrible, she should feel something other than this cold, dispassionate certainty that what she'd done was right.

Behind them Seamus had begun to chant, the green light appearing once more. They were out of time.

She shook her head and stepped back, "Mal, you don't get it. Do you think I wanted to do that to Cormac? That I enjoyed it? Do you have any idea of what he was capable of? What he'd have done to innocent people if I'd just left him?" She sighed. "I did that once, and look what happened: thirty-eight people died. I won't let that happen again."

"But that's just it, who are you to decide?"

"Because there's no one else. Having Iomlan comes with responsibility. I don't get to pick and choose what I want in this; the good bits, the nice bits. Spinning leaves. This is me, the real me, the whole of me, good and bad." She smiled sadly at him. "Iomlan. It's well named."

He looked as though he wanted to say something more, but was struggling to find the words. It was too late.

"Jasmine, we need to go, now!"

The portal was open, ready, the light pulsating, and she could feel Iomlan running through her, throbbing with life. It was exhilarating, like every second of joy and pleasure she'd ever felt had been rolled into one glorious moment that made her want to laugh, shout, sing and run. Malachy still had hold of her hand, and she knew by his face that he could feel it too.

"Jasmine!" Seamus' voice was urgent.

"Wait for me." Letting him go, she joined Seamus in front of the portal.

"Ready?" He squeezed her hand, letting her know he understood.

She looked back. Grainne had joined Malachy, the two of them watching silently.

"Yeah."

Holding hands, they stepped into the light.

Chapter Twenty-Three

Malachy watched them disappear. His arm tingled, as if energised by a small, harmless burst of electricity, but the feeling of elation had already faded, leaving behind a strange absence.

Beside him, Grainne sighed. "Malachy, we must go."

"Yeah." He didn't move.

"She is young; she has much to learn."

His jaw tightened. "I know what you're saying, but it doesn't excuse what she did."

"Perhaps, but when the leg is rotten you cut it off, else let the body perish."

"You agree with her?"

"I would have killed him. Death is kinder." She paused. "You have love for her."

He didn't answer. The light was already shrinking, the sides of the tree trunk reappearing. Soon, the portal would close.

"If she is in need of aid, would you deny her your counsel?"

"She has Seamus, and they don't want me. You heard them."

She didn't answer, but the way she was looking at him, sadly, as if she knew what he was refusing to see.

"What would you do?" he asked, exasperated.

Still, she didn't answer, but she didn't need to; he already knew what she would say, for she was Granuaile, pirate queen, greater than any legend because she was wonderfully flawed and human. And against all tradition, a woman and true chieftain of the O'Malleys, she bowed to no one. The light was almost gone. He had seconds to decide. There was something very wrong with Jasmine, something connected with Iomlan. Grainne was right; even if she didn't realise it, Jasmine needed him.

"Thank you." There was no time for anything else.

Darting forward, he threw himself into the portal just as the light faded.

Turn the page and discover *Of Fire and Stone*,
Book III of Nina Oram's Carrowkeel trilogy!

Of Fire and Stone

Everything spun crazily. Bathed in green light, Malachy's whole body tingled. Remembering Seamus' words in the tomb, he thought of Jasmine, his mind clinging to her, as if she were the last thing in the world. He turned and turned, his stomach churning, until he forgot everything else in the jumbled, chaotic spinning. Abruptly it stopped, a light flashed, its brilliance half blinding him. Then he was through and out the other side, falling through wind and rain. He hit the ground, his body sprawling, with the scent of wet earth and grass in his nostrils. He rolled over and, feeling the rain on his face, opened his eyes. Stars twinkled, the sheer volume of their number lighting up the sky and the ground around him. He staggered to his feet, breathing heavily, and, pulling his cloak tight, lifted the hood over his head. Trees lined three sides; he guessed he was on the edge of forest, although it was hard to tell, even with the light from the stars.

"Jasmine! Seamus!"

No answer. He strained to hear over the wind and rain and the rustling trees. He called again. The wind blew harder, tore through the trees with a whistling, unearthly howl, almost as if to mock his efforts. He groaned. How stupid was he? He probably wasn't even in the right time, and even if he was, Seamus and Jasmine could be anywhere. Who knew how much time had passed since they arrived? He might never find them. He might be stuck here forever.

He shivered. Despite the wind, the rain seemed to be easing, which was just as well, for it was already beginning to soak through the thick wool of his cloak. But it didn't solve the problem of what to do next. He looked around him. Reason said he should find some shelter inside the forest and wait for the night to pass, but that meant getting even further behind Seamus and Jasmine. The other option was to turn away from the forest and look for some kind of settlement and hope to find Jasmine and Seamus there. He frowned, undecided, and then abruptly the weather decided for him. The clouds parted and a large, low moon appeared, illuminating the ground all around him. He was right, stood on the edge of a forest, the ground sloped downwards towards what looked like a river, shining silver in the moonlight. If this was still Sligo, or rather where Sligo was going to be, the river had to be the Garvogue, and where there was a river, there had to be… something, but hopefully it would be people living beside fresh, running water. For a moment, he imagined a fire, warmth and Jasmine's face smiling at him and then, fixing his eyes on the ground, he began to walk towards it.

Wide, the river flowed silently, its smooth, dark surface capturing the moon and reflecting it back. Following its flow, Malachy walked along a riverbank flattened into a rough path. There were people here, or at least, very nearby. Encouraged, he walked faster, and soon dark shapes appeared, tall with round, peaked tops. He grinned to himself. The sky was becoming lighter, turning from dark blue to a dark grey as dawn approached. He was almost there. Ahead, a thick high fence, made from roughly chopped wood, encircled round houses, their roofs made of some kind of thatch. The path turned away from the river and moved towards the village. It circled the fence and he followed it to what he hoped would be the entrance. A tree lay to his right, its trunk over a metre thick and its canopy high and wide. He passed under it. Something flashed towards him; he glimpsed an arm, a torso and then his legs were kicked from underneath him and he fell hard to the ground. Winded, struggling to breathe, he watched helplessly as a man leant over him. Fingers grabbed his hair, twisting as their owner tilted back his head and pressed a knife, the blade shining in the half-light, to his throat.